Flower
of the North

Flower
of the North

A Modern Romance

James Oliver Curwood

MINT EDITIONS

Flower of the North: A Modern Romance was first published in 1912.

This edition published by Mint Editions 2021.

ISBN 9781513280721 | E-ISBN 9781513285740

Published by Mint Editions®

 MINT
EDITIONS

minteditionbooks.com

Publishing Director: Jennifer Newens
Design & Production: Rachel Lopez Metzger
Project Manager: Micaela Clark
Typesetting: Westchester Publishing Services

Contents

I

S uch hair! Such eyes! Such color! Laugh if you will, Whittemore, but I swear that she was the handsomest girl I've ever laid my eyes upon!"

There was an artist's enthusiasm in Gregson's girlishly sensitive face as he looked across the table at Whittemore and lighted a cigarette.

"She wouldn't so much as give me a look when I stared," he added. "I couldn't help it. Gad, I'm going to make a full-page 'cover' of her to-morrow for Burke's. Burke dotes on pretty women for the cover of his magazine. Why, demmit, man, what the deuce are you laughing at?"

"Not at this particular case, Tom," apologized Whittemore. "But—I'm wondering—"

His eyes wandered ruminatively about the rough interior of the little cabin, lighted by a single oil-lamp hanging from a cross-beam in the ceiling, and he whistled softly.

"I'm wondering," he went on, "if you'll ever strike a place where you won't see 'one of the most beautiful things on earth.' The last one was at Rio Piedras, wasn't it, Tom? A Spanish girl, or was she a Creole? I believe I've got your letter yet, and I'll read it to you to-morrow. I wasn't surprised. There are pretty women down in Porto Rico. But I didn't think you'd have the nerve to discover one up here—in the wilderness."

"She's got them all beat," retorted the artist, flecking the ash from the tip of his cigarette.

"Even the Valencia girl, eh?"

There was a chuckling note of pleasure in Philip Whittemore's voice as he leaned half across the table, his handsome face, bronzed by snow and wind, illumined in the lamp-glow. Gregson, in strong contrast, with his round, smooth cheeks, slim hands, and build that was almost womanish, leaned over his side to meet him. For the twentieth time that evening the two men shook hands.

"Haven't forgotten Valencia, eh?" chuckled the artist, gloatingly. "Lord, but I'm glad to see you again, Phil. Seems like a century since we were out raising the Old Ned together, and yet it's less than three years since we came back from South America. Valencia! Will we ever forget it? When Burke handed me his first turn-down a month ago and said, 'Tom, your work begins to show you want a rest,' I thought of Valencia, and was so confoundedly homesick for those old days when you and

I pretty nearly started a revolution, and came within an ace of getting our scalps lifted, that I moped for a week. Gad, do I remember it? You got out by fighting, and I through a pretty girl."

"And your nerve," chuckled Whittemore, crushing the other's hand. "That was when I made up my mind you were the nerviest man alive, Greggy. Did you ever learn what became of Donna Isobel?"

"She appeared twice in Burke's, once as the 'Goddess of the Southern Republics' and again as 'The Girl of Valencia.' She married that reprobate of a Carabobo planter, and I believe they're happy."

"It seems to me there were others," continued Whittemore, pondering for a moment in mock seriousness. "There was one at Rio whom you swore would make your fortune if you could get her to sit for you, and whose husband was on the point of putting six inches of steel into you for telling her so, when I explained that you were young and harmless, and a little out of your head—"

"With your fist," cried Gregson, joyously. "Gad, but that was a mighty blow! I can see that knife now. I was just beginning my paternoster when—chug!—and down he went! And he deserved it. I said nothing wrong. In my very best Spanish I asked her if she would sit for me, and why the devil did he take that as an insult? And she was beautiful."

"Of course," agreed Whittemore. "If I remember, she was 'the loveliest creature you had ever seen.' And after that there were others—a score of them at least, each lovelier than the one before."

"They make up my life," said Gregson, more seriously than he had yet spoken. "They're the only thing I can draw and do well. I'd think an editor was mad if he asked me to do something without a pretty woman in it. God bless 'em, I hope I'll go on seeing them forever. When I can't see beauty in woman I want to die."

"And you always want to see it in the superlative degree."

"I insist upon it. If she lacks something, as Donna Isobel wanted color, I imagine that it is there, and she is perfect! But this one that I saw to-night is perfect! Now what I want to know is this, Who the deuce is she!"

—"where can she be found, and will she sit for a 'Burke,' two or three miscellaneous, and a 'study' for the annual sale," struck in Whittemore. "Is that it?"

"Exactly. You've a natural ability for hitting the nail on the head, Phil."

"And Burke told you to take a rest."

Gregson offered his cigarettes.

"Yes, Burke is a good-natured, poetic old soul who has a horror of spiders, snakes, and sky-scrapers. He said to me: 'Greggy, go and seek nature in some quiet, secluded place, and forget everything for a fortnight or two except your clothes and half a dozen cases of beer.' Rest! Nature! Beer! Think of those cheerful suggestions, Phil, while I was dreaming of Valencia, of Donna Isobels, and places where Nature cuts up as though she had been taking champagne all her life. Gad, your letter came just in time!"

"And I told you little enough in that," said Philip, quickly, rising and pacing uneasily back and forth across the cabin floor. "I gave you promise of excitement, and urged you to join me if you could. And why? Because—"

He turned sharply, and faced Gregson across the table.

"I wanted you to come because the thing that happened down in Valencia, and that other at Rio, isn't a circumstance to the hell that's going to cut loose pretty soon up here—and I'm in need of help. Understand? It's not fun—this time. I'm playing a single hand in what looks like a losing game. If I ever needed a fighter in my life I need one now. That's why I sent for you."

Gregson shoved back his chair and rose to his feet. He was a head shorter than his companion, of almost delicate physique. Yet there was something in the cold gray-blue of his eyes, a peculiar hardness of his chin, that compelled one to look at him twice and rendered first judgment unsafe. His slim fingers closed like steel about Philip's.

"Now you're coming down to business, Phil," he exclaimed. "I've been waiting with the patience of Job—or of little Bobby Tuckett, if you remember him, who began courting Minnie Sheldon seven years ago— and married her the day after I got your letter. I was too busy figuring out what you hadn't written to go to the wedding. I tried to read between the lines, and fell down completely. I've been thinking all the way up from Le Pas, and I'm still at sea. You called. I came. What's up?"

"It's going to sound a little mad—at first, Greggy," chuckled Whittemore, lighting his pipe. "It's going to give your esthetic tastes a jar. Look here!"

He seized Gregson by the arm and led him to the door.

The cold northern sky was brilliant with stars. The cabin, its logs half smothered in dying masses of verdure which had climbed about it during the summer, was built on the summit of one of the wind-cropped ridges which are called mountains in the far north. Into that north swept infinite wilderness, white and gray where the starlit tops of the spruce rose up at their feet, black in the distance. From somewhere out of it there came the low, weeping monotone of surf beating on a shore. Philip, with one hand on Gregson's shoulder, pointed with the other into the lonely desolation which they were facing.

"There isn't much between us and the Arctic Ocean, Greggy," he said. "See that light off there, like a great fire that has half a mind to die out one minute and flares up the next? Doesn't it remind you of the night we got away from Carabobo, when Donna Isobel pointed out our way to us, with the moon coming up over the mountains as a guide? That isn't the moon. It's the aurora borealis. You can hear the wash of the Bay down there, and if you're keen you can catch the smell of icebergs. There's Fort Churchill—a rifle-shot beyond the ridge, asleep. There's nothing but Hudson's Bay Company's posts, Indian camps, and trappers between here and civilization, which is four hundred miles down there. Seems like a quiet and peaceful country, doesn't it? There's something about it that makes you thrill and wonder if this isn't the biggest part of the universe after all. Listen! Hear the Indian dogs wailing down at Churchill! That's the primal voice in this world, the voice of the wild. Even that beating of the surf is filled with the same thing, for it's rolling up mystery instead of history. It is telling what man doesn't know, and in a language which he cannot understand. You're a beauty scientist, Greggy. This must sink deep."

"It does," said Gregson. "What the deuce are you getting at, Phil?"

"I'm arriving gradually and without undue haste to the point, Greggy. I'm about to tell you why I induced you to join me up here. I hesitate at the last word. It seems almost brutal, taking into consideration your philosophy of beauty, to drop from all this—from that blackness and mystery out there, from Donna Isobels and pretty eyes, down to—fish."

"Fish!"

"Yes, fish."

Gregson, lighting a fresh cigarette, held the match so that the tiny flame lighted up his companion's face for a moment.

"Look here," he expostulated, "you haven't got me up here to go—fishing?"

"Yes—and no," said Philip. "But even if I have—"

He caught Gregson by the arm again, and there was a tightness in the grip of his fingers which convinced the other that he was speaking seriously now.

JAMES OLIVER CURWOOD

"Do you remember what started the revolution down in Honduras the second week after we struck Puerto Barrios, Greggy? It was a girl, wasn't it?"

"Yes, and she wasn't half pretty at that."

"It was less than a girl," went on Philip. "Scene: the palm plaza at Ceiba. President Belize is drinking wine with his cousin, the fiancee of General O'Kelly Bonilla, the half Irish, half Latin-American leader of his forces, and his warmest friend. At a moment when their corner of the plaza is empty Belize helps himself to a cousinly kiss. O'Kelly, unperceived, arrives in time to witness the act. From that moment his friendship for Belize turns to hatred and jealousy. Within three weeks he has started a revolution, beats the government forces at Ceiba, chases Belize from the capital, gets Nicaragua mixed up in the trouble, and draws three French, two German, and two American war-ships to the scene. Six weeks after the wine-drinking he is President of the Republic, en facto. And all of this, Greggy, because of a kiss. Now, if a kiss can start a revolution, unseat a President, send a government to smash, what must be the possibilities of a fish?"

"I'm getting interested," said Gregson. "If there's a climax, come to it, Phil. I admit that there must be enormous possibilities in—a fish. Go on!"

II

For a moment the two men stood in silence, listening to the sullen beat of surf beyond the black edge of forest. Then Philip led the way back into the cabin.

Gregson followed. In the light of the big oil-lamp which hung suspended from the ceiling he noticed something in Whittemore's face he had not observed before, a tenseness about the muscles of his mouth, a restlessness in his eyes, rigidity of jaw, an air of suppressed emotion which puzzled him. He was keenly observant of details, and knew that these things had been missing a short time before. The pleasure of their meeting that afternoon, after a separation of nearly two years, had dispelled for a time the trouble which he now saw revealing itself in his companion's face and attitude, and the lightness of Whittemore's manner in beginning his explanation for inducing him to come into the north had helped to complete the mask. There occurred to him, for an instant, a picture which he had once drawn of Whittemore as he had known him in certain stirring times still fresh in the memory of each—a picture of the old, cool, irresistible Whittemore, smiling in the face of danger, laughing outright at perplexities, always ready to fight with a good-natured word on his lips. He had drawn that picture for Burke's, and had called it "The Fighter." Burke himself had criticized it because of the smile. But Gregson knew his man. It was Whittemore.

There was a change now. He had grown older, surprisingly older. There were deeper lines about his eyes. His face was thinner. He saw, now, that Philip's lightness had been but a passing flash of his old buoyancy, that the old life and sparkle had gone from him. Two years, he judged, had woven things into Philip's life which he could not understand, and he wondered if this was why in all that time he had received no word from his old college chum.

They had seated themselves at opposite sides of the table, and from an inside pocket Philip produced a small bundle of papers. From these he drew forth a map, which he smoothed out under his hands.

"Yes, there are possibilities—and more, Greggy," he said. "I didn't ask you up here to help me fight air and moonshine. And I've promised you a fight. Have you ever seen a rat in a trap with a blood-thirsty terrier guarding the little door that is about to be opened? Thrilling sport for the prisoner, isn't it? But when the rat happens to be human—"

JAMES OLIVER CURWOOD

"I thought it was a fish," protested Gregson, mildly. "Pretty soon you'll be having it a girl in a trap—or at the end of a fish-line—"

"And if I should?" interrupted Philip, looking steadily at him. "What if I should say there is a girl—a woman—in this trap—not only one, but a score, a hundred of them? What then, Greggy?"

"I'd say there was going to be a glorious scrap."

"And so there is, the biggest and most unusual scrap of its kind you ever heard of, Greggy. It's going to be a queer kind of fight—and queer fighting. And it's possible—very probable—that you and I will get lost in the shuffle somewhere. We're two, no more. And we're going up against forces which would make a dozen South American revolutions look like thirty cents. More than that, it's likely we'll be in the wrong locality when certain people rise in a wrath which a Helen of Troy aroused in another people some centuries ago. See here—"

He turned the map to Gregson, pointing with his finger.

"See that red line? That's the new railroad to Hudson's Bay. It is well above Le Pas now, and its builders plan to complete it by next spring. It is the most wonderful piece of railroad building on the American continent, Greggy—wonderful because it has been neglected so long. Something like a hundred million people have been asleep to its enormous value, and they're just waking up now. That road, cutting across four hundred miles of wilderness, is opening up a country half as big as the United States, in which more mineral wealth will be dug during the next fifty years than will ever be taken from Yukon or Alaska. It is shortening the route from Montreal, Duluth, Chicago, and the Middle West to Liverpool and other European ports by a thousand miles. It means the making of a navigable sea out of Hudson's Bay, cities on its shores, and great steel-foundries close to the Arctic Circle— where there is coal and iron enough to supply the world for hundreds of years. That's only a small part of what this road means, Greggy. Two years ago—you remember I asked you to join me in the adventure— I came up seeking opportunity. I didn't dream then—"

Whittemore paused, and a flash of his old smile passed over his face.

"I didn't dream that fate had decreed me to stir up what I'm going to tell you about, Greggy. I followed the line of the proposed railroad, looking for chances. All Canada was asleep, or too much interested in its west, and gave me no competition. I was alone west of the surveyed line; east of it steel-corporation men had optioned mountains of iron and another interest had a grip on coal-fields. Six months I spent among the Indians, French, and half-breeds. I lived with them, trapped and hunted with them, and picked up a little Cree and French. The life suited me. I became a northerner in heart and soul, if not quite yet in full experience. Clubs and balls and cities grew to be only memories. You know how I have always hated that hothouse sort of existence, and you know that same world of clubs and balls and cities has gripped at my throat, downing me again and again, as though it returned my sentiment with interest. Up here I learned to hate it more than ever. I was completely happy. And then—"

He had refolded the map, and drew another from the bundle of papers. It was drawn in pencil.

"And then, Greggy," he went on, smoothing out this map where the other had been, "I struck my chance. It fairly clubbed me into recognizing it. It came in the middle of the night, and I sat up with a camp-fire laughing at me through the flap in my tent, stunned by the knockout it had given me. It seemed, at first, as though a gold-mine had walked up and laid itself down at my feet, and I wondered how there could be so many silly fools in this world of ours. Take a look at that map, Greggy. What do you see?"

Gregson had listened like one under a spell. It was one of his careless boasts that situations could not faze him, that he was immune to outward betrayals of sensation. This seeming indifference—his light-toned attitude in the face of most serious affairs would have made a failure of him in many things. But his tense interest did not hide itself now. A cigarette remained unlighted between his fingers. His eyes never took themselves for an instant from his companion's face. Something that Whittemore had not yet said thrilled him. He looked at the map.

"There's not much to see," he said, "but lakes and rivers."

"You're right," exclaimed Philip, jumping suddenly from his chair and beginning to walk back and forth across the cabin. "Lakes and rivers—hundreds of them—thousands of them! Greggy, there are more than three thousand lakes between here and civilization and within forty miles of the new railroad. And nine out of ten of those lakes are so full of fish that the bears along 'em smell fishy. Whitefish, Gregson—whitefish and trout. There is a fresh-water area represented on that map three times as large as the whole of the five Great Lakes, and yet the Canadians and the government have never wakened up to what it means. There's a fish supply in this northland large enough to feed the world, and that little rim of lakes that I've mapped out along the edge of the coming railroad represents a money value of millions. That was the idea that came to me in the middle of the night, and then I thought—if I could get a corner on a few of these lakes, secure fishing privileges before the road came—"

"You'd be a millionaire," said Gregson.

"Not only that," replied Philip, pausing for a moment in his restless pacing. "I didn't think of money, at first; at least, it was a secondary consideration after that night beside the camp-fire. I saw how this big vacant north could be made to strike a mighty blow at those interests which make a profession of cornering meatstuffs on the other side, how it could be made to fight the fight of the people by sending down an unlimited supply of fish that could be sold at a profit in New York, Boston, or Chicago for a half of what the trust demands. My scheme wasn't aroused entirely by philanthropy, mind you. I saw in it a chance to get back at the very people who brought about my father's ruin, and who kept pounding him after he was in a corner until he broke down and died. They killed him. They robbed me a few years later. They made me hate what I was once, a moving, joyous part of—life down there. I went from the north, first to Ottawa, then to Toronto and Winnipeg. After that I went to Brokaw, my father's old partner, with the scheme. I've told you of Brokaw—one of the deepest, shrewdest old fighters in the Middle West. It was only a year after my father's death that he was on his feet again, as strong as ever. Brokaw drew in two or three others as strong as himself, and we went after the privileges. It was a fight from the beginning. Hardly were our plans made public before we were met by powerful opposition. A combination of Canadian capital quickly organized and petitioned for the same privileges. Old Brokaw knew what it meant. It was the hand of the trust—disguised under a veneer of Canadian promoters. They called us 'aliens'—American 'money-grabbers' robbing Canadians of what justly belonged to them. They aroused two-thirds of the press against us, and yet—"

The lines in Whittemore's face softened. He chuckled as he pulled out his pipe and began filling it.

"They had to go some to beat the old man, Greggy. I don't know just how Brokaw pulled the thing off, but I do know that when we won out three members of parliament and half a dozen other politicians were honorary members of our organization, and that it cost Brokaw a hundred thousand dollars! Our opponents had raised such a howl, calling upon the patriotism of the country and pointing out that the people of the north would resent this invasion of foreigners, that we succeeded in getting only a provisional license, subject to withdrawal by the government at any time conditions seemed to warrant it. I saw in this no blow to my scheme, for I was certain that we could carry the thing along on such a square basis that within a year the whole country would be in sympathy with us. I expressed my views with enthusiasm at our final meeting, when the seven of us met to complete our plans. Brokaw and the other five were to direct matters in the south; I was to have full command of affairs in the north. A month later I was at work. Over here"—he leaned over Gregson's shoulder and placed a forefinger on the map—"I established our headquarters, with MacDougall, a Scotch engineer, to help me. Within six months we had a hundred and fifty men at Blind Indian Lake, fifty canoemen bringing in supplies, and another gang putting in stations over a stretch of more than a hundred miles of lake country. Everything was working smoothly, better than I had expected. At Blind Indian Lake we had a shipyard, two warehouses, ice-houses, a company store, and a population of three hundred, and had nearly completed a ten-mile roadbed for narrow-gauge steel, which would connect us with the main line when it came up to us. I was completely lost in my work. At times I almost forgot Brokaw and the others. I was particularly careful of the funds sent up to me, and had accomplished my work at a cost of a little under a hundred thousand. At the end of the six months, when I was about to make a visit into the south, one of our warehouses and ten thousand dollars' worth of supplies went up in smoke. It was our first misfortune, and it was a big one. It was about the first matter that I brought up after I had shaken hands with Brokaw."

Philip's face was set and white as he stood in the middle of the room looking at Gregson.

"And what do you think was his reply, Greggy? He looked at me for a moment, a peculiar twitching around the corners of his mouth, and then said, 'Don't allow a trivial matter like that to worry you, Philip. Why—we've already cleaned up a million on this little fish deal!'"

Gregson sat up with a jerk.

"A million! Great Scott—"

"Yes, a million, Greggy," said Philip, softly, with his old fighting smile. "There was a hundred thousand dollars to my credit in a First National Bank. Pleasant surprise, eh?"

Gregson had dropped his cigarette. His slim hands gripped the edges of the table. He made no reply as he waited for Whittemore to continue.

III

For a full minute Philip paced back and forth without speaking. Then he stopped, and faced Gregson, who was staring at him.

"A million, Greggy," he repeated, in the same soft voice. "A hundred thousand dollars to my credit—in a First National Bank! While I was up here hustling to get affairs on a working basis, eager to show the government and the people what we could do and would do, triumphing in our victory over the trust, and figuring each day on my scheme of making this big, rich north deal a staggering blow to those accursed combinations down there, they were at work, too. While I was dreaming and doing these things, Brokaw and the others had formed the Great Northern Fish and Development Company, had incorporated it under the laws of New Jersey, and had already sold over a million dollars' worth of stock! The thing was in full swing when I reached headquarters. I had authorized Brokaw to act for me, and I found that I was vice-president of one of the biggest legalized robbery combinations of recent years. More money had been spent in advertising than in development work. Hundreds of thousands of copies of my letters from the north, filled to the brim with the enthusiasm I had felt for my work and projects, had been sent out broadcast, luring buyers of stock. In one of these letters I had said that if a half of the lakes I had mapped out were fished the north could be made to produce a million tons of fish a year. Two hundred thousand copies of this letter were sent out, but Brokaw and his associates had omitted the words, 'If a half of the lakes mapped out were fished.' It would take fifteen thousand men, a thousand refrigerator cars, and a capital of five million to bring this about. I was stunned by the enormity of their fraud, and yet when I threatened to bring the whole thing to smash Brokaw only laughed and pointed out that not a single caution had been omitted. In all of the advertising it was frankly stated that our license was provisional, subject to withdrawal if the company did not keep within laws. That very frankness was an advertisement. It was something different. It struck home where it was meant to strike—among small and unfledged investors. It roped them in by thousands. The shares were ten dollars each, and non-assessable. Five out of six orders were from one to five shares; ninety-nine out of every hundred were not above ten shares. It was damnable. The very people for whom I wanted the north to fight had been humbugged to the tune of a million and a quarter dollars. Within a year Brokaw and the others had floated a scheme which was worse than any trust, for the trusts pay back a part of their steals in dividends. And *I* was responsible! Do you realize that, Greggy? It was I who started the project. It was my reports from the north which chiefly induced people to buy. And this company—a company of robbers licensed under the law—I am its founder and its vice-president!"

Philip dropped back into his chair. The face that he turned to Gregson was damp with perspiration, though the room was chilly.

"You stayed in," said Gregson.

"I had to. There wasn't a loophole left open to me. There wasn't a single point at which I could bring attack against Brokaw and the others. They were six veritable Bismarcks of deviltry and shrewdness. They hadn't over-stepped the law. They had sold a million and a quarter of stock on a hundred-thousand-dollar investment, but Brokaw only laughed when I raged at this. 'Why, Philip,' he said, 'we value our license alone at over a million!' And there was no law which could prevent them from placing that value upon it, or more. There was one thing that I could do—and only one. I could resign, decline to accept my stock and the hundred thousand, and publicly announce why I had broken off my connections with the company. I was about to do this when cooler judgment prevailed. It occurred to me that there would have to be an accounting. The company might sell a million and a quarter of stock— but in the end there would have to be an accounting. If I was out of the game it would be easily made. If I was in—well, do you see, Greggy? There was still a chance of making the company win out as a legitimate enterprise, even though it began under the black flag of piratical finance and fraud. Brokaw and the others were astonished at the stand I took. It was like throwing a big, ripe plum into the fire Brokaw was the first to hedge. He came over to my side in a private interview which we had, and for the first time I convinced him completely of the tremendous possibilities before us. To my surprise he began to show actual enthusiasm in my favor. We figured out how the company, if properly developed, could be made to pay a dividend of fifty cents a share on the stock issued within two years. This, I thought, would be at least a partial return of the original steal. Brokaw worked the thing through in his own way. He was authorized to vote for one of the directors, who was in Europe, and he won over two of the others. As a consequence we voted all of the money in the treasury, nearly six hundred thousand dollars, and the remainder of the stock that was on the market, for development purposes. Brokaw then made the proposition that the company buy up any interest that wished to withdraw. The two M. P. 's and a professional promoter from Toronto immediately sold out at fifty thousand each. With their original hundred thousand these three retired with an aggregate steal of nearly half a million. Pretty good work for yours truly, eh, Greggy! Good Heaven, think of it! I started out to strike a blow, to launch a gigantic project for the people, and this was what I had hatched! Robbery, bribery, fraud—"

He paused, his hands clenched until the blue veins stood out on them like whipcords.

"And—"

Gregson spoke, uneasily.

"And what?"

Philip's fingers relaxed their grip on the table.

"If that had been all, I wouldn't have called you up here," he continued. "I've taken a long time in coming down to the real hell of the affair, because I wanted you to understand the situation from the beginning. After I left Brokaw I came north again. I possessed all the funds necessary to make an honest working organization out of the Northern Fish and Development Company. I hired two hundred additional men, added twenty new fishing-stations, began a second road-bed to the main line, and started a huge dam at Blind Indian Lake. We had thirty horses, driven up through the wilderness from Le Pas, and twenty teams on the way. There didn't appear to be an important obstacle in the path of our success, and I had recovered most of my old enthusiasm when Brokaw sprung a new mine under my feet.

"He had written a long letter almost immediately after I left him, which had been delayed at several places. In it he told me that he had discovered a plot to wreck our enterprise, that some powerful force was about to be pitted against us in the very country we were holding. I could see that Brokaw was tremendously worked up when he wrote the letter, and that for once he felt himself outwitted by a rival faction, and realized to the full a danger which it took me some time to comprehend. He had discovered absolute evidence, he said, that the bunch of trust capitalists whom he had beaten were about to attack us in another way. Their forces were already moving into the north country. Their object was to stir up the country against us, to bring about that condition of unrest and antagonism between the people of the north and ourselves which would compel the government to take away our license. Remember, this license was only provisional. It was, in fact, left to the people of the north to decide whether we should remain among them or not. If they turned against us there would be only one thing for the government to do.

"At first Brokaw's letter caused me no very great uneasiness. I knew the people up here. I knew that the Indian, the Breed, the Frenchman, and the White of this God's country were as invulnerable to bribery as Brokaw himself is to the pangs of conscience. I loved them. I had faith in them. I knew them to possess an honor which is not known down there, where we have a church on every four corners, and where the Word of God is preached day and night on the open streets. I felt myself warming with indignation as I replied to Brokaw, resenting his insinuations as to the crimes which a 'half-savage' people might be induced to commit for a little whisky and a little money. And then—"

Whittemore wiped his face. The lines settled deeper about his mouth.

"Greggy, a week after I received this letter two warehouses were burned on the same night at Blind Indian Lake. They were three hundred yards apart. There is absolutely no doubt that it was incendiarism."

He waited in silence, but Gregson still sat watching him in silence.

"That was the beginning—three months ago. Since then some mysterious force has been fighting us at every step. A week after the warehouses burned, a dredge and boat-building yard, which we had constructed at considerable expense at the mouth of the Gray Beaver, was destroyed by fire. A little later a 'premature' explosion of dynamite cost us ten thousand dollars and two weeks' labor of fifty men. I organized a special guard service, composed of fifty of my best men, but it seemed to do no good. Since then we have lost three miles of road-bed, destroyed by a washout. A terrific charge of dynamite had been used to let down upon us the water of a lake which was situated at the top of a ridge near our right of way. Whoever our enemies are, they seem to know our most secret movements, and attack us whenever we leave a vulnerable point open. The most surprising part of the whole affair is this: in spite of my own efforts to keep our losses quiet the rumor has spread for hundreds of miles around us, even reaching Churchill, that the northerners have declared war against our enterprise and are determined to drive us out. Two-thirds of my men believe this. MacDougall, my engineer, believes it. Between my working forces and the Indians, French, and half-breeds about us there has slowly developed a feeling of suspicion and resentment. It is growing—every day, every hour. If it continues it can result in but two things—ruin for ourselves, triumph for those who are getting at us in this dastardly manner. If something is not done very soon—within a month—perhaps less—the country will run with the blood of vengeance from Churchill to the Barrens. If what I expect to happen does happen there will be no government road built to the Bay, the new buildings at Churchill will turn gray with disuse, the treasures of the north will remain undisturbed, the country itself will slip back a hundred years. The forest people will be filled with hatred and suspicion so long as the story of great wrong travels down from father to son. And this wrong, this crime—"

Philip's face was white, cold, almost passionless in the grim hardness that had settled in it. He unfolded a long typewritten letter, and handed it to Gregson.

"That letter is the final word," he explained. "It will tell you what I have not told you. In some way it was mixed in my mail and I did not discover the error until I had opened it. It is from the headquarters of our enemies, addressed to the man who is in charge of their plot up here."

"He waited, scarce breathing, while Gregson bent over the typewritten pages. He noted the slow tightening of the other's fingers as he turned from the first sheet to the second; he watched Gregson's face, the slow ebbing of color, the gray white that followed it, the stiffening of his arms and shoulders as he finished. Then Gregson looked up.

"Good God!" he breathed.

For a full half-minute the two men gazed at each other across the table, without speaking.

IV

P hilip broke the silence.

"Now—you understand."

"It is impossible!" gasped Gregson. "I cannot believe this! It—it might have happened a thousand—two thousand years ago—but not now. My God, man!" he cried, more excitedly. "You do not mean to tell me that you believe this will be done?"

"Yes," replied Philip.

"It is impossible!" exclaimed Gregson again, crushing the letter in his hand. "A man doesn't live—a combination doesn't exist—that would start such a hell loose as this—in this way!"

Philip smiled grimly.

"The man does live, and the combination does exist," he said, slowly. "Greggy, I have known of men, and of combinations who have spent millions, who have sacrificed everything of honor and truth, who have driven thousands of men, women, and children to starvation— and worse—to achieve a victory in high finance. I have known of men and combinations who have broken almost every law of man and God in the fight for money and power. And so have you! You have associated with some of these men. You have laughed and talked with them, smoked with them, and have dined at their tables. You spent a week at Selden's summer borne, and it was Selden who cornered wheat three years ago and raised the price of bread two cents a loaf. It was Selden who brought about the bread riots in New York, Chicago, and a score of other cities, who swung wide the prison doors for thousands, whose millions were gained at a cost of misery, crime, and even death. And Selden is only one out of thousands who live to-day, watching for their opportunities, giving no heed to those who may fall under the juggernaut of their capital. This isn't the age of petty discrimination, Greggy. It's the age of the almighty dollar, and of the fight for it. And there's no chivalry, no quarter shown in this fight. Men of Selden's stamp don't stop at women and children. The scrubwoman's dollar is just as big as yours or mine, and if a scheme could be promoted whereby every scrubwoman in America could be safely robbed of a dollar you'd find thousands of men down there in our cities ready to go into it to-morrow. And to such men as these what is the sacrifice of a few women up here?"

Gregson dropped the letter, crumpled and twisted, upon the table.

"I wonder—if I understand," he said, looking into Philip's white face. "There has undoubtedly been previous correspondence, and this letter contains the final word. It shows that your enemies have already succeeded in working up the forest people against you, and have filled them with suspicion. Their last blow is to be—"

He stopped, and Philip nodded at the horrified question in his eyes.

"Greggy, up here there is one law which reigns above all other law. When I was in Prince Albert a year ago I was sitting on the veranda of the little old Windsor Hotel. About me were a dozen wild men of the north, who had come down for a day or two to the edge of civilization. Most of those men had not been out of the forests for a year. Two of them were from the Barrens, and this was their first glimpse of civilized life in five years. As we sat there a woman came up the street. She turned in at the hotel. About me there was a sudden lowering of voices, a shuffling of feet. As she passed, every one of those twelve rose from their seats and stood with bowed heads and their caps in their hands until she had gone. I was the only one who remained sitting! That, Greggy, is the one great law of life up here, the worship of woman because she is woman. A man may steal, he may kill, but he must not break this law. If he steals or kills, the mounted police may bring the offender to justice; but if he breaks this other law there is but one punishment, and that is the punishment of the people. That is what this letter purposes to do—to break this law in order that its penalty may fall upon us. And if they succeed, God help us!"

It was Gregson who jumped to his feet now. He took half a dozen nervous steps, paused, lighted a cigarette, and looked down into Philip's upturned face.

"I understand now where the fight is coming in," he said. "If this thing goes through, these people will rise and wipe you off the map. They'll lay it to you and your men, of course. And I fancy it won't be a job half done if they feel about it as I'd feel. But," he demanded, sharply, "why don't you put the affair into the hands of the proper authorities— the police or the government? You've got—By George, you must have the name of the man to whom that letter was addressed!"

Philip handed him a soiled white envelope, of the kind in which official documents are usually mailed.

"That's the man."

Gregson gave a low whistle.

"Lord—Fitzhugh—Lee!" he read, slowly, as though scarce believing his eyes. "Great Scott! A British peer!"

The cynical smile on Philip's lips cut his words short.

"Perhaps," he said. "But if there is a British lord up here he isn't very well known, Greggy. No one knows of him. No one has heard a rumor of him. That is why we can't go to the police or the government. They'd give small credence to what we've got to show. This letter wouldn't count the weight of a feather without further evidence, and a lot of it. Besides, we haven't time to go to the government. It is too far away and too slow. And as for the police—I know of three in this territory, and there are fifteen thousand square miles of mountains and plains and forest in their 'beat.' It's up to you and me to find this Lord Fitzhugh. If we can do that we will be in a position to put a kibosh on this plot in a hurry. If we fail to run him down—"

"What then?"

"We'll have to watch our chances. I've told you all that I know, and you're on an even working basis with me. At first I thought that I understood the object of those who are planning to ruin us in this cowardly manner. But I don't now. If they ruin us they also destroy the chances of any other company that may be scheming to usurp our place. For that reason I—"

"There must still be other factors in the game," said Gregson, as Philip hesitated.

"There are. I want you to work out your own suspicions, Greggy, and then we'll compare notes. Lord Fitzhugh is the key to the whole situation. No matter who is at the bottom of this plot, Lord Fitzhugh is the man at the working end of it. We don't care so much about the writer of this letter as the one to whom it was written. It is evident that he had planned to be at Churchill, for the letter is addressed to him here. But he hasn't shown up. He has never been here, so far as I can discover."

"I'd give a year's growth for a copy of the British Peerage or a Who's Who," mused Gregson, flecking the ashes from his cigarette. "Who the deuce can this Lord Fitzhugh be? What sort of an Englishman would mix up in a dirty job of this kind? You might imagine him to be one of the men behind the guns, like Brokaw. But, by George, he's working the dirty end of it himself, according to that letter!"

"You're beginning to use your head already, Greggy," said Philip, a little more cheerfully. "I've asked myself that question a hundred times during the last three days, and I'm more at sea than ever. If it had been plain Tom Brown or Bill Jones, the name would not have suggested anything beyond what you have read in the letter. That's the question: Why should a Lord Fitzhugh Lee be mixed up in this affair?"

The two men looked at each other keenly for a few moments in silence.

"It suggests—" began Gregson.

"What?"

"That there may be a bigger scheme behind this affair than we imagine. In fact, it suggests to me that the northerners are being stirred up against you and your men for some other and more powerful reason than to make you get out of the country and compel the government to withdraw your license. So help me God, I believe there's more behind it!"

"So do I," said Philip, quietly.

"Have you any suspicions of what might be the more powerful motive?"

"None. I know that British capital is heavily interested in mineral lands east of the surveyed line. But there is none at Churchill. All operations have been carried on from Montreal and Toronto."

"Have you written to Brokaw about this letter?"

"You are the first to whom I have revealed its contents," said Philip. "I have neglected to tell you that Brokaw is so worked up over the affair that he is joining me in the north. The Hudson's Bay Company's ship, which comes over twice a year, touches at Halifax, and if Brokaw followed out his intentions he took passage there. The ship should be in within a week or ten days. And, by the way"—Philip stood up and thrust his hands deep in his pockets as he spoke, half smiling at Gregson— "it gives me pleasure to hand you a bit of cheerful information along with that," he added. "Miss Brokaw is coming with him. She is very beautiful."

Gregson held a lighted match until it burnt his finger-tips.

"The deuce you say! I've heard—"

"Yes, you have heard of her beauty, no doubt. I am not a special enthusiast in your line, Greggy, but I will confirm your opinion of Miss Brokaw. You will say that she is the most beautiful girl you have ever seen, and you will want to make heads of her for BURKE's. I suppose you wonder why she is coming up here? So do I."

There was a look of perplexity in Philip's eyes which Gregson might have noticed if he had not gone to the door to look out into the night.

"What makes the stars so big and bright up in this country, Phil?" he asked.

"Because of the clearness of the atmosphere through which you are looking," replied Philip, wondering what was passing through the other's mind. "This air—compared with ours—is just like a piece of glass that has been cleaned of a year's accumulation of dirt."

Gregson whistled softly for a few moments. Then he said, without turning:

"She's got to go some if she beats the girl I saw this evening, Phil." He turned at Philip's silence, and laughed. "I beg your pardon, old man, I didn't mean to speak of her as if she were a horse. I mean Miss Brokaw."

"And I don't particularly like the idea of betting on the merits of a pretty girl," replied Philip, "but I'll break the rule for once, and wager you the best hat in New York that she does beat her."

"Done!" said Gregson. "A little gentle excitement of this sort will relieve the tension of the other thing, Phil. I've heard enough of business for to-night. I'm going to finish a sketch that I have begun of her before I forget the fine points. Any objection?"

"None at all," said Philip. "Meanwhile I'll go out to breathe a spell."

He put on his coat and took down his cap from a peg in the wall. Gregson had seated himself under the lamp and was sharpening a pencil. As Philip went to go out Gregson drew an envelope from his pocket and tossed it on the table.

"If you should happen to see any one that looks like—her," he said, nodding toward the envelope, "kindly put in a word for me, will you? I did that in a hurry. It's not half flattering."

Philip laughed as he picked up the envelope.

"The most beau—" he began.

He caught himself with a jerk. Gregson, looking up from his pencil-sharpening, saw the smile leave his lips and a quick flush leap into his bronzed cheeks. He stared at the face on the envelope for a half a minute, then gazed speechlessly at Gregson.

It was Gregson who laughed, softly and without suspicion.

"How does your wager look now?" he taunted.

"She—is—beautiful," murmured Philip, dropping the envelope and turning to the door, "Don't wait for me, Greggy. Go to bed."

He heard Gregson laugh behind him, and he wondered, as he went out, what Gregson would say if he told him that he had drawn on the back of the old envelope the beautiful face of Eileen Brokaw!

V

A dozen steps beyond the door Philip paused in the shadow of a dense spruce, half persuaded to return. From where he stood he could see Gregson bending over the table, already at work on the picture. He confessed that the sketch had startled him. He knew that it had sent the hot blood rushing to his face, and that only through a fortunate circumstance had Gregson ascribed its effect upon him to something that was wide of the truth. Miss Brokaw was a thousand or more miles away. At this moment she was somewhere in the North Atlantic, if their ship had left Halifax. She had never been in the north. More than that, he knew that Gregson had never seen Miss Brokaw, and had heard of her only through himself and the society columns of the newspapers. How could he explain his possession of the sketch?

He drew a step or two nearer to the open door, and stopped again. If he returned to question Gregson it would draw him perilously near to explanations which he did not care to make, to the one secret which he wished to guard from his friend's knowledge. After all, the picture was only a resemblance. It could be nothing but a resemblance, even though it was so striking and unusual that it had thrown him off his guard at first. When he returned later and looked at it again he would no doubt be able to see his error.

He walked on through the spruce shadows and up a narrow trail that led to the bald knob of the ridge, feeling his way with his right hand before him when the denseness of the forest shut out the light of the stars and the moon, until at last he stood out strong and clear under the glow of the skies, with the world sweeping out in black and gray mystery around him. To the north was the Bay, reaching away like a vast black plain. Half a mile distant two or three lights were burning over Fort Churchill, red eyes peering up out of the deep pool of darkness; to the south and west there swept the gray, starlit distances which lay between him and civilization.

He leaned against a great rock, resting his elbows in a carpet of moss, and his eyes turned into the mystery of those distances. The sea of spruce-tops that rose out of the ragged valley at his feet whispered softly in the night wind; from out of their depths trembled the low hoot of an owl; over the vaster desolation beyond hovered a weird and unbroken silence. More than once the spirit of this world had come to him in the night and had roused him from his slumber to sit alone out under the stars, imagining all that it might tell him if he could read the voice of it in the whispering of the trees, if he could but understand it as he longed to understand it, and could find in it the peace which he knew that it all but held for him. The spirit of it had never been nearer to him than to-night. He felt it close to him, so near that it seemed like the warm, vibrant touch of a presence at his side, something which had come to him in a voiceless loneliness as great as his own, watching and listening with him beside the rock. It seemed nearer to him since he had seen and talked with Gregson. It was much nearer to him since a few minutes ago, when he had looked upon what he had first thought to be the face of Eileen Brokaw.

And this was the world—the spirit—that had changed him. He wondered if Gregson had seen the change which he tried so hard to conceal. He wondered if Miss Brokaw would see it when she came, and if her soft, gray eyes would read to the bottom of him as they had fathomed him once before upon a time which seemed years and years ago. Thoughts like these troubled him. Twice that day he had found stealing over him a feeling that was almost physical pain, and yet he knew that this pain was but the gnawing of a great loneliness in his heart. In these moments he had been sorry that he had brought Gregson back into his life. And with Gregson he was bringing back Eileen Brokaw. He was more than sorry for that. The thought of it made him grow warm and uncomfortable, though the night air from off the Bay was filled with the chill tang of the northern icebergs. Again his thoughts brought him face to face with the old pictures, the old life. With them came haunting memories of a Philip Whittemore who had once lived, and who had died; and with these ghosts of the past there surged upon him the loneliness which seemed to crush and stifle him. Like one in a dream he was swept back. Over the black spruce at his feet, far into the gray, misty distances beyond, over forests and mountains and the vast, grim silences his vision reached out until he saw life as it had begun for him, and as he had lived it for a time. It had opened fair. It had given promise. It had filled him with hope and ambition. And then it had changed.

Unconsciously he clenched his hands as he thought of what had followed, of the black days of ruin, of death, of the dissolution of all that he had hoped and dreamed for. He had fought, because he was born a fighter. He had risen again and again, only to find misfortune still at his face. At first he had laughed, and had called it bad luck. But the bad luck had followed him, dogging him with a persistence which developed in him a new perspective of things. He dropped away from his clubs. He began to measure men and women as he had not measured them before, and there grew in him slowly a revulsion for what those measurements revealed. The spirit that was growing in him called out for bigger things, for the wild freedom which he had tasted for a time with Gregson—for a life which was not warped by the gilded amenities of the crowded ballroom to-night, by the frenzied dollar-fight to-morrow. No one could understand that change in him. He could find no spirit in sympathy with him, no chord in another breast that he could reach out and touch and thrill with understanding. Once he had hoped—and tried—

A deep breath, almost a sigh, fell from his lips as he thought of that last night, at the Brokaw ball. He heard again the laughter and chatter of men and women, the soft rustle of skirts—and then the break, the silence, as the low, sweet music of his favorite waltz began, while he stood screened behind a bank of palms looking down into the clear gray eyes of Eileen Brokaw. He saw himself as he had stood then, leaning over her slim white shoulders, intoxicated by her beauty, his face pale with the fear of what he was about to say; and he saw the girl, with her beautiful head thrown a little back, so that her golden hair almost touched his lips, waiting for him to speak. For months he had fought against the fascination of her beauty. Again and again he had almost surrendered to it, only to pull himself back in time. He had seen this girl, as pure-looking as an angel, strike deeply at the hearts of other men; he had heard her laugh and talk lightly of the wounds she had made. Behind the eyes which gazed up at him, dear and sweet as pools of sunlit water, he knew there lay the consuming passion for power, for admiration, for the froth-like pleasures of the life that was swirling about them. Sincerity was but their mask. He knew that the beautiful gray eyes lied to him when he saw in them all that he held glorious in womanhood.

He laughed softly to himself as the picture grew in his mind, and he saw Ransom come blundering in through the palms, mopping his red face and chattering inane things to little Miss Meesen. Ransom was always blundering. This time his blunder saved Philip. The passionate words died on his lips; and when Ransom and Miss Meesen turned about in a giggling flutter, he spoke no words of love, but opened up his heart to this girl whom he would have loved if she had been like her eyes. It was his last hope—that she would understand him, see with him the emptiness of his life, sympathize with him.

And she had laughed at him!

She had risen to her feet; there had come for an instant a flash like that of fire in her eyes; her voice trembled a little when she spoke. There was resentment in the poise of her white shoulders as Ransom's voice came to them in a loud laugh from behind the palms; her red lips showed disdain and anger. She hated Ransom for breaking in; she despised Philip for allowing the interruption to tear away her triumph. Her own betrayal of herself was like tonic to Philip. He laughed joyously when he was alone out in the cool night air. Ransom never knew why Philip hunted him out and shook his fat hand so warmly at parting.

Philip again felt himself in the fever of that night as he turned from the rock and began picking his way down the side of the ridge toward the Bay. He found himself wondering what had become of good-natured, dense-headed Ransom, who had all he could do to spend his father's allowance. From Ransom his thoughts turned to little Harry Dell, Roscoe, big Dan Philips, and three or four others who had sacrificed their hearts at Miss Brokaw's feet. He grimaced as he thought of young Dell, who had worshiped the ground she walked on, and who had gone straight to the devil when she threw him over. He wondered, too, where Roscoe was. He knew that Roscoe would have won out if it had not been for the financial crash which took his brokerage firm off its feet and left him a pauper. He had heard that Roscoe had gone up into British Columbia to recuperate his fortune in Douglas fir. As for big Dan—

Philip stumbled over a rock, and rose with a bruised knee. The shock brought him back to realities, and a few moments later he stood upon the narrow boulder-strewn beach, rubbing his knee and calling himself a fool for allowing the old thoughts to stir him up. Out there, somewhere, Brokaw and his daughter were coming. That Miss Brokaw was with her father was a circumstance which was of no importance to him. At least he told himself so, and set his face toward Churchill.

To-night the stars and the moon seemed to be more than usually brilliant. About him the great masses of rock, the tumbling surf, the edge of the forest, and the Bay itself were illumined as if by the light of a softly radiant day. He looked at his watch and found that it was past midnight. He had been up since dawn, and yet he felt no touch of fatigue, no need of sleep. He took off his cap and walked bareheaded in the mellow light, his moccasined feet falling lightly, his eyes alert to all that this wonderful night world might hold for him. Ahead of him rose a giant mass of rock, worn smooth and slippery by the water dashed against it in the crashing storms of countless centuries, and this he climbed, panting when he reached the top. His eyes turned to where he saw Fort Churchill sleeping along the edge of the Bay.

In that same spot, a great pool of night-glow between two forest-crowned ridges, it had lain for hundreds of years. He passed the ancient landing-place of rocks, built a hundred and fifty years ago for the first ships that came over the strange sea; he stood upon the tumbled foundations of the Fort, that was still older, and saw the starlight glinting on one of the brass cannon that lay where it had fallen amid the debris, untouched and unmoved since the days, ages-gone, when it had last thundered its welcome or its defiance through the solitudes; he walked slowly along the shore where the sea had lashed wearily for many a year, to reach the wilderness dead, and where now, triumphant, the frothing surf bared gun-case coffins and tumbled the bones of men down into its sullen depths. And such men! Men who had lived and died when the world was unborn in a half of its knowledge and science, when red blood was the great capital, strong hearts the winners of life. And there were women, too, women who had come with these men, and died with them, in the opening-up of a new world. It was such men as these, and such women as these, that Philip loved, and he walked with bared head and swiftly beating heart over the unmarked jungle of the dead.

And then he came to other things, the first low log buildings of Churchill, to the silence of sleeping life. New buildings loomed up— working quarters of men who were grubbing for dollars, the new wharves, the skeletons of elevators, sullen, windowless warehouses, the office-buildings of men who were already fighting and quarreling and gripping at one another's throats in the struggle for supremacy, for the biggest and ripest plums in this new land of opportunity. The dollar-fight had begun, and the things that already marked its presence loomed monstrous and grotesque to Philip, as if jeering at the forgotten efforts of those whom the sea was washing away. And suddenly it struck Philip that the sea, working ceaselessly, digging away at its dead, was not the enemy of the nameless creatures in the gun-case coffins, but that it was a friend, stanch through centuries, rescuing them now from the desecration that was to come; and for a moment he was resistless to the spirit that moved him about and made him face that sea with something that was almost a prayer in his heart.

As he turned he saw that a light had appeared in one of the low log buildings which contained the two offices of the Keewatin Mines and Lands Company. The light, and the bulky shadow of old Pearce, which appeared for a moment on one of the drawn curtains, aroused Philip to other thoughts. Since his arrival at Churchill he had made the acquaintance of Pearce, and it struck him now that just such a man as this might be Lord Fitzhugh Lee. The Keewatin Mines and Lands Company had no mines and few lands, and yet Pearce had told him that they were doing a hustling business down south, selling stock on mineral claims that couldn't be worked for years. After all, was he any better than Pearce?

The old bitterness rose in him. He was no better than Pearce, no better than this Lord Fitzhugh himself, and it was fate—fate and people, that had made him so. He walked swiftly now, following close along the shore in the hard stretch kept bare by the tides, until he came to the red coals of half a dozen Indian fires on the edge of the forest beyond the company's buildings. A dog scented him and howled. He heard a guttural voice break in a word of command from one of the tepees, and there was silence again.

He turned to the right, burying himself deeper and deeper into the great silence of the north, his quick steps keeping pace with the thoughts that were passing through his brain. Fate, bad luck, circumstance—they had been against him. He had told himself this a hundred times, had laughed at them with the confidence of one who knew that some day he would rise above these things in triumph. And yet what were these elements of fortune, as he had called them, but people? A feeling of personal resentment began to oppress him. People had downed him, and not circumstance and bad luck. Men and women had made a failure of him, and not fate. For the first time it occurred to him that the very men and women whom Brokaw and his associates had duped, whom Pearce was duping, would play the game in the same way if they had the opportunity. What if he had played on the winning side, if he had enlisted his fighting energies with men like Brokaw and Pearce, fought for money and power in place of this other thing, which seemed to count so little? Other men would have given much to have been in his favor with Eileen Brokaw. He might have been in the front of this other fight, the winning fight, the possessor of fortune, a beautiful woman—

He stopped suddenly. It seemed to him that he had heard a voice. He had climbed from out of the shadow of the forest until he stood now on a gray cliff of rock that reached out into the Bay, like the point of a great knife guarding Churchill. A block of sandstone rose in his path, and he passed quietly around it. In another instant he had flattened himself against it.

A dozen feet away, full in the moonlight, three figures sat on the edge of the cliff, as motionless as though hewn out of rock. Instinctively Philip's hand slipped to his revolver holster, but he drew it back when he saw that one of the three figures was that of a woman. Beside her crouched a huge wolf-dog; on the other side of the dog sat a man. The man was resting in the attitude of an Indian, with his elbows on his knees, his chin in the palms of his hands, gazing steadily and silently out over the Bay toward Churchill.

It was his companion that held Philip motionless against the face of the rock. She, too, was leaning forward, gazing in that same steady, silent way toward Churchill. She was bareheaded. Her hair fell loose over her shoulders and streamed down her back until it piled itself upon the rock, shining dark and lustrous in the light of the moon. Philip knew that she was not an Indian.

Suddenly the girl sat erect, and then sprang to her feet, partly facing him, the breeze rippling her hair about her face and shoulders, her eyes turned to the vast gray depths of the world beyond the forests. For an instant she turned so that the light of the moon fell full upon her, and in that moment Philip thought that her eyes had searched him out in the shadow of the rock and were looking straight into his own. Never had he seen such a beautiful face among the forest people. He had dreamed of such faces beside camp-fires, in the deep loneliness of long nights in the forests, when he had awakened to bring before him visions of what Eileen Brokaw might have been to him if he had found her one of these people. He drew himself closer to the rock. The girl turned again to the edge of the cliff, her slender form silhouetted against the starlit sky. She leaned over the dog, and he heard her voice, soft and caressing, but he could not understand her words. The man lifted his head, and he recognized the swarthy, clear-cut features of a French half-breed. He moved away as quietly as he had come.

The girl's voice stopped him.

"And that is Churchill, Pierre—the Churchill you have told me of, where the ships come in?"

"Yes, that is Churchill, Jeanne."

For a moment there was silence. Then, clear and low, with a wild, sobbing note in her voice that thrilled Philip, the girl cried:

"And I hate it, Pierre. I hate it—hate it—hate it!"

Philip stepped out boldly from the rock.

"And I hate it, too," he said.

VI

Scarce had he spoken when he would have given much to have recalled his words, wrung from his lips by that sobbing note of loneliness, of defiance, of half pain in the girl's voice. It was the same note, the same spirit crying out against his world that he had listened to in the moaning of the surf as it labored to carry away the dead, and in the wind that sighed in the spruce-tops below the mountain, only now it was the spirit speaking through a human voice. Every fiber in his body vibrated in response to it, and he stood with bared head, filled with a wild desire to make these people understand, and yet startled at the effect which his appearance had produced.

The girl faced him, her eyes shining with sudden fear. Quicker than her own was the movement of the half-breed. In a flash he was upon his feet, his dark face tense with action, his right hand gripping at something in his belt as he bent toward the figure in the center of the rock. His posture was that of an animal ready to spring. Close beside him gleamed the white fangs of the wolf-dog. The girl leaned over and twisted her fingers in the tawny hair that bristled on the dog's neck. Philip heard her speak, but she did not move her eyes from his face. It was the tableau of a moment, tense, breathless. The only thing that moved was the shimmer of steel. Philip caught the gleam of it under the half-breed's hand.

"Don't do that, M'sieur," he said, pointing at the other's belt. "I am sorry that I disturbed you. Sometimes I come up here—alone—to smoke my pipe and listen to the sea down there. I heard you say that you hate Churchill, and I hate it. That is why I spoke."

He turned to the girl.

"I am sorry. I beg your pardon."

He looked at her with new wonderment. She had tossed back her loose hair, and stood tall and straight in the moonlight, her dark eyes gazing at him now calmly and without affright. She was dressed in rich yellow buckskin, as soft as chamois. Her throat was bare. A deep collar of lace fell over her shoulders. One hand, raised to her breast, revealed a wide gauntlet cuff of red or purple plush, of a fashion two centuries old. Her lips were parted, and he saw the faintest gleam of her white teeth, the quick rising and falling of her bosom. He had spoken directly to her, yet she gave no sign of having heard him.

"You startled us, that is all, M'sieur," said Pierre, quietly. His English was excellent, and as he spoke he bowed low to Philip. "It is I whom you must pardon, M'sieur—for betraying so much caution."

Philip held out his hand.

"My name is Whittemore—Philip Whittemore," he said. "I'm staying at Churchill until the ship comes in and—and I hope you'll let me sit here on the rock."

For an instant Pierre's fingers gripped his hand, and he bowed low again like a courtier. Philip saw that he, too, wore the same big, old-fashioned cuffs, and that it was not a knife that hung at his belt, but a short rapier.

"And I am Pierre—Pierre Couchee," he said. "And this—is my sister—Jeanne. We do not belong to Fort Churchill, but come from Fort o' God. Good night, M'sieur!"

The girl had taken a step back, and now she swept him a courtesy so low that her fallen hair streamed over her shoulders. She spoke no word, but passed quickly with Pierre up the rock, and while Philip stood stunned and speechless they disappeared swiftly into the white gloom of the night.

Mutely he gazed after them. For a long time he stood staring beyond the rocks, marveling at the strangeness of this thing that had happened. An hour before he had stood with bared head over the ancient dead at Churchill, and now, on the rock, he had seen the resurrection of what he had dreamed those dead to be in life. He had never seen people like Pierre and Jeanne. Their strange dress, the rapier at Pierre's side, his courtly bow, the low, graceful courtesy that the girl had made him, all carried him back to the days of the old pictures that hung in the factor's room at Churchill, when high-blooded gallants came into the wilderness with their swords at their sides, wearing the favors of court ladies next their hearts. Pierre, standing there on the rock, with his hand on his rapier, might have been Grosellier himself, the prince's favorite, and Jeanne—

Something white on the rock near where the girl had been sitting caught Philip's eyes. In a moment he held in his fingers a small handkerchief and a broad ribbon of finely knit lace. In her haste to get away she had forgotten these things. He was about to run to the crest of the cliff and call loudly for Pierre Couchee when he held the handkerchief and the lace close to his face and the delicate perfume of heliotrope stopped him. There was something familiar about it, something that held him wondering and mystified, until he knew that he had lost the opportunity to recall Pierre and his companion. He looked at the handkerchief more, closely. It was a dainty fabric, so soft that it gave barely the sensation of touch when he crushed it in the palm of his hand. For a few moments he was puzzled to account for the filmy strip of lace. Then the truth came to him. Jeanne had used it to bind her hair!

He laughed softly, joyously, as he wound the bit of fabric about his fingers and retraced his steps toward Churchill. Again and again he pressed the tiny handkerchief to his face, breathing of its sweetness; and the action suddenly stirred his memory to the solution of its mystery. It was this same sweetness that had come to him on the night that he had looked down into the beautiful face of Eileen Brokaw at the Brokaw ball. He remembered now that Eileen Brokaw loved heliotrope, and that she always wore a purple heliotrope at her white throat or in the gold of her hair. For a moment it struck him as singular that so many things had happened this day to remind him of Brokaw's daughter. The thought hastened his steps. He was anxious to look at the picture again, to convince himself that he had been mistaken. Gregson was asleep when he re-entered the cabin. The light was burning low, and Philip turned up the wick. On the table was the picture as Gregson had left it. This time there was no doubt. He had drawn the face of Eileen Brokaw. In a spirit of jest he had written under it, "The Wife of Lord Fitzhugh."

In spite of their absurdity the words affected Philip curiously. Was it possible that Miss Brokaw had reached Fort Churchill in some other way than by ship? And, if not, was it possible that in this remote corner of the earth there was another woman who resembled her so closely? Philip took a step toward Gregson, half determined to awaken him. And yet, on second thought, he knew that Gregson could not explain. Even if the artist had learned of his affair with Miss Brokaw and had secured a picture of her in some way, he would not presume to go this far. He was convinced that Gregson had drawn the picture of a face that he had seen that day. Again he read the words at the bottom of the sketch, and once more he experienced their curious effect upon him—an effect which it was impossible for him to analyze even in his own mind.

He replaced the picture upon the table and drew the handkerchief and bit of lace from his pocket. In the light of the lamp he saw that both were as unusual as had been the picturesque dress of the girl and her companion. Even to his inexperienced eyes and touch they gave evidence of a richness that puzzled him, of a fashion that he had never seen. They were of exquisite workmanship. The lace was of a delicate ivory color, faintly tinted with yellow. The handkerchief was in the shape of a heart, and in one corner of it, so finely wrought that he could barely make out the silken letters, was the word "Camille."

The scent of heliotrope rose more strongly in the closed room, and from the handkerchief Philip's eyes turned to the face of Eileen Brokaw looking at him from out of Gregson's sketch. It was a curious coincidence. He reached over and placed the picture face down. Then he loaded his pipe, and sat smoking, his vision traveling beyond the table, beyond the closed door to the lonely black rock where he had come upon Jeanne and Pierre. Clouds of smoke rose about him, and he half closed his eyes. He saw the girl again, as she stood there; he saw the moonlight shining in her hair, the dark, startled beauty of her eyes as she turned upon him; he heard again the low sobbing note in her voice as she cried out her hatred against Churchill. He forgot Eileen Brokaw now, forgot in these moments all that he and Gregson had talked of that day. His schemes, his fears, his feverish eagerness to begin the fight against his enemies died away in thoughts of the beautiful girl who had come into his life this night. It seemed to him now that he had known her for a long time, that she had been a part of him always, and that it was her spirit that he had been groping and searching for, and could never find. For the space of those few moments on the cliff she had driven out the emptiness and the loneliness from his heart, and there filled him a wild desire to make her understand, to talk with her, to stand shoulder to shoulder with Pierre out there in the night, a comrade.

Suddenly his fingers closed tightly over the handkerchief. He turned and looked steadily at Gregson. His friend was sleeping, with his face to the wall.

Would not Pierre return to the rock in search of these articles which his sister had left behind? The thought set his blood tingling. He would go back—and wait for Pierre. But if Pierre did not return—until to-morrow?

He laughed softly to himself as he drew paper toward him and picked up the pencil which Gregson had used. For many minutes he wrote steadily. When he had done, he folded what he had written and tied it in the handkerchief. The strip of lace with which Jeanne had bound her hair he folded gently and placed in his breast pocket. There was a guilty flush in his face as he stole silently to the door. What would

Gregson say if he knew that he—Phil Whittemore, the man whom he had once idealized as "The Fighter," and whom he believed to be proof against all love of woman—was doing this thing? He opened and closed the door softly.

At least he would send his message to these strange people of the wilderness. They would know that he was not a part of that Churchill which they hated, that in his heart he had ceased to be a thing of its breed. He apologized again for his sudden appearance on the rock, but the apology was only an excuse for other things which he wrote, in which for a few brief moments he bared himself to those whom he knew would understand, and asked that their acquaintance might be continued. He felt that there was something almost boyish in what he was doing; and yet, as he hurried over the ridge and down into Churchill again, he was thrilled as no other adventure had ever thrilled him before. As he approached the cliff he began to fear that the half-breed would not return for the things which Jeanne had left, or that he had already re-visited the rock. The latter thought urged him on until he was half running. The crest of the cliff was bare when he reached it. He looked at his watch. He had been gone an hour.

Where the moonlight seemed to fall brightest he dropped the handkerchief, and then slipped back into the rocky trail that led to the edge of the Bay. He had scarcely reached the strip of level beach that lay between him and Churchill when from far behind him there came the long howl of a dog. It was the wolf-dog. He knew it by the slow, dismal rising of the cry and the infinite sadness with which it as slowly died away until lost in the whisperings of the forest and the gentle wash of the sea. Pierre was returning. He was coming back through the forest. Perhaps Jeanne would be with him.

For the third time Philip climbed back to the great moonlit rock at the top of the cliff. Eagerly he faced the north, whence the wailing cry of the wolf-dog had come. Then he turned to the spot where he had dropped the handkerchief, and his heart gave a sudden jump.

There was nothing on the rock. The handkerchief was gone!

VII

P hilip stood undecided, his ears strained to catch the slightest sound. Ten minutes had not elapsed since he had dropped the handkerchief. Pierre could not have gone far among the rocks. It was possible that he was concealed somewhere near him now. Softly he called his name.

"Pierre—ho, Pierre Couchee!"

There was no answer, and in the next breath he was sorry that he had called. He went silently down the trail. He had come to the edge of Churchill when once more he heard the howl of the dog far back in the forest. He stopped to locate as nearly as he could the point whence the sound came, for he was certain now that the dog had not returned with Pierre, but had remained with Jeanne, and was howling from their camp.

Gregson was awake and sitting on the edge of his bunk when Philip entered the cabin.

"Where the deuce have you been?" he demanded. "I was just trying to make up my mind to go out and hunt for you. Stolen—lost—or something like that?"

"I've been thinking," said Philip, truthfully.

"So have I," said Gregson. "Ever since you came back, wrote that letter, and went out again—"

"You were asleep," corrected Philip. "I looked at you."

"Perhaps I was—when you looked. But I have a hazy recollection of you sitting there at the table, writing like a fiend. Anyway, I've been thinking ever since you went out of the door, and—I'd like to read that Lord Fitzhugh letter again."

Philip handed him the letter. He was quite sure from his friend's manner of speaking that he had seen nothing of the handkerchief and the lace.

Gregson seized the paper lazily, yawned, and slipped it under the blanket which he had doubled up for a pillow.

"Do you mind if I keep it for a few days. Phil?" he asked.

"Not in the least, if you'll tell me why you want it," said Philip.

"I will—when I discover a reason myself," replied his friend, coolly, stretching himself out again in the bunk. "Remember when I dreamed that Carabobo planter was sticking a knife into you, Phil?—and the next day he tried it? Well, I've had a funny dream, I want to sleep on this letter. I may want to sleep on it for a week. Better turn in if you expect to get a wink between now and morning."

For half an hour after he had undressed and extinguished the light Philip lay awake reviewing the incidents of his night's adventure. He was certain that his letter was in the hands of Pierre and Jeanne, but he was not so sure that they would respond to it. He half expected that they would not, and yet he felt a deep sense of satisfaction in what he had done. If he met them again he would not be quite a stranger. And that he would meet them he was not only confident, but determined. If they did not appear in Fort Churchill he would hunt out their camp.

He found himself asking a dozen questions, none of which he could answer. Who was this girl who had come like a queen from out of the wilderness, and this man who bore with him the manner of a courtier? Was it possible, after all, that they were of the forests? And where was Fort o' God? He had never heard of it before, and as he thought of Jeanne's strange, rich dress, of the heliotrope-scented handkerchief, of the old-fashioned rapier at Pierre's side, and of the exquisite grace with which the girl had left him he wondered if such a place as this Fort o' God must be could exist in the heart of the desolate northland. Pierre had said that they had come from Fort o' God. But were they a part of it?

He fell asleep, the resolution formed in his mind to investigate as soon as he found the opportunity. There would surely be those at Churchill who would know these people; if not, they would know of Fort o' God.

Philip found Gregson awake and dressed when he rolled out of his bunk a few hours later. Gregson had breakfast ready.

"You're a good one to have company," growled the artist. "When you go out mooning again please take me along, will you? Chuck your head in that pail of water and let's eat. I'm starved."

Philip noticed that his companion had tacked the sketch against one of the logs above the table.

"Pretty good for imagination, Greggy," he said, nodding. "Burke will jump at that if you do it in colors."

"Burke won't get it," replied Gregson, soberly, seating himself at the table. "It won't be for sale."

"Why?"

Gregson waited until Philip had seated himself before he answered. "Look here, old man—get ready to laugh. Split your sides, if you want to. But it's God's truth that the girl I saw yesterday is the only girl I've ever seen that I'd be willing to die for!"

"To be sure," agreed Philip. "I understand."

Gregson stared at him in surprise. "Why don't you laugh?" he asked.

"It is not a laughing matter," said Philip. "I say that I understand. And I do."

Gregson looked from Philip's face to the picture.

"Does it—does it hit you that way, Phil?"

"She is very beautiful."

"She is more than that," declared Gregson, warmly. "If I ever looked into an angel's face it was yesterday, Phil. For just a moment I met her eyes—"

"And they were—"

"Wonderful!"

"I mean—the color," said Philip, engaging himself with the food.

"They were blue or gray. It is the first time I ever looked into a woman's eyes without being sure of the color of them. It was her hair, Phil—not this tinsel sort of gold that makes you wonder if it's real, but the kind you dream about. You may think me a loon, but I'm going to find out who she is and where she is as soon as I have done with this breakfast."

"And Lord Fitzhugh?"

A shadow passed over Gregson's face. For a few moments he ate in silence. Then he said:

"That's what kept me awake after you had gone—thinking of Lord Fitzhugh and this girl. See here, Phil. She isn't one of the kind up here. There was breeding and blood in every inch of her, and what I am wondering is if these two could be associated in any way. I don't want it to be so. But—it's possible. Beautiful young women like her don't come, traveling up to this knob-end of the earth alone, do they?"

Philip did not pursue the subject. A quarter of an hour later the two young men left the cabin, crossed the ridge, and walked together down into Churchill. Gregson went to the Company's store, while Philip entered the building occupied by Pearce. Pearce was at his desk. He looked up with tired, puffy eyes, and his fat hands lay limply before him. Philip knew that he had not been to bed. His oily face strove to put on an appearance of animation and business as Philip entered.

Philip produced a couple of cigars and took a chair opposite him.

"You look bushed, Pearce," he began. "Business must be rushing. I saw a light in your window after midnight, and I came within an ace of calling. Thought you wouldn't like to be interrupted, so I put off my business until this morning."

"Insomnia," said Pearce, huskily. "I can't sleep. Suppose you saw me at work through the window?" There was almost an eager haste in his question.

"Saw nothing but the light," replied Philip, carelessly. "You know this country pretty well, don't you, Pearce?"

"Been 'squatting' on prospects for eight years, waiting for this damned railroad," said Pearce, interlacing his thick fingers. "I guess I know it!"

"Then you can undoubtedly tell me the location of Fort o' God?"

"Fort o' What?"

"Fort o' God."

Pearce looked blank.

"It's a new one on me," he said, finally. "Never heard of it." He rose from his chair and went over to a big map hanging against the wall. Studiously he went over it with the point of his stubby forefinger. "This is the latest from the government," he continued, with his back to Philip, "but it ain't here. There's a God's Lake down south of Nelson House, but that's the only thing with a God about it north of fifty-three."

"It's not so far south as that," said Philip, rising.

Pearce's little eyes were fixed on him shrewdly.

"Never heard of it," he repeated. "What sort of a place is it, a post—"

"I have no idea," replied Philip. "I came for information more out of curiosity than anything else. Perhaps I misunderstood the name. I'm much obliged."

He left Pearce in his chair and went directly to the factor's quarters. Bludsoe, chief factor of the Hudson's Bay Company in the far north, could give him no more information than had Pearce. He had never heard of Fort o' God. He could not remember the name of Couchee. During the next two hours Philip talked with French, Indian, and half-breed trappers, and questioned the mail runner, who had come in that morning from the south. No one could tell him of Fort o' God.

Had Pierre lied to him? His face flushed with anger as this thought came to him. In the next breath he assured himself that Pierre was not a man who would lie. He had measured him as a man who would fight, and not one who would lie. Besides, he had voluntarily given the information that he and Jeanne were from Fort o' God. There had been no excuse for falsehood.

He purposely directed his movements so that he would not come into contact with Gregson, little dreaming that his artist friend was working under the same formula. He lunched with the factor, and a little later went boldly back to the cliff where he had met Jeanne and Pierre the preceding night. Although he had now come to expect no response to what he had written, he carefully examined the rocks about him. Then he set out through the forest in the direction from which had come the howling of the wolf-dog.

He searched until late in the afternoon, but found no signs of a recent camp. For several miles he followed the main trail that led northward from Fort Churchill. He crossed three times through the country between this trail and the edge of the Bay, searching for smoke from the top of every ridge that he climbed, listening for any sound that might give him a clue. He visited the shack of an old half-breed deep in the forest beyond the cliff, but its aged tenant could give him no information. He had not seen Pierre and Jeanne, nor had he heard the howling of their dog.

Tired and disappointed, Philip returned to Churchill. He went directly to his cabin and found Gregson waiting for him. There was a curious look in the artist's face as he gazed questioningly at his friend. His immaculate appearance was gone. He looked like one who had passed through an uncomfortable hour or two. Perspiration had dried in dirty streaks on his face, and his hands were buried dejectedly in his trousers pockets. He rose to his feet and stood before his companion.

"Look at me, Phil—take a good long look," he urged.

Philip stared.

"Am I awake?" demanded the artist. "Do I look like a man in his right senses? Eh, tell me!"

He turned and pointed to the sketch hanging against the wall.

"Did I see that girl, or didn't I?" he went on, not waiting for Philip to answer. "Did I dream of seeing her? Eh? By thunder, Phil—" He whirled upon his companion, a glow of excitement taking the place of the fatigue in his eyes. "I couldn't find her to-day. I've hunted in every shack and brush heap in and around Churchill. I've hunted until I'm so tired I can hardly stand up. And the devil of it is, I can find no one else who got more than a glimpse of her, and then they did not see her as I did. She had nothing on her head when I saw her, but I remember now that something like a heavy veil fell about her shoulders, and that she was lifting it when she passed. Anyway, no one saw her like— that." He pointed to the sketch. "And she's gone—gone as completely as though she came in a flying-machine and went away in one. She's gone—unless—"

"What?"

"Unless she is in concealment right here in Churchill. She's gone— or hiding."

"You have reason to suspect that she would be hiding," said Philip, concealing the effect of the other's words upon him.

Gregson was uneasy. He lighted a cigarette, puffed at it once or twice, and tossed it through the open door. Suddenly he reached in his coat pocket and pulled out an envelope.

"Deuce take it, if I know whether I have or not!" he cried. "But— look here, Phil. I saw the mail come in to-day, and I walked up as bold as you please and asked if there was anything for Lord Fitzhugh. I showed the other letter, and said I was Fitzhugh's agent. It went. And I got—this!"

Philip snatched at the letter which Gregson held out to him. His fingers trembled as he unfolded the single sheet of paper which he drew forth. Across it was written a single line:

Don't lose an hour. Strike now.

There was nothing more, except a large ink blot under the words. The envelope was addressed in the same hand as the one he had previously received. The men stared into each other's face.

"It's singular, that's all," pursued Gregson. "Those words are important. The writer expects that they will reach Lord Fitzhugh immediately, and as soon as he gets them you can look for war. Isn't that their significance? I repeat that it is singular this girl should come here so mysteriously, and disappear still more so, just at this psychological moment; and it is still more puzzling when you take into consideration the fact that two hours before the runner came in from the south another person inquired for Lord Fitzhugh's mail!"

Philip started.

"And they told you this?"

"Yes. It was a man who asked—a stranger. He gave no name and left no word. Now, if it should happen to be the man who was with the girl when I saw her—and we can find him—we've as good as got this Lord

Fitzhugh. If we don't find him—and mighty soon—it's up to us to start for your camps and put them into fighting shape. See the point?"

"But we've got the letter," said Philip. "Fitzhugh won't receive the final word, and that will delay whatever plot he has ready to spring."

"My dear Phil," said Gregson, softly. "I always said that you were the fighter and I the diplomat, yours the brawn and mine the brain. Don't you see what this means? I'll gamble my right hand that these very words have been sent to Lord Fitzhugh at two or three different points, so that they would be sure of reaching him. I'm just as positive that he has already received a copy of the letter which we have. Mark my words, it's catch Lord Fitzhugh within the next few days—or fight!"

Philip sat down, breathing heavily.

"I'll send word to MacDougall," he said. "But I—I must wait for the ship!"

"Why not leave word for Brokaw and join MacDougall?"

"Because when the ship comes in I believe that a large part of this mystery will be cleared up," replied Philip. "It is necessary that I remain here. That will give us a few days in which to make a further search for these people."

Gregson did not urge the point, but replaced the second letter in his pocket with the first. During the evening he remained at the cabin. Philip returned to Churchill. For an hour he sat among the ruins of the old fort, striving to bring some sort of order out of the chaos of events that had occurred during the past few days. He was almost convinced that he ought to reveal all that he knew to Gregson, and yet several reasons kept him from doing so. If Miss Brokaw was on the London ship when it arrived at Churchill, there would be no necessity of disclosing that part of his own history which he was keeping secret within himself. If Eileen was not on the ship her absence would be sufficient proof to him that she was in or near Churchill, and in this event he knew that it would be impossible for him to keep from associating with her movements not only those of Lord Fitzhugh, but also those of Jeanne and Pierre and of Brokaw himself. He could see but two things to do at present, wait and watch. If Miss Brokaw was not with her father, he would take Gregson fully into his confidence.

The next morning he despatched a messenger with a letter for MacDougall, at Blind Indian Lake, warning him to be on his guard and to prepare the long line of sub-stations for possible attack. All this day Gregson remained in the cabin.

"It won't do for me to make myself too evident," he explained. "I've called for Lord Fitzhugh's mail, and I'd better lie as low as possible until the corn begins to pop."

Philip again searched the forests to the north and west with the hope of finding some trace of Pierre and Jeanne. The forest people were beginning to come into Churchill from all directions to be present at the big event of the year—the arrival of the London ship—and Philip made inquiries on every trail. No one had seen those whom he described. The fourth and fifth days passed without any developments. So far as he could discover there was no Fort o' God, no Jeanne and Pierre Couchee. He was completely baffled. The sixth day he spent in the cabin with Gregson. On the morning of the seventh there came from far out over the Bay the hollow booming of a cannon.

It was the signal which for two hundred years the ships from over the sea had given to the people of Churchill.

By the time the two young men had finished their breakfasts and climbed to the top of the ridge overlooking the Bay, the vessel had dropped anchor half a mile off shore, where she rode safe from the rocks at low tide. Along the shore below them, where Churchill lay, the forest people were gathered in silent, waiting groups. Philip pointed to the factor's big York boat, already two-thirds of the way to the ship.

"We should have gone with Bludsoe," he said. "Brokaw will think this a shabby reception on our part, and Miss Brokaw won't be half flattered. We'll go down and get a good position on the pier."

Fifteen minutes later they were thrusting themselves through the crowd of men, women, children, and dogs congregated at the foot of the long stone pier alongside which the ship would lie for two or three hours at each high tide. Philip stopped among a number of Crees and half-breeds, and laid a detaining hand upon Gregson's arm.

"This is near enough, if you don't want to make yourself conspicuous," he said.

The York boat was returning. Philip pulled a cigar from his pocket and lighted it. He felt his heart throbbing excitedly as the boat drew nearer. He looked at Gregson. The artist was taking short, quick puffs on his cigarette, and Philip wondered at the evident eagerness with which he was watching the approaching craft.

Until the boat ran close up under the pier its sail hid the occupants. While the canvas still fluttered in the light wind Bludsoe sprang from the bow out upon the rocks with a rope. Three or four of his men

JAMES OLIVER CURWOOD

followed. With a rattle of blocks and rings the sheet dropped like a huge white curtain, and Philip took a step forward, scarce restraining the exclamation that forced itself to his lips at the picture which it revealed. Standing on the broad rail, her slender form poised for the quick upward step, one hand extended to Bludsoe, was Eileen Brokaw! In another instant she was upon the pier, facing the strange people before her, while her father clambered out of the boat behind. There was a smile of expectancy on her lips as she scanned the dark, silent faces of the forest people. Philip knew that she was looking for him. His pulse quickened. He turned for a moment to see the effect of the girl's appearance upon Gregson.

The artist's two hands had gripped his arm. They closed now until his fingers were like cords of steel. His face was white, his lips set into thin lines. For a breath he stood thus, while Miss Brokaw's scrutiny traveled nearer to them. Then, suddenly, he released his hold and darted back among the half-breeds and Indians, his face turning to Philip's in one quick, warning appeal.

He was not a moment too soon, for scarce had he gone when Miss Brokaw caught sight of Philip's tall form at the foot of the pier. Philip did not see the signal which she gave him. He was staring at the line of faces ahead of him. Two people had worked their way through that line, and suddenly every muscle in his body became tense with excitement and joy. They were Pierre and Jeanne!

He caught his breath at what happened then. He saw Jeanne falter for a moment. He noticed that she was now dressed like the others about her, and that Pierre, who stood at her shoulder, was no longer the fine gentleman of the rock. The half-breed bent over her, as if whispering to her, and then Jeanne ran out from those about her to Eileen, her beautiful face flushed with joy and welcome as she reached out her arms to the other woman. Philip saw a sudden startled look leap into Miss Brokaw's face, but it was gone as quickly as it appeared. She stared at the forest girl, drew herself haughtily erect, and, with a word which he could not hear, turned to Bludsoe and her father. For an instant Jeanne stood as if some one had struck her a blow. Then, slowly, she turned. The flush was gone from her face. Her beautiful mouth was quivering, and Philip fancied that he could hear the low sobbing of her breath. With a cry in which he uttered no name, but which was meant for her, he sprang forward into the clear space of the pier. She saw him, and darted back among her people. He would have followed, but

Miss Brokaw was coming to him now, her hand held out to him, and a step behind were Brokaw and the factor.

"Philip!" she cried.

He spoke no word as he crushed her hand. The hot grip of his fingers, the deep flush in his face, was interpreted by her as a welcome which it did not require speech to strengthen. He shook hands with Brokaw, and as the three followed after the factor his eyes sought vainly for Pierre and Jeanne.

They were gone, and he felt suddenly a thrill of repugnance at the gentle pressure of Eileen Brokaw's hand upon his arm.

VIII

Philip did not see the hundred staring eyes that followed in wonderment the tall, beautiful girl who walked at his side. He knew that Miss Brokaw was talking and laughing, and that he was nodding his head and answering her, while his brain raged for an idea that would give him an excuse for leaving her to follow Jeanne and Pierre. The facts that Gregson had left him so strangely, that Eileen had come with her father, and that, instead of clearing up the mystery in which they were so deeply involved, the arrival of the London ship had even more hopelessly entangled them, were forgotten for the moment in the desire to intercept Jeanne and Pierre before they could leave Churchill. Miss Brokaw herself unconsciously gave him the opportunity for which he was seeking.

"You don't look very happy, Philip," she exclaimed, in a chiding voice, meant only for his ears. "I thought—perhaps—my coming would make you glad."

Philip caught eagerly at the half question in her voice.

"I feared you would notice it," he said, quickly. "I was afraid you would think me indifferent because I did not go out to meet you in the boat, and because I stood hidden at the end of the pier when you landed. But I was looking for a man. I have been hunting for him for a long time. And I saw his face just as we came through the crowd. That is why I am—am rattled," he laughed. "Will you excuse me if I go back? Can you find some excuse for the others? I will return in a few minutes, and then you will not say that I am unhappy."

Miss Brokaw drew her hand from his arm.

"Surely I will excuse you," she cried. "Hurry, or you may lose him. I would like to go with you if it is going to be exciting."

Philip turned to Brokaw and the factor, who were close behind them.

"I am compelled to leave you here," he explained. "I have excused myself to Miss Brokaw, and will rejoin you almost immediately."

He lost no time in hurrying back to the shore of the Bay. As he had expected, Jeanne and her companion were no longer in sight. There was only one direction in which they could have disappeared so quickly, and this was toward the cliff. Once hidden by the fringe of forest, he hastened his steps until he was almost running. He had reached the base of the huge mass of rock that rose up from the sea, when down the narrow trail that led to the cliff there came a figure to meet him. It was an Indian boy, and he advanced to question him. If Jeanne and Pierre had passed that way the boy must surely have seen them.

Before he had spoken the lad ran toward him, holding out something in his hand. The question on Philip's lips changed to an exclamation of joy when he recognized the handkerchief which he had dropped upon the rock a few nights before, or one so near like it that he could not have told them apart. It was tied into a knot, and he felt the crumpling of paper under the pressure of his fingers. He almost tore the bit of lace and linen in his eagerness to rescue the paper, which a moment later he held in his fingers. Three short lines, written in a fine, old-fashioned hand, were all that it held for him. But they were sufficient to set his heart, beating wildly.

Will Monsieur come to the top of the rock to-night, some time between the hours of nine and ten.

There was no signature to the note, but Philip knew that only Jeanne could have written it, for the letters were almost of microscopic smallness, as delicate as the bit of lace in which they had been delivered, and of a quaintness of style which added still more to the bewildering mystery which already surrounded these people. He read the lines half a dozen times, and then turned to find that the Indian boy was slipping sway through the rocks.

"Here—you," he commanded, in English. "Come back!"

The boy's white teeth gleamed in a laugh as he waved his hand and leaped farther away. From Philip his eyes shifted in a quick, searching glance to the top of the cliff. In a flash Philip followed its direction. He understood the meaning of the look. From the cliff Jeanne and Pierre had seen his approach, and their meeting with the Indian boy had made it possible for them to intercept him in this manner. They were probably looking down upon him now, and in the gladness of the moment Philip laughed up at the bare rocks and waved his cap above his head as a signal of his acceptance of the strange invitation he had received.

Vaguely he wondered why they had set the meeting for that night, when in three or four minutes he could have joined them up there in broad day. But the central tangle of the mystery that had grown up about him during the past few days was too perplexing to embroider with such a minor detail as this, and he turned back toward Churchill with the feeling that everything was working in his favor. During the next few hours he would clear up the tangle, and in addition to that he

JAMES OLIVER CURWOOD

would meet Jeanne and Pierre. It was the thought of Jeanne, and not of the surprises which he was about to explain, that stirred his blood as he hurried back to the Fort.

It was his intention to return to Eileen and her father. But he changed this. He would first hunt up Gregson and begin his work there. He knew that the artist would be expecting him, and he went directly to the cabin, escaping notice by following along the fringe of the forest.

Gregson was pacing back and forth across the cabin floor when Philip arrived. His steps were quick and excited. His hands were thrust deep in his trousers pockets. The butts of innumerable half-smoked cigarettes lay scattered under his feet. He ceased his restless movement upon his companion's interruption, and for a moment or two gazed at Philip in blank silence.

"Well," he said, at last, "have you got anything to say?"

"Nothing," said Philip. "It's beyond me, Greggy. For Heaven's sake give me an explanation!"

There was nothing womanish in the hard lines of Gregson's face now. He spoke with the suggestion of a sneer.

"You knew—all the time," he said, coldly. "You knew that Miss Brokaw and the girl whom I drew were one and the same person. What was the object of your little sensation?"

Philip ignored his question. He stepped quickly up to Gregson and seized him by the arm.

"It is impossible!" he cried, in a low voice. "They cannot be the same person. That ship out there has not touched land since she left Halifax. Until she hove in sight off Churchill she hasn't been within two hundred miles of a coast this side of Hudson's Strait. Miss Brokaw is as new to this country as you. It is beyond all reason to suppose anything else."

"Nevertheless," said Gregson, quietly, "it was Miss Brokaw whom I saw the other day, and that is Miss Brokaw's picture."

He pointed to the sketch, and freed his arm to light another cigarette. There was a peculiar tone of finality in his voice which warned Philip that no amount of logic or arguing on his part would change his friend's belief. Gregson looked at him over his lighted match.

"It was Miss Brokaw," he said again. "Perhaps it is within reason to suppose that she came to Churchill in a balloon, dropped into town for luncheon, and departed in a balloon, descending by some miraculous chance aboard the ship that was bringing her father. However it may have happened, she was in Churchill a few days ago. On that hypothesis I am going to work, and as a consequence I am going to ask you for the indefinite loan of the Lord Fitzhugh letter. Will you give me your word to say nothing of that letter—for a few days?"

"It is almost necessary to show it to Brokaw," hesitated Philip.

"Almost—but not quite," Gregson caught him up. "Brokaw knows the seriousness of the situation without that letter. See here, Phil—you go out and fight, and let me handle this end of the business. Don't reveal me to the Brokaws. I don't want to meet—her—yet, though God knows if it wasn't for my confounded friendship for you I'd go over there with you this minute. She was even more beautiful than when I saw her—before."

"Then there is a difference," laughed Philip, meaningly.

"Not a difference, but a little better view," corrected the artist.

"Now, if we could only find the other girl, what a mess you'd be in, Greggy! By George, but this is beginning to have its humorous as well as its tragic side. I'd give a thousand dollars to have this other golden-haired beauty appear upon the scene!"

"I'll give a thousand if you produce her," retorted Gregson.

"Good!" laughed Philip, holding out a hand. "I'll report again this afternoon or to-night."

Inwardly he felt himself in no humorous mood as he retraced his steps to Churchill. He had thought to begin his work of clearing up the puzzling situation with Gregson, and Gregson had failed him completely by his persistence in the belief that Miss Brokaw was the girl whose face he had seen more than a week before. Was it possible, after all, that the ship had touched at some point up the coast? The supposition was preposterous. Yet before rejoining the Brokaws he sought out the captain and found that the company's vessel had come directly from Halifax without a change or stop in her regular course. The word of the company's captain cleared up his doubts in one direction; it mystified him more than ever in another. He was convinced that Gregson had not seen Miss Brokaw until that morning. But who was Eileen's double? Where was she at this moment? What peculiar combination of circumstance had drawn them both to Churchill at this particularly significant time? It was impossible for him not to associate the girl whom Gregson had encountered, and who so closely resembled Eileen, with Lord Fitzhugh and the plot against his company. And it struck him with a certain feeling of dread that, if his suspicions were true, Jeanne and Pierre must also be mixed up in the affair. For had not Jeanne, in her error, greeted Eileen as though she were a dear friend?

He went directly to the factor's house, and knocked at the door opening into the rooms occupied by Brokaw and his daughter. Brokaw admitted him, and at Philip's searching glance about the room he nodded toward a closed inner door and said:

"Eileen is resting. It's been a hard trip on her, Phil, and she hasn't slept for two consecutive nights since we left Halifax."

Philip's keen glance told him that Brokaw himself had not slept much. The promoter's eyes were heavy, with little puffy bags under them. But otherwise he betrayed no signs of unrest or lack of rest. He motioned Philip to a chair close to a huge fireplace in which a pile of birch was leaping into flame, offered him a cigar, and plunged immediately into business.

"It's hell, Philip," he said, in a hard, quiet voice, as though he were restraining an outburst of passion with effort. "In another three months we'd have been on a working basis, earning dividends. I've even gone to the point of making contracts that show us five hundred per cent, profit. And now—this!"

He dashed his half-burned cigar into the fire, and viciously bit the end from another.

Philip was lighting his own, and there was a moment's silence, broken sharply by the financier.

"Are your men prepared to fight?"

"If it's necessary," replied Philip. "We can at least depend upon a part of them, especially the men at Blind Indian Lake. But—this fighting— Why do you think it will come to that? If there is fighting we are ruined."

"If the people rise against us in a body—yes, we are ruined. That is what we must not permit. It is our one chance. I have done everything in my power to beat this movement against us down south, and have failed. Our enemies are completely masked. They have won popular sentiment through the newspapers. Their next move is to strike directly at us. Whatever is to happen will happen soon. The plan is to attack us, to destroy our property, and the movement is to be advertised as a retaliation for heinous outrages perpetrated by our men. It is possible that the attack will not be by northerners alone, but by men brought in for the purpose. The result will be the same—if it succeeds. The attack is planned to be a surprise. Our one chance is to meet it, to completely frustrate it—to strike an overwhelming blow, and to capture enough of our assailants to give us the evidence we must have."

Brokaw was excited. He emphasized his words with angry sweeps of his arms. He clenched his fists, and his face grew red. He was not like the old, shrewd, indomitable Brokaw, completely master of himself, never revealing himself beyond the unruffled veil of his self-possession, and Philip was surprised. He had expected that Brokaw's wily brain would bring with it half a dozen schemes for the quiet undoing of their enemies. And now here was Brokaw, the man who always hedged himself in with legal breast-works—who never revealed himself to the shot of his enemies—enlisting himself for a fight in the open! Philip had told Gregson that there would be a fight. He was firmly convinced that there would be a fight. But he had never believed that Brokaw would come to join in it. He leaned toward the financier, his face flushed a little by the warmth of the fire and by the knowledge that Brokaw was relinquishing the situation entirely into his hands. If it came to fighting, he would win. He was confident of himself there. But—

"What will be the result if we win?" he asked.

"If we secure those who will give the evidence we need—evidence that the movement against us is a plot to destroy our company, the government will stand by us," replied Brokaw. "I have sounded the situation there. I have filed a formal declaration to the effect that such a movement is on foot, and have received a promise that the commissioner of police will investigate the matter. But before that happens our enemies will strike. There is no time for red tape or investigations. We must achieve our own salvation. And to achieve that we must fight."

"And if we lose?"

Brokaw lifted his hands and shoulders with a significant gesture.

"The moral effect will be tremendous," he said. "It will be shown that the entire north is inimical to our company, and the government will withdraw our option. We will be ruined. Our stockholders will lose every cent invested."

In moments of mental energy Philip was restless. He rose from his chair now and moved softly back and forth across the carpeted floor of the big room, shrouded in tobacco smoke. Should he break his word to Gregson and tell Brokaw of Lord Fitzhugh? But, on second thought, what good would come of it? Brokaw was already aware of the seriousness of the situation. In some one of his unaccountable ways he had learned that their enemies were to strike almost immediately, and his own revelation of the Fitzhugh letters would but strengthen this evidence. He would keep his faith with Gregson for the promised day or two. For an hour the two men were alone in the room. At the end of that time their plans were settled. The next morning Philip would leave for Blind Indian Lake and prepare for war. Brokaw would follow two or three days later.

A heavy weight seemed lifted from Philip's shoulders when he left Brokaw. After months of worry and weeks of physical inaction he saw his way clear for the first time. And for the first time, too, something seemed to have come into his life that filled him with a strange exhilaration, and made him forgetful of the gloom that had settled over him during these last months. That night he would see Jeanne. His body thrilled at the thought, until for a time he forgot that he would also see and talk with Eileen. A few days before he had told Gregson that it would be suicidal to fight the northerners; now he was eager for action, eager to begin and end the affair—to win or lose. If he had stopped to analyze the change in himself he would have found that the beautiful girl whom he had first seen on the moonlit rock was at the bottom of it. And yet Jeanne was a northerner, one of those against whom his actions must be directed. But he had confidence in himself, confidence in what that night would bring forth. He was like one freed from a bondage that had oppressed him for a long time, and the fact that he might be compelled to fight Jeanne's own people did not destroy his hopefulness, the new joy and excitement that he had found in life. As he hurried back to his cabin he told himself that both Jeanne and Pierre had read what he had sent to them in the handkerchief; their response was a proof that they understood him, and deep down a voice kept telling him that if it came to fighting they three, Pierre, Jeanne, and himself, would rise or fall together. A few hours had transformed him into Gregson's old appreciation of the fighting man. Long and tedious months of diplomacy, of political intrigue, of bribery and dishonest financiering, in which he had played but the part of a helpless machine, were gone. Now he held the whip-hand; Brokaw had acknowledged his own surrender. He was to fight—a clean, fair fight on his part, and his blood leaped in every vein like marshaling armies. That nights on the rock, he would reveal himself frankly to Pierre and Jeanne. He would tell them of the plot to disrupt the company, and of the work ahead of him. And after that—

He thrust open the door of his cabin, eager to enlist Gregson in his enthusiasm. The artist was not in. Philip noticed that the cartridge-belt and the revolver which usually hung over Gregson's bunk were gone. He never entered the cabin without looking at the sketch of Eileen Brokaw. Something about it seemed to fascinate him, to challenge his presence. Now it was missing from the wall.

He threw off his coat and hat, filled his pipe, and began gathering up his few possessions, ready for packing. It was noon before he was through, and Gregson had not returned. He boiled himself some coffee and sat down to wait. At five o'clock he was to eat supper with the Brokaws and the factor; Eileen, through her father, had asked him to join her an hour or two earlier in the big room. He waited until four, and then left a brief note for Gregson upon the table.

It was growing dusk in the forest. From the top of the ridge Philip caught the last red glow of the sun, sinking far to the south and west. A faint radiance of it still swept over his head and mingled with the thickening gray gloom of the northern sea. Across the dip in the Bay the huge, white-capped cliff seemed to loom nearer and more gigantic in the whimsical light. For a few moments a red bar shot across it, and as the golden fire faded and died away Philip could not but think it was like a torch beckoning to him. A few hours more, and where that light had been he would see Jeanne. And now, down there, Eileen was waiting for him.

His pulse quickened as he passed beyond the ancient fort, over the burial-place of the dead, and into Churchill. He met no one at the factor's, and the door leading into Miss Brokaw's room was partly ajar. A great fire was burning in the fireplace, and he saw Eileen seated in the rich glow of it, smiling at him as he entered. He closed the door, and when he turned she had risen and was holding out her hands to him. She had dressed for him, almost as on that night of the Brokaw ball. In the flashing play of the fire her exquisite arms and shoulders shone with dazzling beauty; her eyes laughed at him; her hair rippled in a golden flood. Faintly there came to him, filling the room slowly, tingling his nerves, the sweet scent of heliotrope—the perfume that had filled his nostrils on that other night, a long time ago, the sweet scent that had come to him in the handkerchief dropped on the rock, the breath of the bit of lace that had bound Jeanne's hair!

Eileen moved toward him. "Philip," she said, "now are you glad to see me?"

IX

H er voice broke the spell that had held him for a moment.

"I am glad to see you," he cried, quickly, seizing both her hands. "Only I haven't quite yet awakened from my dream. It seems too wonderful, almost unreal. Are you the old Eileen who used to shudder when I told you of a bit of jungle and wild beasts, and who laughed at me because I loved to sleep out-of-doors and tramp mountains, instead of decently behaving myself at home? I demand an explanation. It must be a wonderful change—"

"There has been a change," she interrupted him. "Sit down, Philip—there!" She nestled herself on a stool, close to his feet, and looked up at him, her hands clasped under her chin, radiantly lovely. "You told me once that girls like me simply fluttered over the top of life like butterflies; that we couldn't understand life, or live it, until somewhere—at some time—we came into touch with nature. Do you remember? I was consumed with rage then—at your frankness, at what I considered your impertinence. I couldn't get what you said out of my mind. And I'm trying it."

"And you like it?" He put the question almost eagerly.

"Yes." She was looking at him steadily, her beautiful gray eyes meeting his own in a silence that stirred him deeply. He had never seen her more beautiful. Was it the firelight on her face, the crimson leapings of the flames, that gave her skin a richer hue? Was it the mingling of fire and shadow that darkened her cheeks? An impulse made him utter the words which passed through his mind.

"You have already tried it," he said. "I can see the effects of it in your face. It would take weeks in the forests to do that."

The gray eyes faltered; the flush deepened.

"Yes, I have tried it. I spent a half of the summer at our cottage on the lake."

"But it is not tan," he persisted, thrilled for a moment by the discoveries he was making. "It is the wind; it is the open; it is the smoke of camp-fires; it is the elixir of balsam and cedar and pine. That is what I see in your face—unless it is the fire."

"It is the fire, partly," she said. "And the rest is the wind and the open of the seas we have come across, and the sting of icebergs. Ugh: my face feels like nettles!"

She rubbed her cheeks with her two hands, and then held up one hand to Philip.

"Look," she said. "It's as rough as sand-paper. Isn't that a change? I didn't even wear gloves on the ship. I'm an enthusiast. I'm going down there with you, and I'm going to fight. Now have you got anything to say against me, Mr. Philip?"

There was a lightness in her words, and yet not in her voice. In her manner was an uneasiness, mingled with an almost childish eagerness for him to answer, which Philip could not understand. He fancied that once or twice he had caught the faintest sign of a break in her voice.

"You really mean to hazard this adventure?" he cried, softly, in his astonishment. "You, whom wild horses couldn't drag into the wilderness, as you once told me!"

"Yes," she affirmed, drawing her stool back out of the increasing heat of the fire. Her face was almost entirely in shadow now, and she did not look at Philip. "I am beginning to—to love adventure," she went on, in an even voice. "It was an adventure coming up. And when we landed down there something curious happened. Did you see a girl who thought that she knew me—"

She stopped, and a sudden flash of the fire lit up her eyes, fixed on him intently from between her shielding hands.

"I saw her run out and speak to you," said Philip, his heart beating at double-quick. He leaned over so that he was looking squarely into Miss Brokaw's face.

"Did you know her?" she asked.

"I have seen her only twice—once before she spoke to you."

"If I meet her again I shall apologize," said Eileen. "It was her mistake, and she startled me. When she ran out to me like that, and held out her hands I—I thought of beggars."

"Beggars!" almost shouted Philip. "A beggar!" He caught himself with a laugh, and to cover his sudden emotion turned to lay a fresh piece of birch on the fire. "We don't have beggars up here."

The door opened behind them and Brokaw entered. Philip's face was red when he greeted him. For half an hour after that he cursed himself for not being as clever as Gregson. He knew that there was a change in Eileen Brokaw, a change which nature had not worked alone, as she wished him to believe. Then, and at supper, he tried to fathom her. At times he detected the metallic ring of what was unreal and make-believe in what she said; at other times she seemed stirred by emotions which

JAMES OLIVER CURWOOD

added immeasurably to the sweetness and truthfulness of her voice. She was nervous. He found her eyes frequently seeking her father's face, and more than once they were filled with a mysterious questioning, as if within Brokaw's brain there lurked hidden things which were new to her, and which she was struggling to understand. She no longer held the old fascination for Philip, and yet he conceded that she was more beautiful than ever. Until to-night he had never seen the shadow of sadness in her eyes; he had never seen them darken as they darkened now, when she listened with almost feverish interest to the words which passed between himself and Brokaw. He was certain that it was not a whim that had brought her into the north. It was impossible for him to believe that he had piqued at her vanity until she had leaped into action, as she had suggested to him while they were sitting before the fire. Could it be that she had accompanied her father because he—Philip Whittemore—was in the north?

The thought drew a slow flush into his face, and his uneasiness increased when he knew that she was looking at him. He was glad when it came time for cigars, and Eileen excused herself. He opened the door for her, and told her that he probably would not see her again until morning, as he had an important engagement for the evening. She gave him her hand, and for a moment he felt the clinging of her fingers about his own.

"Good night," she whispered.

"Good night."

She drew her hand half away, and then, suddenly, raised her eyes straight to his own. They were calm, quiet, beautiful, and yet there came a quick little catch in her throat as she leaned so close to him that she touched his breast, and said:

"It will be best—best for everything—everybody—if you can influence father to stay at Fort Churchill."

She did not wait for him to reply, but hurried toward her room. For a moment Philip stared after her in amazement. Then he took a step as if to follow her, to call her back. The impulse left him as quickly as it came, and he rejoined Brokaw and the factor.

He looked at his watch. It was seven o'clock. At half-past seven he shook hands with the two men, lighted a fresh cigar, and passed out into the night. It was early for his meeting with Pierre and Jeanne, but he went down to the shore and walked slowly in the direction of the cliff. He was still an hour early when he arrived at the great rock, and sat down, with his face turned to the sea.

It was a white, radiant night, such as he had seen in the tropics. Only here, in the north, his vision reached to greater distances. Churchill lay lifeless in its pool of light; the ship hung like a black silhouette in the distance, with a cloud of jet-black smoke rising straight up from its funnels, and spreading out high up against the sky, a huge, ebon monster that cast its shadow for half a mile over the Bay. The shadow held Philip's eyes. Now it was like a gigantic face, now like a monster beast—now it reached out in the form of a great threatening hand, as though somewhere in the mystery of the north it sought a spirit-victim as potent as itself.

Then the spell of it was broken. From the end of the shadow, which reached almost to the base of the cliff on which Philip sat, there came a sound. It was a clear, metallic sound that left the vibration of steel in the air, and Philip leaned over the edge of the rock. Below him the shadow was broken into a pool of rippling starlight. He heard the faint dip of paddles, and suddenly a canoe shot from the shadow out into the clear light of the moon and stars.

It was a large canoe. In it he could make out four figures. Three of them were paddling; the fourth sat motionless in the bow. They passed under him swiftly, guiding their canoe so that it was soon hidden in the shelter of the cliff. By the faint reflections cast by the disturbed water, Philip saw that the occupants of the canoe had made an effort to conceal themselves by following the course of the dense shadow. Only the chance sound had led him to observe them.

Under ordinary circumstances the passing of a strange canoe at night would have had no significance for him. But at the present time it troubled him. The manner of its approach through the shadow, the strange quiet of its occupants, the stealth with which they had shot the canoe under the cliff, were all unusual. Could the incident have anything to do with Jeanne and Pierre?

He waited until he heard the tiny bell in his watch tinkle the half-hour, and then he set out slowly over the moonlit rocks to the north. Jeanne and Pierre would surely come from that direction. It was impossible to miss them. He walked without sound in his moccasins, keeping close to the edge of the cliff so that he could look out over the Bay. Two or three hundred yards beyond the big rock the sea-wall swung in sharply, disclosing the open water, like a still, silvery sheet, for a mile or more. Philip scanned it for the canoe, but as far as he could see there was not a shadow.

For a quarter of a mile he walked over the rocks, then returned. It was nine o'clock. The moment had arrived for the appearance of Jeanne and Pierre. He resumed his patrol of the cliff, and with each moment his nervousness increased. What if Jeanne failed him? What if she did not come to the rock? The mere thought made his heart sink with a sudden painful throb. Until now the fear that Jeanne might disappoint him, that she might not keep the tryst, had not entered his head. His faith in this girl, whom he had seen but twice, was supreme.

A second and a third time he patrolled the quarter mile of cliff. Again his watch tinkled the half-hour, and he knew that the last minutes of the appointed time had come.

The third and last time he went beyond the quarter-mile limit, searching in the white distances beyond. A low wind was rising from the Bay; it rustled in the spruce and balsam tops of the forest that reached up to the barren whiteness of the rock plateau on which he stood; under him he heard, growing more and more distinct, the moaning wash of the swelling tide. A moment of despair possessed him, and he felt that he had lost.

Suddenly the wind brought to him a different sound—a shout far down the cliff, a second cry, and then the scream of a woman, deadened by the wash of the sea and the increasing sweep of the wind among the trees.

He stood for a moment powerless, listening. The wind lulled, and the woman's cry now came to him again—a voice that was filled with terror rising in a wild appeal for help. With an answering shout he ran like a swift-footed animal along the cliff. It was Jeanne who was calling! Who else but Jeanne would be out there in the gray night—Jeanne and Pierre? He listened as he ran, but there came no other sound. At last he stopped, and drew in a great breath, to send out a shout that would reach their ears.

Above the fierce beating of his heart, the throbbing intake of his breath, he heard sounds which were not of the wind or the sea. He ran on, and suddenly the cliff dropped from under his feet, and he found himself on the edge of a great rift in the wall of rock, looking across upon a strange scene. In the brilliant moonlight, with his back against a rock, stood Pierre, his glistening rapier in his hand, his thin, lithe body bent for the attack of three men who faced him. It was but a moment's tableau. The men rushed in. Muffled cries, blows, a single clash of steel, and Pierre's voice rose above the sound of conflict. "For the love of God, give me help, M'sieur!" He had seen Philip rush up to the edge of the break in the cliff, and as he fought he cried out again.

"Shoot, M'sieur! In a moment it will be too late!"

Philip had drawn his heavy revolver. He watched for an opportunity. The men were fighting now so that Pierre had been forced between his assailants and the breach in the wall. There was no chance to fire without hitting him.

"Run, Pierre!" shouted Philip. "Run—"

He fired once, over the heads of the fighters, and as Pierre suddenly darted to one side in obedience to his command there came for the first time a shot from the other side. The bullet whistled close to his ears. A second shot, and Pierre fell down like one dead among the rocks. Again Philip fired—a third and a fourth time, and one of the three who were disappearing in the white gloom stumbled over a rock, and fell as Pierre had fallen. His companions stopped, picked him up, and staggered on with him. Philip's last shot missed, and before he could reload they were lost among the upheaved masses of the cliff.

"Pierre!" he called. "Ho! Pierre Couchee!"

There was no answer from the other side.

He ran along the edge of the break, and in the direction of the forest he found a place where he could descend. In his haste he fell; his hands were scratched, blood flowed from a cut in his forehead when he dragged himself up to the face of the cliff again. He tried to shout when he saw a figure drag itself up from among the rocks, but his almost superhuman exertions had left him voiceless. His wind whistled from between his parted lips when he came to Pierre.

Pierre was supporting himself against a rock. His face was streaming with blood. In his hand he held what remained of the rapier, which had broken off close to the hilt. His eyes were blazing like a madman's, and his face was twisted with an agony that sent a thrill of horror through Philip.

"My hurt is nothing—nothing-M'sieur!" he gasped, understanding the look in Philip's face. "It is Jeanne! They have gone—gone with Jeanne!" The rapier slipped from his hand and he slid weakly down against the rock. Philip dropped upon his knees, and with his handkerchief began wiping the blood from the half-breed's face. For a few moments Pierre's head hung limp against his shoulder.

"What is it, Pierre?" he urged. "Tell me—quick! They have gone with Jeanne!"

Pierre's body grew rigid. With one great effort he seemed to marshal all of his strength, and straightened himself.

"Listen, M'sieur," he said, speaking calmly. "They set upon us as we were going to meet you at the rock. There were four. One of them is dead—back there. The others—with Jeanne—have gone in the canoe. It is death—worse than death—for her—"

His body writhed. In a passion he strove to rise to his feet. Then with a groan he sank back, and for a moment Philip thought he was dying.

"I will go, Pierre," he cried. "I will bring her back. I swear it."

Pierre's hand detained him as he went to rise.

"You swear—"

"Yes."

"At the next break—there is a canoe. They have gone for the Churchill—"

Pierre's voice was growing weaker. In a spasm of sudden fear at the dizziness which was turning the night black for him he clutched at Philip's arm.

"If you save her, M'sieur, do not bring her back," he whispered, hoarsely. "Take her to Fort o' God. Lose not an hour—not a minute. Trust no one. Hide yourselves. Fight—kill—but take her to Fort o' God! You will do this—M'sieur—you promise—"

He fell back limp. Philip lowered him gently, holding his head so that he could look into the staring eyes that were still open and understanding.

"I will go, Pierre," he said. "I will take her to Fort o' God. And you—"

A shadow was creeping over Pierre's eyes. He was still fighting to understand, fighting to hold for another breath or two the consciousness that was fast slipping from him.

"Listen," cried Philip, striving to rouse him. "You will not die. The bullet grazed your head, and the wound has already stopped bleeding. To-morrow you must go to Churchill and hunt up a man named Gregson—the man I was with when you and Jeanne came to see the ship. Tell him that an important thing has happened, and that he must tell the others I have gone to the camps. He will understand. Tell him—tell him—"

He struggled to find some final word for Gregson. Pierre still looked at him, his eyes half closed now.

Philip bent close down.

"Tell him," he said, "that I am on the trail of Lord Fitzhugh!"

Scarcely had he uttered the name when Pierre's closing eyes shot open. A groaning cry burst from his lips, and, as if that name had aroused the last spark of life and strength within him into action, he wrenched himself from Philip's arms, striving to speak. A trickle of fresh blood ran over his face. Incoherent sounds rattled in his throat, and then, overcome by his effort, he dropped back unconscious. Philip wound his handkerchief about the wounded man's head and straightened out his limbs. Then he rose to his feet and reloaded his revolver. His hands were steady now. His brain was clear; the enervating thrill of excitement had gone from his body. Only his heart beat like a racing engine.

He turned and ran in the direction which Pierre's assailants had taken, his head lowered, his revolver held in front of him, on a level with his breast. He had not gone a hundred yards when something stopped him. In his path, with its face turned straight up to the moonlit sky, lay the body of a man. For an instant Philip bent over it. The broken blade of Pierre's rapier glistened under the man's throat. One lifeless hand clutched at it, as though in the last moment of life he had tried to draw it forth. The face was distorted, the eyes were still open, the lips parted. Death had come with terrible suddenness.

Philip bent lower, and stared into the face of the dead man. Where had he seen that face before?

Suddenly he remembered. He drew back, and a cold sweat seemed to break out all at once over his face and body. This man who lay with the broken blade of Pierre Couchee's rapier in his breast had come ashore from the London ship that day in company with Eileen and her father!

For a space he was overwhelmed by the discovery. Everything that had happened—the scene upon the rock when he first met Jeanne, the arrival of the ship, the moment's tableau on the pier when Jeanne and Eileen stood face to face—rushed upon him now as he gazed down into the staring eyes at his feet. What did it all mean? Why had Lord Fitzhugh's name been sufficient to drag the half-breed back from the brink of unconsciousness? What significance was there in this strange combination of circumstances that persisted in drawing Pierre and Jeanne into the plot that threatened himself? Had there been truth, after all, in those last words that he impressed upon the fainting senses of Pierre Couchee's message to Gregson?

He waited to answer none of the questions that leaped through his brain. To-morrow some one would find Pierre, or Pierre would crawl down into Churchill. And then there would be the dead man to account for. He shuddered as he returned his revolver into his holster and braced his limbs. It was an unpleasant task, but he knew that it must be done—to save Pierre. He lifted the body clear of the rocks, and bending under its weight carried it to the edge of the cliff. Far below sounded the wash of the sea. He shoved his burden over the edge, and listened. After a moment there came a dull splash.

Then he hastened on, as Pierre had guided him.

X

Soon Philip slackened his pace, and looked anxiously ahead of him. From where he stood the cliff sloped down to a white strip of beach that reached out into the night as far as he could see, hemmed close in by the black gloom of the forest. Half-way down the slope the moonlight was cut by a dark streak, and he found this to be the second break. He had no difficulty in descending. Its sides were smooth, as though worn by water. At the bottom white, dry sand slipped under his feet. He made his way between the walls, and darkness shut him in. The trail grew rougher. Near the shore he stumbled blindly among huge rocks and piles of crumbling slate, wondering why Jeanne and Pierre had come this way when they might have taken a smoother road. Close to the stony beach, where the light was a little better, he made out the canoe which Pierre had drawn into the shadows.

Not until he had dragged it into the moonlight at the edge of the water did he see that it was equipped as if for a long journey. Close to the stern was a bulging pack, with a rifle strapped across it. Two or three smaller caribou-skin bags lay in the center of the canoe. In the bow was a thick nest of bearskin, and he knew that this was for Jeanne.

Cautiously Philip launched himself, and with silent sweeps of the paddle that made scarcely the sound of a ripple in the water set out in the direction of Churchill. Jeanne's captors had a considerable start of him, but he felt confident of his ability to overtake them shortly if Pierre had spoken with truth when he said that they would head for the Churchill River. He had observed the caution with which Pierre's assailants had approached the cliff, and he was sure that they would double that caution in their return, especially as their attack had been interrupted at the last moment. For this reason he paddled without great haste, keeping well within the concealment of the precipitous shore, with his ears and eyes keenly alive to discover a sign of those who were ahead of him.

Opposite the rock where Pierre and Jeanne were to have met him he stopped and stood up in the canoe. The wind had dispelled the smoke shadow. Between him and the distant ship lay an unclouded sea. Two-thirds of the distance to the vessel he made out the larger canoe, rising and falling with the smooth undulations of the tide. He sank upon his knees again and unstrapped Pierre's rifle. There was a cartridge in the chamber. He made sure that the magazine was loaded, and resumed his paddling.

His mind worked rapidly. Within half an hour, if he desired, he could overtake the other canoe. And what then? There were three to one, if it came to a fight—and how could he rescue Jeanne without a fight? His blood was pounding eagerly, almost with pleasure at the promise of what was ahead of him, and he laughed softly to himself as he thought of the odds.

The ship loomed nearer; the canoe vanished behind it. A brief stop, a dozen words of explanation, and Philip knew that he could secure assistance from the vessel. After all, would that not be the wisest course for him to pursue? For a moment he hesitated, and paddled more slowly. If others joined with him in the rescue of Jeanne what excuse could he offer for not bringing her back to Churchill? What would happen if he returned with her? Why had Pierre roused himself from something that was almost death to entreat him to take Jeanne to Fort o' God?

At the thought of Fort o' God a new strength leaped into his arms and body, urging him on to cope with the situation single-handed. If he rescued Jeanne alone, and went on with her as he had promised Pierre, many things that were puzzling him would be explained. It occurred to him again that Jeanne and Pierre might be the key to the mysterious plot that promised to crash out the life of the enterprise he had founded in the north. He found reasons for this belief. Why had Lord Fitzhugh's name had such a startling effect upon Pierre? Why was one of his assailants a man fresh from the London ship that had borne Eileen Brokaw and her father as passengers? He felt that Jeanne could explain these things, as well as her brother. She could explain the strange scene on the pier, when for a moment she had stood crushed and startled before Eileen. She could clear up the mystery of Gregson's sketch, for if there were two Eileen Brokaws, Jeanne would know. With these arguments he convinced himself that he should go on alone. Yet, behind them there was another and more powerful motive. He confessed to himself that he would willingly accept double the chances against him to achieve Jeanne's rescue without assistance and to accompany her to Fort o' God. The thought of their being together, of the girl's companionship—perhaps for days—thrilled him with exquisite anticipation. An hour or so ago he had been satisfied in the assurance that he would see her for a few minutes on the cliff. Since then fate had played his way. Jeanne was his own, to save, to defend, to carry on to Fort o' God.

Not for a moment did he hesitate at the danger ahead of him, and yet his pursuit was filled with caution. Gregson, the diplomat, would have seen the necessity of halting at the ship for help; Philip was confident in himself. He knew that he would have at least three against him, for he was satisfied that the man whom he had wounded on the cliff was still in fighting trim. There might be others whom he had not taken into account.

He passed so close under the stern of the ship that his canoe scraped against her side. For a few minutes the vessel had obstructed his view, but now he saw again, a quarter of a mile distant, the craft which he was pursuing. Jeanne's captors were heading straight for the river, and as the canoe was now partly broadside to him he could easily make out the figures in her, but not distinctly enough to make sure of their number. He shoved out boldly into the moonlight, and, instead of following in his former course, he turned at a sharp angle in the direction of the shore. If the others saw him, which was probable, they would think that he was making a landing from the ship. Once he was in the deep fringe of shadow along the shore he could redouble his exertions and draw nearer to them without being observed.

No sooner had he readied the sheltering gloom than he bent to his paddle and the light birch-bark fairly hissed through the water. Not until he found himself abreast of the pursued did it occur to him that he could beat them out to the mouth of the Churchill and lie in wait for them. Every stroke of his paddle widened the distant between him and the larger canoe. Fifteen minutes later he reached the edge of the huge delta of wild rice and reeds through which the sluggish volume of the river emptied into the Bay. The chances were that the approaching canoe would take the nearest channel into the main stream, and Philip concealed himself so that it would have to pass within twenty yards of him.

From his ambuscade he looked out upon the approaching canoe. He was puzzled by the slowness of its progress. At times it seemed to stand still, and he could distinguish no movement at all among its occupants. At first he thought they were undecided as to which course to pursue, but a few minutes more sufficed to show that this was not the reason for their desultory advance. The canoe was headed for the first channel. The solution came when a low but clear whistle signaled over the

JAMES OLIVER CURWOOD

water. Almost instantly there came a responsive whistle from up the channel.

Philip drew a quick breath, and a new sensation brought his teeth together in sudden perplexity. It looked as though he had a bigger fight before him than he had anticipated.

At the signal from up-stream he heard the quick dip of paddles, and the canoe cut swiftly toward him. He drew back the hammer of Pierre's rule, and cleared a little space through the reeds and grass so that his view into the channel was unobstructed. Three or four well-directed shots, a quick dash out into the stream, and he would possess Jeanne. This was his first thought. It was followed by others, rapid as lightning, that restrained his eagerness. The night-glow was treacherous to shoot by. What if he should miss, or hit Jeanne—or in the sudden commotion and destruction of his shots the canoe should be overturned? A single error, the slightest mishap to himself, would mean the annihilation of his hopes. Even if he succeeded in directing his shots with accuracy, both himself and Jeanne would almost immediately be under fire from those above.

He dropped back again behind the screen of reeds. The canoe drew nearer. A moment more and it was almost abreast of him, and his heart pounded like a swiftly beating hammer when he saw Jeanne in the stern. She was leaning back as though unconscious. He could see nothing of her face, but as the canoe passed within ten yards of his hiding-place he saw the dark glow of her disheveled hair, which fell thickly over the object against which she was resting. It was but a moment's view, and they were gone. He had not looked at the three men in the canoe. His whole being was centered upon Jeanne. He had seen no sign of life— no movement in her body, not the flutter of a hand, and all his fears leaped like brands of burning fire into his brain. He thought of the inhuman plot which Lord Fitzhugh's letter had revealed; in the same breath Pierre Couchee's words rang in his ears—"It is death—worse than death—for her—"

Was Jeanne the first victim of that diabolical scheme to awaken the wrath of the northland? In the madness which possessed him now Philip shoved out his canoe while there was still danger of discovery. Fortunately none of the pursued glanced back, and a turn in the channel soon hid them from view. Philip had recovered his self-possession by the time he reached the turn. He assured himself that Jeanne was unharmed as yet, and that when he saw her she had probably fainted from excitement and terror. Her fate still lay before her, somewhere in the deep and undisturbed forests up the Churchill. His one hope was to remain undiscovered and to rescue her at the last moment when she was taken ashore by her captors.

He followed, close up against the reeds, never trusting himself out of the shadows. After a little he heard voices, and a second canoe appeared. There was a short pause, and the two canoes continued side by side up the channel. A quarter of an hour brought both the pursuers and the pursued into the main stream, which lay in black gloom between forest walls that cut out all light but the shimmer of the stars.

No longer could Philip see those ahead of him, but he guided himself by occasional voices and the dip of paddles. At times, when the stream narrowed and the forest walls gave him deeper shelter, he drew perilously near with the hope of overhearing what was said, but he caught only an occasional word or two. He listened in vain for Jeanne's voice. Once he heard her name spoken, and it was followed by a low laugh from some one in the canoe that had waited at the mouth of the Churchill. A dozen times during the first half-hour after they entered the main stream Philip heard this same laughing voice.

After a time there fell a silence upon those ahead. No sound rose above the steady dip of paddles, and the speed of the two canoes increased. Suddenly, from far up the river, there came a voice, faintly at first, but growing steadily louder, singing one of the wild half-breed songs of the forest. The voice broke the silence of those in the canoes. They ceased paddling, and Philip stopped. He heard low words, and after a few moments the paddling was resumed, and the canoes turned in toward the shore. Philip followed their movement, dropping fifty yards farther down the stream, and thrust big birch-bark alongside a thick balsam that had fallen into the river.

The singing voice approached rapidly. Five minutes later a long company canoe floated down out of the gloom. It passed so near that Philip could see the picturesque figure in the stern paddling and singing. In the bow kneeled an Indian working in stoic silence. Between them, in the body of the canoe, sat two men whom he knew at a glance were white men. The strangers and their craft slipped by with the quickness of a shadow.

Again Philip heard movements above him, and once more he took up the pursuit. He wondered why Jeanne had not called for help when the company canoe passed. If she was not hurt or unconscious, her

JAMES OLIVER CURWOOD

captors had been forced to hold a handkerchief or a brutal hand over her mouth, perhaps at her throat! His blood grew hot with rage at the thought.

For three-quarters of an hour longer the swift paddling up-stream continued without interruption. Then the river widened into a small lake, and Philip was compelled to hold back until the two canoes, which he could see clearly now, had passed over the exposed area.

By the time he dared to follow, Jeanne's captors were a quarter of a mile ahead of him. He no longer heard their paddles when he entered the stream at the upper end of the lake, and he bent to his work with greater energy and less caution. Five minutes—ten minutes passed, and he saw nothing, heard nothing. His strokes grew more powerful and the canoe shot through the water with the swift cleavage of a knife. A perspiration began to gather on his face, and a sudden chilling fear entered him. Another five minutes and he stopped. The river swept out ahead of him, broad and clear, for a quarter of a mile. There was no sign of the canoes!

For a few moments he remained motionless, drifting back with the slow current of the stream, stunned by the thought that he had allowed Jeanne's captors to escape him. Had they heard him and dropped in to shore to let him pass? He swung his canoe about and headed down-stream. In that case he could not miss them, if he used caution. But if they had turned into some creek hidden in the gloom—were even now picking their way through a secret channel that led back from the river—

A groan burst from his lips as he thought of Jeanne. In that half mile of river he could surely find where the canoes had gone, but it might be too late. He went down in mid-stream, searching the shadows of both shores. His heart sank like lead when he came to the lake. There was but one thing to do now, and he ran his canoe close along the right-hand shore, looking for an opening. His progress was slow. A dozen times he entangled himself in masses of reeds and rice, or thrust himself under over-hanging tree-tops and vines to investigate the deeper gloom beyond. He had returned two-thirds of the distance to the straight-water where he had given up the pursuit when the bow of his canoe ran upon a smooth, sandy bar that shelved out thirty or forty feet from the shore. Scarcely had he felt the grate of sand when with a powerful shove he sent his canoe back, and almost in the same instant Pierre's rifle leveled menacingly shoreward. Drawn up high and dry on the sand-bar were the two canoes.

For a space Philip expected that his appearance would be the signal for some movement ashore; but as he drifted slowly away, his rifle still leveled, he was filled more and more with the belief that he had not been discovered. He allowed himself to drift until he knew that he was hidden in the shadows, and then quietly worked himself in to shore. Making no sound, he pulled himself up the bank and crept among the trees toward the bar. There was no one guarding the canoes. He heard no sound of voice, no crackling of brush or movement of reeds. For a full minute he crouched and listened. Then he crept nearer and found where both reeds and brush were trampled down into a path that led away from the river.

His heart gave a bound of joy, and he darted along the path, holding his rifle ready for instant use. The trail wound through the tall grass of a dry swamp meadow and, two hundred yards beyond the river, plunged into a forest. He had barely entered this when he saw the glow of a fire. It was only a short distance ahead, hidden in a deep hollow that completely concealed its existence from the keenest eyes that might pass along the river. Stealing cautiously to the crest of the little knoll between him and the light, Philip found himself within fifty feet of a camp.

A big canvas tent was the first thing to come within his vision. The fire was built against this face of a rock in front of this, and over the fire hovered a man dragging out beds of coals with a forked stick. Almost at the same moment a second man appeared from the tent, bearing two huge skillets in one hand and a big pot in the other. At a glance Philip knew that they were preparing to cook a meal, and that it was for many instead of two. Wildly he searched the firelit spaces and the shadows for a sign of Jeanne. He saw nothing. She was not in the camp. The five or six men who had fled up the river with her were not there. His fingers dug deep in the earth under him at the discovery, and once more appalling fears overwhelmed him. Perhaps she had already met her fate a little deeper in the forest.

He crept over the edge of the knoll and worked himself down through the low bush on the opposite side, which would bring him within a dozen feet of the man over the fire. There he would have them at his mercy, and at the point of his revolver would compel them to tell him where Jeanne had been taken. The advantage was all in his favor. It would not be difficult to make them prisoners and leave them secured while he followed after their companions.

JAMES OLIVER CURWOOD

He was intent only upon his plan, and did not take his eyes from the men over the fire. He came to the end of the bush, and crouched with head and shoulders exposed, his revolver in his hand. Suddenly a sound close to the tent startled him. It was a low cough. The men over the fire made no movement to look behind them, but Philip turned.

In the shadow of a tree, which had concealed her until now, sat Jeanne. She was tense and straight. Her white face was turned to him. Her beautiful eyes glowed like stars. Her lips were parted; he could see her quick, excited breathing. She saw him! She knew him! He could see the joy of hope in her face and that she was crushing back an impulse to cry out to him, even as he was restraining his own mad desire to shout out his defiance and joy. And there in the firelight, his face illumined, and oblivious for the moment of the presence of the two men, Philip straightened himself and held out his arms with a glad smile to Jeanne.

Hardly had he turned to the men, ready to spring out upon them, when there came a terrific interruption. There was a sudden crash in the brush behind him, a menacing snarl, and a huge wolfish brute launched itself at his throat. The swift instinct of self-preservation turned the weapon intended for the men over the fire upon this unexpected assailant. The snarling fangs of the husky were gleaming in his face and the animal's body was against the muzzle of his revolver when Philip fired. Though he escaped the fangs, he could not ward off the impact of the dog's body, and in another moment he was sprawling upon his back in the light of the camp. Before Philip could recover himself Jeanne's startled guards were upon him. Flung back, he still possessed his pistol, and pulled the trigger blindly. The report was muffled and sickening. At the same moment a heavy blow fell upon his head, and a furious weight crushed him back to the ground. He dropped his revolver. His brain reeled; his muscles relaxed. He felt his assailant's fingers at his throat, and their menace brought back every ounce of fighting strength in his body. For a moment he lay still, his eyes closed, the warm blood flowing over his face. He had worked this game once before, years ago. He even thought of that time now, as he lay upon his back. It had worked then, and it worked now. The choking fingers at his throat loosened; the weight lifted itself a little from his chest. The lone guard thought that he was unconscious, and Jeanne, who had staggered to her feet, thought that he was dead.

It was her cry, terrible, filled with agony and despair, that urged him into action an instant too soon. His foe was still partly on his guard, rising with a caution born of more than one wilderness episode, when with a quick movement Philip closed with him. Locked in a deadly grip, they rolled upon the ground; and, with a feeling of despair which had never entered into his soul before, the terrible truth came to Philip that the old strength was gone from his arms and that with each added exertion he was growing weaker. For a moment he saw Jeanne. She stood almost above them, her hands clutched at her breast. And as he looked, she suddenly turned and ran to the fire. An instant more and she was back, a red-hot brand in her hand. Philip saw it flash close to his eyes, felt the heat of it; and then a scream, animal-like in its ferocity and pain, burst from the lips of his antagonist. The man reeled backward, clutching at his thick neck, where Jeanne had thrust the burning stick. Philip rose to his knees. His fist shot out like lightning against the other's jaw, and the second guard fell back in a limp heap.

Even as the blow fell, a loud shout came from close back in the forest, followed by the crashing of many feet tearing through the underbrush.

JAMES OLIVER CURWOOD

XI

P hilip and Jeanne stood face to face in the firelight.

"Quick!" he cried. "We must hurry!"

He bent over to pick up his revolver from the ground. His movement was followed by a low sob of pain. Jeanne was swaying as though about to faint. She fell in a crumpled heap before he could reach her side.

"You are hurt!" he exclaimed. "Jeanne! Jeanne!"

He was upon his knees beside her, crying out her name, half holding her in his arms.

"No, no! I am not hurt—much," she replied, trying to recover herself. "It is my ankle. I sprained it—on the cliff. Now—"

She became heavier against his arm. Her eyes were limpid with pain.

Rising, Philip caught her in his arms. The crashing of brush was within pistol-shot distance of them, but in that moment he felt no fear. Life leaped back into his veins. He wanted to shout back his defiance as he ran with Jeanne along the path to the river. He could feel her pulsing against him. His lips were in her hair. Her heart was beating wildly against his own. One of her arms was about his shoulder, her hand against his neck. Life, love, the joy of possession swept through him in burning floods, and it seemed in these first moments of his contact with Jeanne, in the first sound of her voice speaking to him, that the passionate language of his soul must escape through his lips. For this moment he had risked his life, had taken a hundred chances; he had anticipated, and yet he had not dreamed beyond a hundredth part of what it would mean for him. He looked down into the white face of the girl as he ran. Her beautiful eyes were open to him. Her lips were parted; her cheek lay against his breast. He did not realize how close he was holding her until, at last, he stopped where he had hidden the canoe. Then he felt her beating and throbbing against him, as he had felt the quivering life of a frightened bird imprisoned in his hands. She drew a deep breath when he opened his arms, and lifted her head. Her loose hair swept over his breast and hands.

He spoke no word as he placed her in the canoe. Not a whisper passed between them as the canoe sped swiftly from the shore. A hundred yards down the stream Philip headed straight across the river and plunged into the shadows along the opposite bank.

Jeanne was close to him. He could hear her breathing. Suddenly he felt the touch of her hand.

"M'sieur, I must ask—about Pierre!"

There was the thrill of fear in the low words. She leaned back, her face a pale shadow in the deep gloom; and Philip bent over until he felt her breath, and the sweetness of her hair filled his nostrils. Quickly he whispered what had happened. He told her that Pierre was hurt, but not badly, and that he had promised to take her on to Fort o' God.

"It is up the Churchill?" he questioned.

"Yes," she whispered.

They heard voices now, and almost opposite them they saw shadowy figures running out to the canoes upon the sand-bar.

"They will think that we are escaping toward Churchill," said Philip, gloatingly. "It is the nearest refuge. See—"

One of the canoes was launched, and shot swiftly down the river. A moment later the second followed. The dip of paddles died away, and Philip laughed softly and joyously.

"They will hunt for us from now until morning between here and the Bay. And then they will look for you again in Churchill."

Philip was conscious, almost without seeing, that Jeanne had bowed her head in her arms and that she was giving way now to the terrific strain which she had been under. Not until he heard a low sob, which she strove hard to choke back in her throat, did he dare to lean over again and touch her. Whatever was throbbing in his heart, he knew that he must hide it now.

"You read the letter?" he asked, softly.

"Yes, M'sieur."

"Then you know—that you are safe with me!"

There was pride and strength, the ring of triumph in his voice. It was the voice of a man thrilled by his own strength, by the warmth of a great love, by the knowledge that he was the protector of a creature dearer to him than all else on earth. The truth of it set Jeanne quivering. She reached out until in the darkness her two hands found one of Philip's, and for a moment she held his paddle motionless in midair.

"Thank you, M'sieur," she whispered. "I trust you, as I would trust Pierre."

All the words that women had ever spoken to him were as nothing to those few that fell softly from Jeanne's lips; in the clinging pressure of her fingers as she uttered them were the concentrated joys of all that he had dreamed of in the touch of women. He knelt silent, motionless, until her hands left his own.

"I am to take you to Fort o' God," he said, fighting to keep the tremble of joy out of his voice. "And you—you must guide me."

"It is far up the Churchill," she replied, understanding the question he intended. "It is two hundred miles from the Bay."

He put his strength into his paddle for ten minutes, and then ran the canoe into shore fully half a mile above the sand-bar. He stepped out into water up to his knees.

"We must risk a little time here to attend to your injured ankle," he explained. "Then you can arrange yourself comfortably among these robes in the bow. Shall I carry you?"

"You can—help," said Jeanne. She gave him her hand and made an effort to rise. Instantly she sank back with a sob of pain.

It was strange that her pain should fill him with a wonderful joy. He knew that she was suffering, that she could not walk or stand alone. And yet, back at the camp, she had risen in her torture and had come to his rescue. She could not bear her own weight now, but then she had run to him and had fought for him. The knowledge that she had done this, and for him, filled him with an exquisite sensation.

"I must carry you," he said, speaking to her with the calm decision that he might have voiced to a little child. His tone reassured her, and she made no remonstrance when he lifted her in his arms. For a brief moment she lay against him again, and when he lowered her upon the bank his hand accidentally touched the soft warmth of her face.

"My specialty is sprains," he said, speaking a little lightly to raise her spirits for the instant's ordeal through which she must pass. "I have doctored half a dozen during the last three months. You must take off your moccasin and your stocking, and I will make a bandage."

He drew a big handkerchief from his pocket and dipped it in the water. Then he searched along the shore for a dozen paces, until he found an Indian willow. With his knife he scraped off a handful of bark, soaked it in water, crushed it between his hands, and returned to her. Jeanne's little foot lay naked in the starlight.

"It will hurt just a moment," he said, gently. "But it is the only cure. To-morrow it will be strong enough for you to stand upon. Can you bear a little hurt?"

He knelt before her and looked up, scarce daring to touch her foot before she spoke.

"I may cry," she said.

Her voice fluttered, but it gave him permission. He folded the wet handkerchief in the form of a bandage, with the willow bark spread over it. Then, very gently, he seized her foot in one hand and her ankle in the other.

"It will hurt just a little," he soothed. "Only a moment."

His fingers tightened. He put into them the whole strength of his grip, pulling downward on the foot and upward on the ankle until, with a low cry, Jeanne flung her hands over his.

"There, it is done," he laughed, nervously. He wrapped the bandage around so tightly that Jeanne could not move her foot, and tied it with strips of cloth. Then he turned to the canoe while she drew on her stocking and moccasin.

He was trembling. A maddening joy pounded in his brain. Jeanne's voice came to him sweetly, with a shyness in it that made him feel like a boy. He was glad that the night concealed his face. He would have given worlds to have seen Jeanne's.

"I am ready," she said.

He carried her to the bow of the canoe and fixed her among the robes, arranging a place for her head so that she might sleep if she wished. For the first time the light was so that he could see her plainly as she nestled back in the place made for her. Their eyes met for a moment.

"You must sleep," he urged. "I shall paddle all night."

"You are sure that Pierre is not badly hurt?" she asked, tremulously. "You—you would not—keep the truth from me?"

"He was not more than stunned," assured Philip. "It is impossible that his wound should prove serious. Only there was no time to lose, and I came without him. He will follow us soon."

He took his position in the stern, and Jeanne lay back among the bearskins. For a long time after that Philip paddled in silence. He had hoped that Jeanne would give him an opportunity to continue their conversation, in spite of his advice to her to secure what rest she could. But there came no promise from the bow of the canoe. After half an hour he guessed that Jeanne had taken him at his word, and was asleep.

It was disappointing, and yet there came a pleasurable throb with his disappointment. Jeanne trusted him. She was sleeping under his protection as sweetly as a child. Fear of her enemies no longer kept her awake or filled her with terror. This night, under these stars, with the wilderness all about them, she had given herself into his keeping. His cheeks burned. He dipped his paddle noiselessly, so that he might not interrupt her slumber. Each moment added to the fullness of his joy, and he wished that he might only see her face, hidden in the darkness of her hair and the bear-robes.

The silence no longer seemed a silence to him. It was filled with the beating of his heart, the singing of his love, a gentle sigh now and then that came like a deeper breath between Jeanne's sweet lips. It was a silence that pulsated with a voiceless and intoxicating life for him, and he was happy. In these moments, when even their voices were stilled, Jeanne belonged to him, and to him alone. He could feel the warmth of her presence. He felt still the thrill of her breast against his own, the touch of her hair upon his lips, the gentle clinging of her arms. The spirit of her moved, and sat awake, and talked with him, just as the old spirit of his dreams had communed with him a thousand times in his loneliness. Dreams were at an end. Now had come reality.

He looked up into the sky. The moon had dropped below the southwestern forests, and there were only the stars above him, filling a gray-blue vault in which there was not even the lingering mist of a cloud. It was a beautifully clear night, and he wondered how the light fell so that it did not reveal Jeanne in her nest. The thought that came to him then set his heart tingling and made his face radiant. Even the stars were guarding Jeanne, and refused to disclose the mystery of her slumber. He laughed within himself. His being throbbed, and suddenly a voice seemed to cry softly, trembling in its joy:

"Jeanne! Jeanne! My beloved Jeanne!"

With horror Philip caught himself too late. He had spoken the words aloud. For an instant reality had transformed itself into the old dream, and his dream-spirit had called to its mate for the first time in words. Appalled at what he had said, Philip bent over and listened. He heard Jeanne's breathing. It was deeper than before. She was surely asleep!

He straightened himself and resumed his paddling. He was glad now that he had spoken. Jeanne seemed nearer to him after those words.

Before this night he never realized how beautiful the wilderness was, how complete it could be. It had offered him visions of new life, but these visions had never quite shut out the memories of old pain. He watched and listened. The water rippled behind his canoe; it trickled in a soothing cadence after each dip of his paddle; he heard the gentle murmur of it among the reeds and grasses, and now and then the gurgling laughter of it, like the faintest tinkling of dainty bells. He had never understood it before; he had never joined in its happiness. The night sounds came to him with a different meaning, filled him with different sensations. As he slipped quietly around a bend in the river he heard a splashing ahead of him, and knew that a moose was feeding, belly-deep, in the water. At other times the sound would have set his fingers itching for a rifle, but now it was a part of the music of the night. Later he heard the crashing of a heavy body along the shore and in the distance the lonely howl of a wolf. He listened to the sounds with a quiet pleasure instead of creeping thrills which they once sent through him. Every sound spoke of Jeanne—of Jeanne and her world, into which each stroke of his paddle carried them a little deeper.

And yet the truth could not but come to him that Jeanne was but a stranger. She was a creature of mystery, as she lay there asleep in the bow of the canoe; he loved her, and yet he did not know her. He confessed to himself, as the night lengthened, that he would be glad when morning came. Jeanne would clear up a half of his perplexities then, perhaps all of them. He would at least learn more about herself and the reason for the attack at Fort Churchill.

He paddled for another hour, and then looked at his watch by the light of a match. It was three o'clock.

Jeanne had not moved, but as the match burned out between his fingers she startled him by speaking.

"Is it nearly morning, M'sieur?"

"An hour until dawn," said Philip. "You have been sleeping a long time—" Her name was on his lips, but he found it a little more difficult to speak now. And yet there was a gentleness in Jeanne's "M'sieur" which encouraged him. "Are you getting hungry?" he asked.

"Pierre and my father always ask me that when THEY are starving," replied Jeanne, sitting erect in her nest so that Philip saw her face and the shimmer of her hair. "There is everything to eat in the pack, M'sieur Philip, even to a bottle of olives."

"Good!" cried Philip, delighted, "But won't you please cut out that 'm'sieur?' My greatest weakness is a desire to be called by my first name. Will you?"

"If it pleases you," said Jeanne. "There is everything there to eat, and I will make you a cup of coffee, M'sieur—"

"What?"

"Philip."

There was a ripple of laughter in the girl's voice. Philip fairly trembled.

"You were prepared for this journey," he said. "You were going to leave after you saw me on the rock. I have been wondering why—why you took enough interest in me—"

He knew that he was blundering, and in the darkness his face turned red. Jeanne's tact was delightful.

"We were curious about you," she said, with bewitching candor. "Pierre is the most inquisitive creature in the world, and I wanted to thank you for returning my handkerchief. I'm sorry you didn't find a bit of lace which I lost at the same time!"

"I did!" exclaimed Philip.

He bit his tongue, and cursed himself at this fresh break. Jeanne was silent. After a moment she said:

"Shall I make you some coffee?"

"Will you be able to do it? Your foot—"

"I had forgotten that," she said. "It doesn't hurt any more. But I can show you how."

Her unaffected ingenuousness, the sweetness of her voice, the simplicity and ease of her manner delighted Philip, and at the same time filled him with amazement. He had never met a forest girl like Jeanne. Her beauty, her queen-like bearing, when she had stood with Pierre on the rock, had puzzled him and filled him with admiration. But now her voice, the music of her words, her quickness of perception added tenfold to those impressions. It might have been Miss Brokaw who was sitting there in the bow talking to him, only Jeanne's voice was sweeter than Miss Brokaw's; and even in the lightest of the words she had spoken there was a tone of sincerity and truth. It flashed upon Philip that Jeanne might have stepped from a convent school, where gentle voices had taught her and language was formed in the ripe fullness of music. In a moment he believed that something like this had happened.

"We will go ashore," he said, searching for an open space. "This must be tedious to you, if you are not accustomed to it."

"Accustomed to it, M'sieur—Philip!" exclaimed Jeanne, catching herself. "I was born here!"

"In the wilderness?"

"At Fort o' God."

"You have not always lived there?"

For a brief space Jeanne was silent.

"Yes, always, M'sieur. I am eighteen years old, and this is the first time that I have ever seen what you people call civilization. It is my first visit to Fort Churchill. It is the first time I have ever been away from Fort o' God."

Jeanne's voice was low and subdued. It rang with truth. In it there was something that was almost tragedy. For a breath or two Philip's heart seemed to stop its beating, and he leaned far over, looking straight and questioningly into the beautiful face that met his own. In that moment the world had opened and engulfed him in a wonder which at first his mind could not comprehend.

XII

The canoe ran among the reeds, with its bow to the shore. Philip's astonishment still held him motionless.

"A little while ago you asked me if I would tell you anything but—but—the truth," he stammered, trying to find words to express himself, "and this—"

"Is the truth," interrupted Jeanne, a little coolly. "Why should I tell you an untruth, M'sieur?"

Philip had asked himself that same question shortly after their first meeting on the cliff. And now in the girl's question there was sounded a warning for him to be more discreet.

"I did not mean that," he cried, quickly. "Please forgive me. Only—it is so wonderful, so almost IMPOSSIBLE to believe. Do you know what I thought of for three-quarters of the night after I left you and Pierre on the rock? It was of years—centuries ago. I put you and Pierre back there. It seemed as though you had come to me from out of another world, that you had strayed from the chivalry and beauty of some royal court, that a queen's painter might have known and made a picture of you, as I saw you there, but that to me you were only the vision of a dream. And now you say that you have always lived here!"

He saw Jeanne's eyes glowing. She had lifted herself from among the bearskins and was leaning toward him. Her face was quivering with emotion; her whole being seemed concentrated on his words.

"M'sieur—Philip—did we seem—like that?" she asked, tremulously.

"Yes, or I would not have written the letter," replied Philip. He leaned forward over the pack, and his face was close to Jeanne's. "I had just passed over the place where men and women of a century or two ago were buried, and when I saw you and Pierre I thought of them; of Mademoiselle D'Arcon, who left a prince to follow her lover to a grave back there at Churchill, and I wondered if Grosellier—"

"Grosellier!" cried the girl.

She was breathing quickly, excitedly. Suddenly she drew back with a little, nervous laugh.

"I am glad you thought of us like THAT," she added. "It was Grosellier, le grand chevalier, who first lived at Fort o' God!"

Philip could no longer restrain himself. He forgot that the canoe was lying motionless among the reeds and that they were to go ashore.

In a voice that trembled with his eagerness to be understood, to win her confidence, he told her fully of what had happened that night on the cliff. He repeated Pierre's instructions to him, described his terrible fear for her, and in it all withheld but one thing—the name of Lord Fitzhugh Lee. Jeanne listened to him without a word. She sat as erect as one of the slender reeds among which the canoe was hidden. Her dark eyes never left his face. They seemed to have grown darker when he finished.

"May the great God reward you for what you have done," she said, in a low voice, quivering with a suppressed passion. "You are brave, M'sieur Philip—as brave as I have dreamed of men being."

Philip's heart throbbed with delight, and yet he said quickly:

"It isn't THAT. I have done nothing—nothing more than Pierre would have done for me. But don't you understand? If there is to be a reward for the little I have given—I could ask for nothing greater than your confidence and Pierre's. There are reasons, and perhaps if I told you those you would understand."

"I do understand, without further explanation," answered Jeanne, in the same low, strained voice. "You fought for Pierre on the cliff, and you have saved—me. We owe you everything, even our lives. I understand, M'sieur Philip," she said, more softly, leaning still nearer to him; "but I can tell you nothing."

"You prefer to leave that to Pierre," he said a little hurt. "I beg your pardon."

"No, no! I don't mean that!" she cried, quickly. "You misunderstand me. I mean that you know as much of this whole affair as I do, that you know what I know, and perhaps more."

The emotion which she had suppressed burst forth now in a choking sob. She recovered herself in an instant, her eyes still upon Philip.

"It was only a whim of mine that took us to Churchill," she went on, before he could find words to say. "It is Pierre's secret why we lived in our own camp and went down into Churchill but once—when the ship came in. I do not know the reason for the attack. I can only guess—"

"And your guess—"

Jeanne drew back. For a moment she did not speak. Then she said, without a note of harshness in her voice, but with the finality of a queen:

"Father may tell you that when we reach Fort o' God!"

And then she suddenly leaned toward him again and held out both her hands.

"If you only could know how I thank you!" she exclaimed, impulsively.

For a moment Philip held her hands. He felt them trembling. In Jeanne's eyes he saw the glisten of tears.

"Circumstances have come about so strangely," he said, his heart palpitating at the warm pressure of her fingers, "that I half believed you and Pierre could help me in—in an affair of my own. I would give a great deal to find a certain person, and after the attack on the cliff, and what Pierre said, I thought—"

He hesitated, and Jeanne gently drew her hands from him.

"I thought that you might know him," he finished. "His name is Lord Fitzhugh Lee."

Jeanne gave no sign that she had heard the name before. The question in her eyes remained unchanged.

"We have never heard of him at Fort o' God," she said.

Philip shoved the canoe more firmly upon the shore and stepped over the side.

"This Fort o' God must be a wonderful place," he said, as he bent over to help her. "You have aroused something in me I never thought I possessed before—a tremendous curiosity."

"It is a wonderful place, M'sieur Philip," replied the girl, holding up her hands to him. "But why should you guess it?"

"Because of you," laughed Philip. "I am half convinced that you take a wicked delight in bewildering me."

He found Jeanne a comfortable spot on the bank, brought her one of the bearskins, and began collecting a pile of dry reeds and wood.

"I am sure of it," he went on. He struck a match, and the reeds flared into flame, lighting up his face.

Jeanne gave a startled cry.

"You are hurt!" she exclaimed. "Your face is red with blood."

Philip jumped back.

"I had forgotten that. I'll wash my face."

He waded into the edge of the water and began scrubbing himself. When he returned, Jeanne looked at him closely. The fire illumined her pale face. She had gathered her beautiful hair in a thick braid, which fell over her shoulder. She appeared lovelier to him now than when he had first seen her in the night-glow on the cliff. She was dressed the same. He observed that the filmy bit of lace about her slender throat was torn, and that one side of her short buckskin skirt was covered with half-dried splashes of mud. His blood rose at these signs of the rough treatment of those who had attacked her. It reached fever-heat when, coming nearer, he saw a livid bruise on her forehead close up under her hair.

"They struck you?" he demanded.

He stood with his hands clenched. She smiled up at him.

"It was my fault," she explained. "I'm afraid I gave them a good deal of trouble on the cliff."

She laughed outright at the fierceness in Philip's face, and so sweet was the sound of it to him that his hands relaxed and he laughed with her.

"So help me, you're a brick!" he cried.

"There are pots and kettles and coffee and things to eat in the pack, M'sieur Philip," reminded Jeanne, softly, as he still remained staring down upon her.

Philip turned to the canoe, with a laugh that was like a boy's. He threw the pack at Jeanne's feet and unstrapped it. Together they sorted out the things they wanted, and Philip cut crotched sticks on which he suspended two pots of water over the fire. He found himself whistling as he gathered an armful of wood along the shore. When he came back Jeanne had opened a bottle of olives and was nibbling at one, while she held out another to him on the end of a fork.

"I love olives," she said. "Won't you have one?"

He accepted the thing, and ate it joyously, though he hated olives.

"Where did you acquire the taste?" he asked. "I thought it took a course at college to make one like 'em."

"I've been to college," answered Jeanne, quietly. There was a glow in her cheeks now, a swift flash of tantalizing fun in her eyes, as she fished after another olive. "I have been a student—a Teneris Annis," she added, and he stood stupefied.

"That's Latin!" he gasped.

"Oui, M'sieur. Wollen Sie noch eine Olive haben?"

Laughter rippled in her throat. She held out another olive to him, her face aglow. Firelight danced in her hair, flooding its darker shadows with lights of red and gold.

"I was sure of it," he exclaimed, convinced. "That's post-graduate Latin and senior German, or I'm as mad as a March hare! Where—where did you go to school?"

"At Fort o' God. Quick, M'sieur Philip, the water is boiling over!"

Philip sprang to the fire. Jeanne handed him coffee, and set out cold meat and bread. For the first time that night he pulled out his pipe and filled it with tobacco.

"You don't mind if I smoke, do you, Miss Jeanne?" he groaned. "Under some circumstances tobacco is the only thing that will hold me up. Do you know that you are shaking my confidence in you?"

"I have told you nothing but the truth," retorted Jeanne, innocently. She was still busying herself over the pack, but Philip caught the slightest gleam of her laughing teeth.

"You are making fun of me," he remonstrated. "Tell me—where is this Fort o' God, and what is it?"

"It is far up the Churchill, M'sieur Philip. It is a log chateau, built hundreds and hundreds of years ago, I guess. My father, Pierre, and I, with one other, live there alone among the savages. I have never been so far away from home before."

"I suppose," said Philip, "that the savages up your way converse in Latin, Greek, and German—"

"Latin, French, and German," corrected Jeanne. "We haven't added a Greek course yet."

"I know of a girl," mused Philip, as though speaking to himself, "who spent five years in a girls' college, and she can talk nothing but light English. Her name is Eileen Brokaw."

Jeanne looked up, but only to point to the coffee.

"It is done," she advised, "unless you like it bitter."

XIII

Philip knew that Jeanne was watching him as he lifted the coffee from the fire and placed the pot on the ground to cool. His mind was in a hopeless tangle—a riot of things he would like to say, throbbing with a hundred questions he would like to ask, one after another. And yet Jeanne seemed bewitchingly unconscious of his uneasiness. Not one of his references to names and events so vital to himself had in any way produced a change in her. Was she, after all, innocent of all knowledge in the things he wished to know? Was it possible that she was entirely ignorant as to the identity of the men who had attacked Pierre and herself on the cliff? Was it true that she did not know Eileen Brokaw, that she had never heard of Lord Fitzhugh Lee, and that she had always lived among the wild people of the north? By what miracle performed here in the heart of a savage world could this girl talk to him in German and Latin? Was she making fun of him? He turned to look at her and found her dark, clear eyes upon him. She smiled at him in a tired little way, and he saw nothing but sweetness and truth in her face. In an instant every suspicion was swept away. He felt like a criminal for having doubted her; and for a moment he was on the point of confessing to her what had been in his thoughts. He restrained himself, and went to the river to wash the pot-black from his hands. Jeanne was a mystery to him, a mystery that delighted him and filled him each moment with a deeper love. He saw the life and freedom of the forests in her every movement—in the gesture of her hands, the bird-like poise of her pretty head, the lithe grace of her slender body. She breathed the forests. It glowed in her eyes, in the rich red of her lips, and revealed its beauty and strength in the unconfined wealth of her gold-brown hair. In a dozen ways he could see her primitiveness, her kinship to the wilderness. She had told him the truth. Her eyes smiled truth at him as he came up the bank. No other woman's eyes had ever looked at him like hers; none had he seen so beautiful. And yet in them he saw nothing that she would not have expressed in words—companionship, trust, thankfulness that he was there to care for her. Such eyes as those belonged only to the wilderness, brimming with the flawless beauty of an undefiled nature. He had seen them, but not so beautiful, in Cree women. He thought of Eileen Brokaw's eyes as he looked at Jeanne's. They were very beautiful, but they were DIFFERENT. Jeanne's could not lie.

On a white napkin Jeanne had spread out cold meat, bread, pickles, and cheese, and Philip brought her the coffee. He noticed that she was resting a little of her weight upon her injured ankle.

"Better?" he asked, indicating the bandaged ankle with a nod of his head.

"Much," replied Jeanne, as tersely. "I'm going to try standing upon it in a few minutes. But not now. I'm starved."

She gave him his coffee and began eating with a relish that made him want to sit back and watch her. Instead, he joined her; and they ate like two hungry children. It was when she turned him out a second cup of coffee that Philip noticed her hand tremble a little.

"If Pierre was here we would be quite happy, M'sieur Philip," she said, uneasily. "I can't understand why he asked you to run away with me to Fort o' God. If he is not badly hurt, as you have told me, why do we not hide and wait for him? He would overtake us to-morrow."

"There—there was no time to talk over plans," answered Philip, inwardly embarrassed for a moment by the unexpectedness of Jeanne's question. A vision of Pierre, bleeding and unconscious on the cliff, leaped into his mind, and the thought that he had lied to Jeanne and must still make her believe what was half false sickened him. There was, after all, a chance that Pierre would never again come up the Churchill. "Perhaps Pierre thought we would be hotly pursued," he went on, seeing no escape from the demand in the girl's eyes. "In that event it would be best for me to get you to Fort o' God as quickly as possible. You must remember that Pierre was thinking of you. He can care for himself. It may take him two or three days to get back the strength of—of his arm," he finished, blindly.

"He was wounded in the arm?"

"And on the head," said Philip. "It was only a scalp wound, however— nothing at all, except that it dazed him a little at the time."

Jeanne pointed to the reflection of the fire on the river.

"If we should be pursued?" she suggested.

"There is no danger," assured Philip, though he had left the flap of his revolver holster unbuttoned. "They will search for us between their camp and Churchill."

"Citius venit periculum cum contemnitur," remonstrated Jeanne, half smiling.

She was pale, but Philip saw that she was making a tremendous effort to appear brave and cheerful.

"Perhaps you are right," laughed Philip, "but I swear that I don't know what you mean. I suppose you picked that lingo up among the Indians."

He caught the faintest gleam of Jeanne's white teeth again as she bent her head.

"I have a tutor at home," she explained, softly. "You shall meet him when we reach Fort o' God. He is the most wonderful man in the world."

Her words sent a strange chill through Philip. They were filled with an exquisite tenderness, a pride that sent her eyes back to his, glowing. The questions that he had meant to ask died and faded away. He thought of her words of a few minutes before, when he had asked about Fort o' God. She had said, "My father, Pierre, and I, WITH ONE OTHER, live there alone." The OTHER was the tutor, the man who had come from civilization to teach this beautiful girl those things which had amazed him, and this man was THE MOST WONDERFUL MAN IN THE WORLD. He had no excuse for the feelings which were aroused in him. Only he knew, as he rose to his feet, that a part of his old burden seemed suddenly to have returned to his shoulders, and the old loneliness was beating at the door of his heart. He rearranged the pack in silence, and the strength and joy of life were gone from his arms when he helped Jeanne back to her place among the bear-skins. He did not notice that her eyes were watching him curiously, or that her lips trembled once or twice, as if about to speak words which never came. Jeanne, as well as he, seemed to have discovered something which neither dared to reveal in that last five minutes on the shore.

"There is one thing that I must know," said Philip, when they were about to start, "and that is where to find Fort o' God? Is it on the Churchill?"

"It is on the Little Churchill, M'sieur, near Waskiaowaka Lake."

Darkness concealed the effect of her words upon Philip. For a moment he stared like one struck dumb. He stifled the exclamation that rose to his lips. He felt himself trembling. He knew that if he spoke his voice would betray him.

NEAR WASKIAOWAKA LAKE! And Waskiaowaka was within thirty miles of his own camp on the Blind Indian! If a bomb had burst under his feet he could not have been more amazed than at this information, given to him in Jeanne's quiet voice. Fort o' God—within thirty miles of the scene where very soon he was to fight the great battle of his life! He dug his paddle into the water and sent the canoe hissing up the river. His blood pounded like that of a racehorse on the home-stretch. Of all the things that had happened, of all he had learned, this was the most significant. Every thought ran like a separate powder-flash to a single idea, to one great, overpowering question. Were Fort o' God and its people the key to the plot against himself and his company? Was it the rendezvous of those who were striving to work his ruin? Doubt, suspicion, almost belief came to him in those few moments, in spite of himself.

He looked at Jeanne. The gray dawn was breaking, and now light followed swiftly and dissolved the last mist. In the chill of early morning, when with the approach of the sun a cold, uncomfortable sweat rises heavily from the earth and water, Jeanne had drawn one of the bearskins closely about her. Her head was bare. Her hair, glistening with damp, clung in heavy masses about her face. There was a bewitching childishness about her, a pathetic appeal to him in the forlorn little picture she made—so helpless, and yet so confident in him. Every energy in him leaped up in defiance of the revolution which for a few moments had stirred within him. And Jeanne, as though she had read the working of his mind, looked straight at him and smiled, with a little purring note in her throat that took the place of a thousand words. It was such a smile, and yet not one of love, which puts the strength of ten men in one man's arms; and Philip laughed back at her, every chord in his body responding in joyous vibration to the delicate note that had come with it. No matter what events might find their birth at Fort o' God, Jeanne was innocent of all knowledge of plot or wrong-doing. Once for all Philip convinced himself of this.

The thought that came to him, as he looked at Jeanne, found voice through his lips.

"Do you know," he said, "if I never saw you again I would always have three pictures of you in my memory. I would never forget how you looked when I first saw you on the cliff—or as I see you now, wrapped in your bearskins. Only—I would think of you—as you smiled."

"And the third picture?" questioned Jeanne, little guessing what was in his mind. "Would that be at the fire, when I burned the bad man's neck—or—or when—"

She stopped herself, and pouted her mouth in sudden vexation, while a flush which Philip could easily see rose in her cheeks.

"When I doctored your foot?" he finished, rather unchivalrously, chuckling in his delight at her pretty discomfiture. "No, that wouldn't be the third, Miss Jeanne. The other scene which I shall never forget was that on the stone pier at Churchill, when you met a beautiful girl who was coming off the ship."

The blood leaped to Jeanne's face. Her soft lips tightened. A sudden movement, and the bearskin slipped from her shoulders, leaving her leaning a little forward, her eyes blazing. A dozen words had transformed her from the child he had fancied her to a woman quivering with some powerful emotion, her beautiful head proud and erect, her nostrils dilating with the quickness of her breath.

"That was a mistake," she said. There was no sign of passion in her voice. It trembled a little, but that was all. "It was a mistake, M'sieur Philip. I thought that I knew her, and—and I was wrong. You—you must not remember THAT!"

"I am no better than a wild beast," groaned Philip, hating himself. "I'm the biggest idiot in the world when it comes to saying the wrong thing, I never miss a chance. I didn't mean to say anything—that would hurt—"

"You haven't," interrupted the girl, quickly, seeing the distress in his face. "You haven't said a thing that's wrong. Only I don't want you to remember THAT picture. I want you to think of me as—as—I burned the bad man's neck."

She was laughing now, though her breast was rising and falling a little excitedly and the deep color was still in her cheeks.

"Will you?" she entreated.

"Until I die," he exclaimed.

She was fumbling under the luggage, and dragged forth a second paddle.

"I've had an easy time with you, M'sieur Philip," she said, turning so that she was kneeling with her back to him. "Pierre makes me work. Always I kneel here, in the bow, and paddle. I am ashamed of myself. You have worked all night."

"And I feel as fresh as though I had slept for a week," declared Philip, his eyes devouring the slim figure a paddle's length in front of him.

For an hour they continued up the river, with scarcely a word between them to break the silence. Their paddles rose and fell with a rhythmic motion; the water rippled like low music under their canoe; the spell of the silent shores, of voiceless beauty, of the wilderness awakening into day appealed to them both and held them quiet. The sun broke faintly through the drawn mists behind. Its first rays lighted up Jeanne's rumpled hair, so that her heavy braid, partly undone and falling upon the luggage behind her, shone in rich and changing colors that fascinated Philip. He had thought that Jeanne's hair was very dark, but he saw now that it was filled with the rare life of a Titian head, running from red to gold and dark brown, with changing shadows and flashes of light. It was beautiful. And Jeanne, as he looked at her, he thought to be the most beautiful thing on earth. The movement of her arms, the graceful, sinuous twists of her slender body as she put her strength upon the paddle, the poise of her head, the piquant tilt to her chin whenever she turned so that he caught a half profile of her flushed, eager face all filled his cup of admiration to overflowing. And he found himself wondering, suddenly, how this girl could be a sister to Pierre Couchee. He saw in her no sign of French or half-breed blood. Her hair was fine and soft, and waved about her ears and where it fell loose upon the back. The color in her cheeks was as delicate as the tints of the bakneesh flower. She had rolled up her broad cuffs to give her greater freedom in paddling, and her arms shone white and firm, glistening with the wet drip of the paddle. He was marveling at her relationship to Pierre when she looked back at him, her face aglow with exercise and the spice of the morning, and he saw the sunlight as blue as the sky above him in her eyes. If he had not known, he would have sworn that there was not a drop of Pierre's blood in her veins.

"We are coming to the first rapids, M'sieur Philip," she announced. "It is just beyond that ugly mountain of rock ahead of us, and we will have a quarter-mile portage. It is filled with great stones and so swift that Pierre and I nearly wrecked ourselves coming down."

It was the most that had been said since the beginning of that wonderful hour that had come before the first gleam of sunrise, and Philip, laying his paddle athwart the canoe, stretched himself and yawned, as though he had just awakened.

"Poor boy," said Jeanne; and it struck him that her words were strangely like those which Eileen might have spoken had she been there, only an artless comradeship replaced what would have been Miss Brokaw's tone of intimacy. She added, with genuine sympathy in her face and voice: "You must be exhausted, M'sieur Philip. If you were Pierre I should insist upon going ashore for a number of hours. Pierre obeys me when we are together. He calls me his captain. Won't you let me command you?"

"If you will let me call you—my captain," replied Philip. "Only there is one thing—one reservation. We must go on. Command me in everything else, but we must go on—for a time. To-night I will sleep. I will sleep like the dead. So, My Captain," he laughed, "may I have your permission to work to-day?"

Jeanne was turning the bow shoreward. Her back was turned to him again.

"You have no pity on me," she pouted. "Pierre would be good to me, and we would fish all day in that pretty pool over there. I'll bet it's full of trout."

Her words, her manner of speaking them, was a new revelation to Philip. She was delightful. He laughed, and his voice rang out in the clear morning like a school-boy's. Jeanne pretended that she saw nothing to laugh at, and no sooner had the canoe touched shore than she sprang lightly out, not waiting for his assistance. With a laughing cry, she stumbled and fell. Philip was at her side in an instant.

"You shouldn't have done that," he objected. "I am your doctor, and I insist that your foot is not well."

"But it is!" cried Jeanne, and he saw that there was laughter instead of pain in her eyes. "It's the bandage. My right foot feels like that of a Chinese debutante. Ugh! I'm going to undo it."

"You've been to China, too," mused Philip, half to himself.

"I know that it's filled with yellow girls, and that they squeeze their feet like this," said Jeanne, unlacing her moccasin. "My tutor and I have just finished a delightful trip along the Great Wall. We'd go to Peking, in an automobile, if I wasn't afraid."

Philip's groan was audible. He went to the canoe, and Jeanne's red lips curled in a merriment which it was hard for her too suppress. Philip did not see. When he had unloaded the canoe and turned, Jeanne was walking slowly back and forth, limping a little.

"It's all right," she said, answering the question on his lips. "I don't feel any pain at all, but my foot's asleep. Won't you please unstrap the small pack? I'm going to make my toilet while you are gone with the canoe."

Half an hour later Philip unshouldered the canoe at the upper end of the rapids. His own toilet articles were back in the cabin with Gregson, but he took a wash in the river and combed his hair with his fingers. When he returned, there was a transformation in Jeanne. Her beautiful hair was done up in shining coils. She had changed her bedraggled skirt for another of soft, yellow buckskin. At her throat she wore a fluffy mass of crimson stuff which seemed to reflect a richer rose-flush in her cheeks. A curious thought came to Philip as he looked at her. Like a flash the memory of a certain night came to him—when it had taken Miss Brokaw and her maid two hours to make a toilet for a ball. And Jeanne, in the heart of a wilderness, had made herself more beautiful than Eileen. He imagined, as she stood before him, a little embarrassed by the admiration in his eyes, the sensation Jeanne would create in a ballroom at home. And then he laughed—laughed joyously at thoughts which he could not reveal to Jeanne, and which she, by some quick intuition, knew that she should not ask him to express.

Twice again Philip made the portage, accompanied the second time by Jeanne, who insisted on carrying a small pack and two paddles. In spite of his determination and splendid physique, Philip began to feel the effects of the tremendous strain which he had been under for so long. He counted back and found that he had slept but six hours in the last forty-eight. There was a warning ache in his shoulders and a gnawing pain in the bones of his forearms. But he knew that he had not yet made sufficient headway up the Churchill. It would not be difficult for him to make a camp far enough back in the bush to avoid discovery; but, at the same time, if he and Jeanne were pursued, the stop would give their enemies a chance to get ahead of them. This danger he wished to escape.

He flattered himself that Jeanne saw no signs of his weakening. He did not know that Jeanne put more and more effort into her paddle, until her arms and body ached, because she saw the truth.

The Churchill narrowed and its current became swifter as they progressed. Five portages were made between sunrise and eleven o'clock. They ate dinner at the fifth, and rested for two hours. Then the journey was resumed. It was three o'clock when Jeanne dropped her paddle and turned to Philip. There were deep lines in his face. He smiled, but there was more of haggard misery than cheer in the smile. There was an unnatural flush in his cheeks, and he began to feel a burning pain where the blow had fallen upon his head before. For a full half-minute Jeanne looked at him without speaking. "Philip," she said—and it was the first time she had spoken his name in this way, "I insist upon going ashore immediately. If you do not land—now—in that opening ahead, I shall jump out, and you can go on alone."

"As you say—my Captain Jeanne," surrendered Philip, a little dizzily.

Jeanne guided the canoe to the shore, and was the first to spring out, while Philip steadied the light craft with his paddle. She pointed to the luggage.

"We will want the tent—everything," she said, "because we are going to camp here until to-morrow."

Once on shore, Philip's dizziness left him. He pulled the canoe high up on the bank, and then Jeanne and he set off, side by side, to explore the high, wooded ground back from the river. They followed a well-worn moose trail, and two or three hundred yards from the stream came upon a small opening cluttered by great rocks and surrounded by clumps of birch, spruce, and banskian pine. The moose trail crossed this rough open space; and, following it to the opposite side, Philip and Jeanne came upon a clear, rippling little stream, scarcely two yards in width, hidden in places under thick caribou moss and jungles of seedling pines. It was an ideal camping spot, and Jeanne gave a little cry of delight when they found the cold water of the creek.

Philip then returned to the river, concealed the canoe, covered up all traces of their landing, and began to carry the camping outfit back to the open. The small silk tent for Jeanne's use he set up in a little grassy corner of the clearing, and built their fire a dozen paces from it. With a sort of thrilling pleasure he began cutting balsam boughs for Jeanne's bed. He cut armful after armful, and it was growing dusk in the forest by the time he was done. In the glow and the heat of the fire Jeanne's cheeks were as pink as an apple. She had turned a big flat rock into a table, and as she busied herself about this she burst suddenly into a soft ripple of song; then, remembering that it was not Pierre who was near her, she stopped. Philip, with his last armful of bedding, was directly behind her, and he laughed happily at her over the green mass of balsam when she turned and saw him looking at her.

"You like this?" he asked.

"It is glorious!" cried Jeanne, her eyes flashing. She seemed to grow taller before him, and stood with her head thrown back, lips parted, gazing upon the wilderness about her. "It is glorious!" she repeated, breathing deeply. "There is nothing in the whole world that could make me give this up, M'sieur Philip. I was born in it. I want to die in it. Only—"

Her face clouded for a moment as her eyes rested upon his.

"Your civilization is coming north to spoil it all," she added, and turned to the rock table.

Philip dropped his load.

"Supper is ready," she said, and the cloud had passed.

It was Jeanne's first reference to his own people, to the invasion of civilization into the north, and there recurred to Philip the words in which she had cried out her hatred against Churchill. But Jeanne did not betray herself again. She was quiet while they were eating, and Philip saw that she was very tired. When they had finished, they sat for a few minutes watching the lowering flames of the fire. Darkness had gathered about them. Their faces and the rock were illumined more and more faintly as the embers died down. A silence fell upon them. In the banskians close behind them an owl hooted softly, a cautious, drumming note, as though the night-bird possessed still a fear of the newly dead day. The brush gave out sound—voices infinitesimally small, strange quiverings, rustlings that might have been made by wind, by breath, by shadows, almost. Overhead the tips of the spruce and tall pines whispered among themselves, as they never commune by day. Spirits seemed to move among them, sending down to Jeanne's and Philip's listening ears a restful, sleepy murmur. Farther back there sounded a deep sniff, where a moose, traveling the well-worn trail, stopped in sudden fear and wonder at the strange man-scent which came to its nostrils. And still farther, from some little lake nameless and undiscovered in the black depths of the forest to the south, a great northern loon sent out its cowardly cry of defiance to all night things, and then plunged deep under water, as though frightened into the depths by its own mad jargon. The fire died lower. Philip moved a little nearer to the girl, whose breathing he could hear.

"Jeanne," he said, softly, fighting to keep himself from touching her hand, "I know what you mean—I understand. Two years ago I gave up civilization for this. I am glad that I wrote to you as I did, for now you will believe me and know that I understand. I love this world up here as you love it. I am never going back again."

Jeanne was silent.

"But there is one thing, at least one—which I cannot understand in you," he went on, nerving himself for what might come a moment later. "You are of this world—you hate civilization—and yet you have brought a man into the north to teach you its ways. I mean this man who you say is the most wonderful man in the world."

He waited, trembling. It seemed an eternity before Jeanne answered. And then she said:

"He is my father, M'sieur Philip."

Philip could not speak. Darkness hid him from Jeanne. She did not see that which leaped into his face, and that for a moment he was on the point of flinging himself at her feet.

"You spoke of yourself, of Pierre, of your father, and of one other at Fort o' God," said Philip. "I thought that he—the other—was your tutor."

"No, it is Pierre's sister," replied Jeanne.

"Your sister! You have a sister?"

He could hear Jeanne catch her breath.

"Listen, M'sieur,'" she said, after a moment. "I must tell you a little about Pierre, a story of something that happened a long, long time ago. It was in the middle of a terrible winter, and Pierre was then a boy. One day he was out hunting and he came upon a trail—the trail of a woman who had dragged herself through the snow in her moccasined feet. It was far out upon a barren, where there was no life, and he followed. He found her, M'sieur, and she was dead. She had died from cold and starvation. An hour sooner he might have saved her, for, wrapped up close against her breast, he found a little child—a baby girl, and she was alive. He brought her to Fort o' God, M'sieur—to a noble man who lived there almost alone; and there, through all these years, she has lived and grown up. And no one knows who her mother was, or who her father was, and so it happens that Pierre, who found her, is her brother, and the man who has loved her and cared for her is her father."

"And she is the other at Fort o' God—Pierre's sister," said Philip.

Jeanne rose from the rock and moved toward the tent, glimmering indistinctly in the night. Her voice came back chokingly.

"No, M'sieur. Pierre's real sister is at Fort o' God. I am the one whom he found out on the barren."

To the night sounds there was added a heart-broken sob, and Jeanne disappeared in the tent.

XIV

Philip sat where Jeanne had left him. He was powerless to move or to say a word that might have recalled her. Her own grief, quivering in that one piteous sob, overwhelmed him. It held him mute and listening, with the hope that each instant the tent-flap might open and Jeanne reappear. And yet if she came he had no words to say. Unwittingly he had probed deep into one of those wounds that never heal, and he realized that to ask forgiveness would be but another blunder. He almost groaned as he thought of what he had done. In his desire to understand, to know more about Jeanne, he had driven her into a corner. What he had forced from her he might have learned a little later from Pierre or from the father at Fort o' God. He thought that Jeanne must despise him now, for he had taken advantage of her helplessness and his own position. He had saved her from her enemies; and in return she had opened her heart, naked and bleeding, to his eyes. What she had told him was not a voluntary confidence; it was a confession wrung from her by the rack of his questionings—the confession that she was a waif-child, that Pierre was not her brother, and that the man at Fort o' God was not her father. He had gone to the very depths of that which was sacred to herself and those whom she loved.

He rose and stirred the fire, and stray ends of birch leaped into flame, lighting his pale face. He wanted to go to the tent, kneel there where Jeanne could hear him, and tell her that it was all a mistake. Yet he knew that this could not be, neither the next day nor the next, for to plead extenuation for himself would be to reveal his love. Two or three times he had been on the point of revealing that love. Only now, after what had happened, did it occur to him that to disclose his heart to Jeanne would be the greatest crime he could commit. She was alone with him in the heart of a wilderness, dependent upon him, upon his honor. He shivered when he thought how narrow had been his escape, how short a time he had known her, and how in that brief spell he had given himself up to an almost insane hope. To him Jeanne was not a stranger. She was the embodiment, in flesh and blood, of the spirit which had been his companion for so long. He loved her more than ever now, for Jeanne the lost child of the snows was more the earthly revelation of his beloved spirit than Jeanne the sister of Pierre. But—what was he to Jeanne?

He left the fire and went to the pile of balsam which he had spread out between two rocks for his bed. He lay down and pulled Pierre's blanket over him, but his fatigue and his desire for sleep seemed to have left him, and it was a long time before slumber finally drove from him the thought of what he had done. After that he did not move. He heard none of the sounds of the night. A little owl, the devil-witch, screamed horribly overhead and awakened Jeanne, who sat up for a few moments in her balsam bed, white-faced and shivering. But Philip slept. Long afterward something warm awakened him, and he opened his eyes, thinking that it was the glow of the fire in his face. It was the sun. He heard a sound which brought him quickly into consciousness of day. It was Jeanne singing softly over beyond the rocks.

He had dreaded the coming of morning, when he would have to face Jeanne. His guilt hung heavily upon him. But the sound of her voice, low and sweet, filled with the carroling happiness of a bird, brought a glad smile to his lips. After all, Jeanne had understood him. She had forgiven him, if she had not forgotten.

For the first time he noticed the height of the sun, and he sat bolt upright. Jeanne saw his head and shoulders pop over the top of the rocks, and she laughed at him from their stone table.

"I've been keeping breakfast for over an hour, M'sieur Philip," she cried. "Hurry down to the creek and wash yourself, or I shall eat all alone!"

Philip rose stupidly and looked at his watch.

"Eight o'clock!" he gasped. "We should have been ten miles on the way by this time!"

Jeanne was still laughing at him. Like sunlight she dispelled his gloom of the night before. A glance around the camp showed him that she must have been awake for at least two hours. The packs were filled and strapped. The silken tent was down and folded. She had gathered wood, built the fire, and cooked breakfast while he slept. And now she stood a dozen paces from him, blushing a little at his amazed stare, waiting for him.

"It's deuced good of you, Miss Jeanne!" he exclaimed. "I don't deserve such kindness from you."

"Oh!" said Jeanne, and that was all. She bent over the fire, and Philip went to the creek.

He was determined now to maintain a more certain hold upon himself. As he doused his face in the cold water his resolutions formed

JAMES OLIVER CURWOOD

themselves. For the next few days he would forget everything but the one fact that Jeanne was in his care; he would not hurt her again or compel her confidence.

It was after nine o'clock before they were upon the river. They paddled without a rest until twelve. After lunch Philip confiscated Jeanne's paddle and made her sit facing him in the canoe.

The afternoon passed like a dream to Philip, He did not refer again to Fort o' God or the people there; he did not speak again of Eileen Brokaw, of Lord Fitzhugh, or of Pierre. He talked of himself and of those things which had once been his life. He told of his mother and his father, who had died, and of the little sister, whom he had worshiped, but who had gone with the others. He bared his loneliness to her as he would have told them to the sister, had she lived; and Jeanne's soft blue eyes were filled with tenderness and sympathy. And then he talked of Gregson's world. Within himself he called it no longer his own.

It was Jeanne who questioned now. She asked about cities and great people, about books and WOMEN. Her knowledge amazed Philip. She might have visited the Louvre. One would have guessed that she had walked in the streets of Paris, Berlin, and London. She spoke of Johnson, of Dickens, and of Balzac as though they had died but yesterday. She was like one who had been everywhere and yet saw everything through a veil that bewildered her. In her simplicity she unfolded herself to Philip, leaf by leaf, petal by petal, like the morning apios that surrenders its mysteries to the sun. She knew the world which he had come from, its people, its cities, its greatness; and yet her knowledge was like that of the blind. She knew, but she had never seen; and in her wistfulness to see as HE could see there was a sweetness and a pathos which made every fiber in his body sing with a quiet and thrilling joy. He knew, now, that the man who was at Fort o' God must, indeed, be the most wonderful man in the world. For out of a child of the snows, of the forest, of a savage desolation, he had made Jeanne. And Jeanne was glorious!

The afternoon passed, and they made thirty miles before they camped for the night. They traveled the next day, and the one that followed. On the afternoon of the fourth they were approaching Big Thunder Rapids, close to the influx of the Little Churchill, sixty miles from Fort o' God.

These days, too, passed for Philip with joyous swiftness; swiftly because they were too short for him. His life, now, was Jeanne. Each day she became a more vital part of him. She crept into his soul until there was no longer left room for any other thought than of her. And yet his happiness was tampered by a thing which, if not grief, depressed and saddened him at times. Two days more and they would be at Fort o' God, and there Jeanne would be no longer his own, as she was now. Even the wilderness has its conventionality, and at Fort o' God their comradeship would end. A day of rest, two at the most, and he would leave for the camp on Blind Indian Lake. As the time drew nearer when they would be but friends and no longer comrades, Philip could not always hide the signs of gloom which weighed upon him. He revealed nothing in words; but now and then Jeanne had caught him when the fears at his heart betrayed themselves in his face. Jeanne became happier as their journey approached its end. She was alive every moment, joyous, expectant, looking ahead to Fort o' God; and this in itself was a bitterness to Philip, though he knew that he was a fool for allowing it to be so. He reasoned, with dull, masculine wit, that if Jeanne cared for him at all she would not be so anxious for their comradeship to end. But these moods, when they came, passed quickly. And on this afternoon of the fourth day they passed away entirely, for in an instant there came a solution to it all. They had known each other but four days, yet that brief time had encompassed what might not have been in as many years. Life, smooth, uneventful, develops friendship slowly; an hour of the unusual may lay bare a soul. Philip thought of Eileen Brokaw, whose heart was still a closed mystery to him; who was a stranger, in spite of the years he had known her. In four days he had known Jeanne a lifetime; in those four days Jeanne had learned more of him than Eileen Brokaw could ever know. So he arrived at the resolution which made him, too, look eagerly ahead to the end of the journey. At Fort o' God he would tell Jeanne of his love.

Jeanne was looking at him when the determination came. She saw the gloom pass, a flush mount into his face; and when he saw her eyes upon him he laughed, without knowing why.

"If it is so funny," she said, "please tell me."

It was a temptation, but he resisted it.

"It is a secret," he said, "which I shall keep until we reach Fort o' God."

Jeanne turned her face up-stream to listen. A dozen times she had done this during the last half-hour, and Philip had listened with her. At first they had heard a distant murmur, rising as they advanced, like an autumn wind that grows stronger each moment in the tree-tops. The murmur was steady now, without the variations of a wind. It was the distant roaring of the rocks and rushing floods of Big Thunder Rapids. It grew steadily from a murmur to a moan, from a moan to rumbling thunder. The current became so swift that Philip was compelled to use all his strength to force the canoe ahead. A few moments later he turned into shore.

From where they landed, a worn trail led up to one of the precipitous walls of rock and shut in the Big Thunder Rapids. Everything about them was rock. The trail was over rock, worn smooth by the countless feet of centuries—clawed feet, naked feet, moccasined feet, the feet of white men. It was the Great Portage, for animal as well as man. Philip went up with the pack, and Jeanne followed behind him. The thunder increased. It roared in their ears until they could no longer hear their own voices. Directly above the rapids the trail was narrow, scarcely eight feet in width, shut in on the land side by a mountain wall, on the other by the precipice. Philip looked behind, and saw Jeanne hugging close to the wall. Her face was white, her eyes shone with terror and awe. He spoke to her, but she saw only the movement of his lips. Then he put down his pack and went close to the edge of the precipice.

Sixty feet below him was the Big Thunder, a chaos of lashing foam, of slippery, black-capped rocks bobbing and grimacing amid the rushing torrents like monsters playing at hide-and-seek. Now one rose high, as though thrust up out of chaos by giant hands; then it sank back, and milk-white foam swirled softly over the place where it had been. There seemed to be life in the chaos—a grim, terrible life whose voice was a thunder that never died. For a few moments Philip stood fascinated by the scene below him. Then he felt a touch upon his arm. It was Jeanne. She stood beside him quivering, dead-white, Almost daring to take the final step. Philip caught her hands firmly in his own, and Jeanne looked over. Then she darted back and hovered, shuddering, near the wall.

The portage was a short one, scarce two hundred yards in length, and at the upper end was a small green meadow in which river voyagers camped. It still lacked two hours of dusk when Philip carried over the last of the luggage.

"We will not camp here," he said to Jeanne pointing to the remains of numerous fires and remembering Pierre's exhortation. "It is too public, as you might say. Besides, that noise makes me deaf."

Jeanne shuddered.

"Let us hurry," she said. "I'm—I'm afraid of THAT!"

Philip carried the canoe down to the river, and Jeanne followed with the bearskins. The current was soft and sluggish, with tiny maelstroms gurgling up here and there, like air-bubbles in boiling syrup. He only half launched the canoe, and Jeanne remained while he went for another load. The dip, kept green by the water of a spring, was a pistol-shot from the river. Philip looked back from the crest and saw Jeanne leaning over the canoe. Then he descended into the meadow, whistling. He had reached the packs when to his ears there seemed to come a sound that rose faintly above the roar of the water in the chasm. He straightened himself and listened.

"Philip! Philip!"

The cry came twice—his own name, piercing, agonizing, rising above the thunder of the floods. He heard no more, but raced up the slope of the dip. From the crest he stared down to where Jeanne had been. She was gone. The canoe was gone. A terrible fear swept upon him, and for an instant he turned faint. Jeanne's cry came to him again.

"Philip! Philip!"

Like a madman he dashed up the rocky trail to the chasm, calling to Jeanne, shrieking to her, telling her that he was coming. He reached the edge of the precipice and looked down. Below him was the canoe and Jeanne. She was fighting futilely against the resistless flood; he saw her paddle wrenched suddenly from her hands, and as it went swirling beyond her reach she cried out his name again. Philip shouted, and the girl's white face was turned up to him. Fifty yards ahead of her were the first of the rocks. In another minute, even less, Jeanne would be dashed to pieces before his eyes. Thoughts, swifter than light, flashed through his mind. He could do nothing for her, for it seemed impossible that any living creature could exist amid the maelstroms and rocks ahead. And yet she was calling to him. She was reaching up her arms to him. She had faith in him, even in the face of death.

"Philip! Philip!"

There was no M'sieur to that cry now, only a moaning, sobbing prayer filled with his name.

"I'm coming, Jeanne!" he shouted. "I'm coming! Hold fast to the canoe!"

He ran ahead, stripping off his coat. A little below the first rocks a stunted banskian grew out of an earthy fissure in the cliff, with its lower branches dipping within a dozen feet of the stream. He climbed out on this with the quickness of a squirrel, and hung to a limb with both hands, ready to drop alongside the canoe. There was one chance, and only one, of saving Jeanne. It was a chance out of a thousand— ten thousand. If he could drop at the right moment, seize the stern of the canoe, and make a rudder of himself, he could keep the craft from turning broadside and might possibly guide it between the rocks below. This one hope was destroyed as quickly as it was born. The canoe crashed against the first rock. A smother of foam rose about it and he saw Jeanne suddenly engulfed and lost. Then she reappeared, almost under him, and he launched himself downward, clutching at her dress with his hands. By a supreme effort he caught her around the waist with his left arm, so that his right was free.

Ahead of them was a boiling sea of white, even more terrible than when they had looked down upon it from above. The rocks were hidden by mist and foam; their roar was deafening. Between Philip and the awful maelstrom of death there was a quieter space of water, black, sullen, and swift—the power itself, rushing on to whip itself into ribbons among the taunting rocks that barred its way to the sea. In that space Philip looked at Jeanne. Her face was against his breast. Her eyes met his own, and In that last moment, face to face with death, love leaped above all fear. They were about to die, and Jeanne would die in his arms. She was his now—forever. His hold tightened. Her face came nearer. He wanted to shout, to let her know what he had meant to say at Fort o' God. But his voice would have been like a whisper in a hurricane. Could Jeanne understand? The wall of foam was almost in their faces. Suddenly he bent down, crushed his face to hers, and kissed her again and again. Then, as the maelstrom engulfed them, he swung his own body to take the brunt of the shock.

He no longer reasoned beyond one thing. He must keep his body between Jeanne and the rocks. He would be crushed, beaten to pieces, made unrecognizable, but Jeanne would be only drowned. He fought to keep himself half under her, with his head and shoulders in advance. When he felt the floods sucking him under, he thrust her upward. He fought, and did not know what happened. Only there was the crashing of a thousand cannon in his ears, and he seemed to live through an eternity. They thundered about him, against him, ahead of him, and then more and more behind. He felt no pain, no shock. It was the Sound that he seemed to be fighting; in the buffeting of his body against the rocks there was the painlessness of a knife-thrust delivered amid the roar of battle. And the sound receded. It was thundering in retreat, and a curious thought came to him. Providence had delivered him through the maelstrom. He had not struck the rocks. He was saved. And in his arms he held Jeanne.

It was day when he began the fight, broad day. And now it was night. He felt earth, under his feet, and he knew that he had brought Jeanne ashore. He heard her voice speaking his name; and he was so glad that he laughed and sobbed like a babbling idiot. It was dark, and he was tired. He sank down, and he could feel Jeanne's arms striving to hold him up, and he could still hear her voice. But nothing could keep him from sleeping. And during that sleep he had visions. Now it was day, and he saw Jeanne's face over him; again it was night, and he heard only the roaring of the flood. Again he heard voices, Jeanne's voice and a man's, and he wondered who the man could be. It was a strange sleep filled with strange dreams. But at last the dreams seemed to go. He lost himself. He awoke, and the night had turned into day. He was in a tent, and the sun was gleaming on the outside. It had been a curious dream, and he sat up astonished.

There was a man sitting beside him. It was Pierre.

"Thank God, M'sieur!" he heard. "We have been waiting for this. You are saved!"

"Pierre!" he gasped.

Memory returned to him. He was awake. He felt weak, but he knew that what he saw was not the vision of a dream.

"I came the day after you went through the rapids," explained Pierre, seeing his amazement. "You saved Jeanne. She was not hurt. But you were badly bruised, M'sieur, and you have been in a fever."

"Jeanne—was not—hurt?"

"No. She cared for you until I came. She is sleeping now."

"I have not been this way—very long, have I, Pierre?"

"I came yesterday," said Pierre. He bent over Philip, and added: "You must remain quiet for a little longer, M'sieur. I have brought you a letter from M'sieur Gregson, and when you read that I will have some broth made for you."

Philip took the letter and opened it as Pierre went quietly out of the tent. Gregson had written him but a few lines. He wrote:

My Dear Phil,

I hope you'll forgive me. But I'm tired of this mess. I was never cut out for the woods, and so I'm going to dismiss myself, leaving all best wishes behind for you. Go in and fight. You're a devil for fighting, and will surely win. I'll only be in the way. So I'm going back with the ship, which leaves in three or four days. Was going to tell you this on the night you disappeared. Am sorry I couldn't shake hands with you before I left. Write and let me know how things come out. As ever,

Tom

Stunned, Philip dropped the letter. He lifted his eyes, and a strange cry burst from his lips. Nothing that Gregson had written could have wrung that cry from him. It was Jeanne. She stood in the open door of the tent. But it was not the Jeanne he had known. A terrible grief was written in her face. Her lips were bloodless, her eyes lusterless; deep suffering seemed to have put hollows in her cheeks. In a moment she had fallen upon her knees beside him and clasped one of his hands in both of her own.

"I am so glad," she whispered, chokingly.

For an instant she pressed his hands to her face.

"I am so glad—"

She rose to her feet, swaying slightly. She turned to the door, and Philip could hear her sobbing as she left him.

XV

Not until the silken flap of the tent had fallen behind Jeanne did power of movement and speech return to Philip. He called her name and straggled to a sitting posture. Then he staggered to his feet. He could scarcely stand. Shooting pains passed like flashes of electricity through his body. His right arm was numb and stiff, and he found that it was thickly bandaged. His head ached, his legs could hardly support him. He went to raise his left hand to his head, but stopped it in front of him, while a slow smile of understanding crept over his face. It was swollen and covered with livid bruises. He wondered if his body looked that way, and sank down exhausted upon his balsam bed. A minute later Pierre returned with a cup of broth in his hand.

Philip looked at him with less feverish eyes now. There was an unaccountable change in the half-breed's appearance, as there had been in Jeanne's. His face seemed thinner. There was a deep gloom in his eyes, a dejected droop to his shoulders. Philip accepted the broth, and drank it slowly, without speaking. He felt strengthened. Then he looked steadily at Pierre. The old pride had fallen from Pierre like a mask. His eyes dropped under Philip's gaze.

Philip held up a hand.

"Pierre!"

The half-breed grasped it and waited. His lips tightened.

"What is the matter?" demanded Philip. "What has happened to Jeanne? You say she was not hurt—"

"By the rocks, M'sieur," interrupted Pierre, quickly, kneeling beside Philip. "Listen. It is best that I tell you. You are a man, you will understand, without being told all. From Churchill I brought news which it was necessary for me to tell Jeanne. It was terrible news, and she is distressed under its weight. Your honor will not allow you to inquire further, M'sieur. I can tell you no more than this—that it is a grief which belongs to but one person on earth—herself. I ask you to help me. Be blind to her unhappiness, M'sieur. Believe that it is the distress of the peril through which she has passed. A little later I will tell you all, and you will understand. But it is impossible now. I confide this much in you—I ask you this—because—"

Pierre's eyes were half closed, and he looked as though unseeing over Philip's head.

"I ask you this," he repeated, softly, "because I have guessed—that you love her."

A cry of joy burst from Philip's lips.

"I do, Pierre—I do—I do—"

"I have guessed it," said Pierre. "You will help me—to save her!"

"Until death!"

"Then you will go with us to Fort o' God, and from there you will go at once to your camp on Blind Indian Lake."

Philip felt the sweat breaking out over his face. He was still weak. His voice was unnatural, and trembled.

"You know—" he gasped.

"Yes, I know, M'sieur," replied Pierre. "I know that you are in charge there, and Jeanne knows. We knew who you were before we appointed to meet you on the cliff. You must return to your men."

Philip was silent. For the moment every hope was crushed within him.

He looked at Pierre. The half-breed's eyes were glowing, his haggard cheeks were flushed.

"And this is necessary?"

"It is absolutely necessary, M'sieur."

"Then I will go. But first, Pierre, I must know a little more. I cannot go entirely blind. Do they fear my men—at Fort o' God?"

"No, M'sieur."

"One more question, Pierre. Who is Lord Fitzhugh Lee?"

For an instant Pierre's eyes widened. They grew black, and burned with a strange, threatening fire. He rose slowly to his feet, and placed both hands upon Philip's shoulders. For a full minute the two men stared into each other's face. Then Pierre spoke. His voice was soft and low, scarcely above a murmur, but it was filled with something that struck a chill to Philip's heart.

"I would kill you before I would answer that question, M'sieur," he said. "No other person has ever done for Jeanne and I what you have done. We owe you more than we can ever repay. Yet if you insist upon an answer to that question you make of me an enemy; if you breathe that name to Jeanne, you turn her away from you forever."

Without another word he left the tent.

For many minutes Philip sat motionless where Pierre had left him. The earth seemed suddenly to have dropped from under his feet, leaving him in an illimitable chaos of mind. Gregson had deserted him, with almost no word of explanation, and he would have staked his life upon

Gregson's loyalty. Under other circumstances his unaccountable action would have been a serious blow. But now it was overshadowed by the mysterious change that had come over Jeanne. A few hours before she had been happy, laughing and singing as they drew nearer to Fort o' God; each hour had added to the brightness of her eyes, the gladness in her voice. The change had come with Pierre, and at the bottom of it all was Lord Fitzhugh Lee. Pierre had warned him not to mention Lord Fitzhugh's name to Jeanne, and yet only a short time before he had spoken the name boldly before Jeanne, and she had betrayed no sign of recognition or of fear. More than that, she had assured him that she had never heard the name before, that it was not known at Fort o' God.

Philip bowed his head in his hands, and his fingers clutched in his hair. What did it all mean? He went back to the scene on the cliff, when Pierre had roused himself at the sound of the name; he thought of all that had happened since Gregson had come to Churchill, and the result was a delirium of thought that made his temples throb. He was sure—now—of but few things. He loved Jeanne—loved her more than he had ever dreamed that he could love a woman, and he believed that it would be impossible for her to tell him a falsehood. He was confident that she had never heard of Lord Fitzhugh until Pierre overtook them in their flight from Churchill. He could see but one thing to do, and that was to follow Pierre's advice, accepting his promise that in the end everything would come out right. He had faith in Pierre.

He rose to his feet and went to the tent-flap. An embarrassing thought came to him, and he stopped, a flush of feverish color suddenly mounting into his pale cheeks. He had kissed Jeanne in the chasm, when death thundered in their faces. He had kissed her again and again, and in those kisses he had declared his love. He was glad, and yet sorry; the knowledge that she must know of his love filled him with happiness, and yet with it there was the feeling that it would place a distance between him and Jeanne.

Jeanne was the first to see him when he came out of the tent. She was sitting beside a small balsam shelter, and Pierre was busy over a fire, with his back turned to them. For a moment the two looked at each other in silence, and then Jeanne came toward him, holding out one of her hands. He saw that she was making a strong effort to appear natural, but there was something in his own face that made her attempt a poor one. The hand that she gave him trembled. Her lips quivered. For the first time her eyes failed to meet his own in their limpid frankness.

"Pierre has told you what happened," she said. "It was a miracle, and I owe you my life. I have had my punishment for being so careless." She tried to laugh at him now, and drew her hand away. "I wasn't beaten against the rocks, like you, but—"

"It was terrible," interrupted Philip, remembering Pierre's words, and eager to put her at ease. "You have stood up under it beautifully. I am afraid of after effects. You must not collapse under the strain now."

Pierre heard his last words and a smile flashed over his dark face as he encountered Philip's glance.

"It is true, M'sieur," he said. "I know of no other woman who would have stood up under such a thing as Jeanne has done. Mon Dieu, when I found a part of the canoe wreckage far below I thought that both of you were dead!"

Philip began to feel that he had foolishly overestimated his strength. There was a weakness in his limbs that surprised him, and a sudden chill replaced the fever in his blood. Jeanne placed her hand upon his arm and thrust him gently toward the tent.

"You must not exert yourself," she said, watching the pallor in his face. "You must be quiet, until after dinner."

He obeyed the pressure of her hand. Pierre followed into the tent, and for a moment he was compelled to lean heavily upon the half-breed.

"It is the reaction, M'sieur," said Pierre. "You are weak after the fever. If you could sleep—"

"I can," murmured Philip, dizzily, dropping upon his balsam. "But, Pierre—"

"Yes, M'sieur."

"I have something—to say to you—no questions—"

"Not now, M'sieur."

Philip heard the rustling of the flap, and Pierre was gone. He felt more comfortable lying down. Dizziness and nausea left him, and he slept. It was the deep, refreshing sleep that always follows the awakening from fever. When he awoke he felt like his old self, and went outside. Pierre was alone; a blanket was drawn across the front of the balsam shelter, and the half-breed nodded toward it in response to Philip's inquiring glance.

Philip ate lightly of the food which Pierre had ready for him. When he had finished he leaned close to him, and said:

"You have warned me to ask no questions, and I am going to ask none. But you have not forbidden me to tell you things which I know. I am going to talk to you about Lord Fitzhugh Lee."

Pierre's dark eyes flashed.

"M'sieur—"

"Listen!" demanded Philip. "I seek your confidence no further. But I shall tell you what I know of Lord Fitzhugh Lee, if it makes us fight. Do you understand? I insist upon this because you have as good as told me that this man is your enemy, and that he is at the bottom of Jeanne's trouble. He is also my enemy. And after I have told you why—you may change your determination to keep me a stranger to your trouble. If not—well, you can hold your tongue then as well as now."

Quickly, without moving his eyes from Pierre's face, Philip told his own story of Lord Fitzhugh Lee. And as he continued a strange change came over the half-breed. When he came to the letters revealing the plot to turn the northerners against his company a low cry escaped Pierre's lips. His eyes seemed starting from his head. Drops of sweat burst out upon his face. His fingers worked convulsively, something rose in his throat and choked him. When Philip had done he buried his face in his hands. For a few moments he remained thus, and then suddenly looked up. Livid spots burned in his cheeks, and he fairly hissed at Philip.

"M'sieur, if this is not the truth—if this is a lie—"

He stopped. Something in Philip's eyes told him to go no further. He was fearless, and he saw more than fearlessness in Philip's face. Such men believe, when they come together.

"It is the truth," said Philip.

With a low, strained laugh Pierre held out his hand as a pledge of his faith.

"I believe in you, M'sieur," he said, and it seemed an effort for him to speak. "Do you know what I would have thought, if you had told this to Jeanne before I came?"

"No."

"I would have thought, M'sieur, that she threw herself purposely into the death of the Big Thunder rocks."

"My God, you mean—"

"That is all, M'sieur. I can say no more. Ah, there is Jeanne!" he cried, more loudly. "Now we will take down the tent, and go."

Jeanne stood a dozen steps behind them when Philip turned. She greeted him with a smile, and hastened to assist Pierre in gathering up the things about the camp. Philip was not blind to her efforts to evade him. He could see that it was a relief to her when they were at last in Pierre's canoe, and headed up the river. They traveled till late in the evening, and set up Jeanne's tent by starlight. The journey was continued at dawn. Late the following afternoon the Little Churchill swept through a low, woodless country, called the White Fox Barren. It was a narrow barren and across it lay the forest and the ridge mountains. Behind these mountains and the forest the sun was setting. Above all else there rose out of the gathering gloom of evening a single ridge, a towering mass of rock which caught the last glow of the sun, and blazed like a signal-fire.

The canoe stopped. Jeanne and Pierre both gazed toward the great rock.

Then Jeanne, who was in the bow, turned her face to Philip, and the glow of the rock itself suffused her cheeks as she pointed over the barren.

"M'sieur Philip," she said, "there is Fort o' God!"

XVI

There was a low tremble in Jeanne's voice. The canoe swung broadside to the slow current, and Philip looked in astonishment at the change in Pierre. The tired half-breed had uncovered his head, and knelt with his face turned to that last crimson glow in the sky, like one in prayer. But his eyes were open, there was a smile on his lips, and he was breathing quickly. Pride and joy came where there had been the lines of grief and exhaustion. His shoulders were thrown back, his head erect, and the fire of the distant rock reflected itself in his eyes. From him Philip turned, so that he could look into Jeanne's face. The girl, too, had changed. Again these two were the Pierre and Jeanne whom he had seen that first night on the moonlit cliff. Pierre seemed no longer the half-breed, but the prince of the rapier and broad cuffs; and Jeanne, smiling proudly at Philip, made him an exquisite little courtesy from her cramped seat in the bow, and said:

"M'sieur Philip, welcome to Fort o' God!"

"Thank you," he said, and stared toward the sun-capped rock.

He could see nothing but the rock, the black forests, and the desolate barren stretching between. Fort o' God, unless it was the rock itself, was still a mystery hidden in the gathering gloom. The canoe began moving slowly onward, and Jeanne turned so that her eyes searched the stream ahead. A thick wall of stunted forest shut out the barren from their view; the stream grew narrower, and on the opposite side a barren ridge, threatening them with torn and upheaved masses of rock, flung the heavy shadows of evening down upon them. No one spoke. Philip could hear Pierre breathing behind him: something in the intense quiet—in the awesome effect which their approach to Fort o' God had upon these two—sent strange little thrills shooting through his body. He listened, and heard nothing, not even the howl of a dog. The stillness was oppressive, and the darkness thickened about them. For half an hour they continued, and then Pierre headed the canoe into a narrow creek, thrusting it through a thick growth of wild rice and reeds.

Balsam and cedar and swamp hazel shut them in. Overhead the tall cedars interlaced, and hid the pale light of the sky. Philip could just make out Jeanne ahead of him.

And then, suddenly, there came a wonderful change. They shot out of the darkness, as if from a tunnel, but so quietly that one a dozen feet away could not have heard the ripple of Pierre's paddle. Almost in their faces rose a huge black bulk, and in that blackness three or four yellow lights gleamed like mellow stars. The canoe touched noiselessly upon sand. Pierre sprang out, still without sound. Jeanne followed, with a whispered word. Philip was last.

Pierre pulled the canoe up, and Jeanne came to Philip. She held out her two hands. Her face shone white in the gloom, and there was a look in her beautiful eyes, as she stood for a moment almost touching him, that set his heart jumping. She let her hands lie in his while she spoke.

"We have not even alarmed the dogs, M'sieur Philip," she whispered. "Is not that splendid? I am going to surprise father, and you will go with Pierre. I will see you a little later, and—"

She rose on tiptoe, and her face was dangerously close to his own.

"And you are very, very welcome to Fort o' God, M'sieur."

She slipped away into the darkness, and Pierre stood beside Philip. His white teeth were gleaming strangely, and he said in a soft voice:

"M'sieur, that is the first time that I have ever heard those words spoken at Fort o' God. We welcome no man here who has your blood and your civilization in his veins. You are greater than a king!"

With a sudden exclamation Philip turned upon Pierre.

"And that is the reason for Jeanne's surprise?" he said. "She wishes to pave a way for me. I begin to understand!"

"It is true that you might not have received that welcome which you are certain to receive now from the master of Fort o' God," replied Pierre, frankly. "So we will go in quietly, and make no disturbance, while your way is being paved, as you call it."

He walked ahead, with Philip following so closely that he could have touched him. He made out more distinctly now the lines of the huge black edifice from which the lights shone. It was a massive structure of logs, two stories high, a half of it almost completely hidden in the impenetrable shadow of a great wall of rock. Philip's eyes traveled up this wall, and he was convinced that he stood under the rock upon whose towering crest he had seen the last reflection of the evening sun. About him there were no signs of life or of other habitation. Pierre moved swiftly. They passed under a small lighted window that was a foot above Philip's head, and turned around the corner of the building. Here all was blackness.

Pierre went straight to a door, and uttered at low word of satisfaction when he found that it was not barred. He opened it, and reached out a guiding hand to Philip's arm. Philip entered, and the door closed softly behind him. He felt the flow of warm air in his face, and his moccasined feet trod upon something soft and velvety. Faintly, as though coming from a great distance, he heard a voice singing. It was a woman's voice, but he knew that it was not Jeanne's.

In spite of himself his heart was beating excitedly. The mystery of Fort o' God was about him, warm and subtle, like a strange spirit, sending through him the thrill of anticipation, a hundred fancies, little fears. Pierre advanced, still guiding him; then he stopped, and chuckled softly in the darkness. The distant voice had stopped singing, and there came in place of it the loud barking of a dog, an unintelligible sound of a voice, and then quiet. Jeanne had sprung her surprise.

Pierre led the way to another room.

"This is to be your room, M'sieur," he explained. "Make yourself comfortable. I have no doubt that the master of Fort o' God will wish to see you very soon."

He struck a match as he spoke, and lighted a lamp. A moment more and he was gone.

Philip looked about him. He was in a room fully twenty feet square, furnished in a manner that drew from him an audible gasp of astonishment. At one end of the room was a massive mahogany bed, screened by heavy curtains which were looped back by silken cords. Near the bed was an old-fashioned mahogany dresser, with a diamond-shaped mirror, and in front of it a straight-backed chair adorned with the grotesque carving of an ancient and long-dead fashion. About him, everywhere, were the evidences of luxury and of age. The big lamp, which gave a brilliant light, was of hammered brass; the base of its square pedestal was partly hidden in the rumples of a heavy damask spread which covered the table on which it rested. The table itself was old, spindle-legged, glowing with the mellow luster endowed by many passing generations—a relic of the days when the originator of its fashion became the favorite of a capricious and beautiful queen. Soft rugs were upon the floor; from the walls, papered and hung with odd bits of tapestry, strange faces looked down upon Philip from out of heavy gilded frames; faces grim, pale, shadowed; men with plaited ruffles and curls; women with powdered hair, who gazed down upon him haughtily, as if they wondered at his intrusion.

　　　　　　　　　　JAMES OLIVER CURWOOD

One picture was turned with its face to the wall.

Philip sank into a huge arm-chair, cushioned with velvet, and dropped his cap upon the floor. And this was Fort o' God! He scarcely breathed. He was back two centuries, and he stared, as if each moment he expected some manifestation of life in what he saw. He had dreamed his dream over the dead at Churchill; here it was reality—almost; it lacked but a breath, a movement, a flutter of life in the dead faces that looked down upon him. He gazed up at them again, and laughed a little nervously. Then he fixed his eyes on the opposite wall. One of the pictures was moving. The thought in his brain had given birth to the movement he had imagined. It was a woman's face in the picture, young and beautiful, and it nodded to him, one moment radiant with light, the next caught in shadows that cast over it a gloom. He jumped from his chair and went so that he stood directly under it.

A current of warm air shot up into his face from the floor. It was this air that was causing movement in the picture, and he looked down. What he discovered broke the spell he was under. About him were the relics of age, of a life long dead. Rubens might have sat in that room, and mourned over his handiwork, lost in a wilderness. The stingy Louis might have recognized in the spindle-legged table a bit of his predecessor's extravagance, which he had sold for the good of the exchequer of France; a Gobelin might have reclaimed one of the woven landscapes on the wall, a Grosellier himself have issued from behind the curtained bed. Philip himself, in that environment, was the stranger. It was the current of warm air which brought him back from the eighteenth to the twentieth century. Under his feet was a furnace!

Even the master of Fort o' God, stern and forbidding as Philip began to imagine him, might have laughed at the look which came into his face. Grosellier, the cavalier, had he appeared, Philip would have accepted with the same confidence that he had accepted Jeanne and Pierre. But—a furnace! He thrust his hands deep in his pockets, a trick which was always the last convincing evidence of his perplexity, and walked slowly around the room. There were two books on the table. One, bound in faded red vellum, was a Greek Anthology, the other Drummond's Ascent of Man. There were other books on a quaintly carved shelf, under the picture which had been turned to the wall. He ran over the titles. There were a number of French novels, Ely's Socialism, Sir Thomas More's Utopia, St. Pierre's Paul and Virginia, and a dozen other volumes; there were Balzac and Hugo, and Dante's

Divine Comedy. Amid this array, like a black sheep lost among the angels, was a finger-worn and faded little volume bearing the name Camille. Something about this one book, so strangely out of place in its present company, aroused Philip's curiosity. It bore the name, too, which he had found worked in the corner of Jeanne's handkerchief. In a way, the presence of this book gave him a sort of shock, and he took it in his hands, and opened the cover. Under his fingers were pages yellow and frayed with age, and in an ancient type, once black, the title, The Meaning of God. In a large masculine hand some one had written under this title the accompanying words; "A black skin often contains a white soul; a woman's beauty, hell."

Philip replaced the book with a feeling of awe. Something in those words, brutal in their truth—something in the strange whim that had placed a pearl of purity within the faded and worn mask of the condemned, seemed to speak to him of a tragedy that might be a key to the mystery of Fort o' God. From the books he looked up at the picture which had been turned to the wall. The temptation to see what was hidden overcame him, and he turned the frame over. Then he stepped back with a low cry of pleasure.

From out of the proscribed canvas there smiled down upon him a face of bewildering beauty. It was the face of a young woman, a stranger among its companions, because it was of the present. Philip stepped to one side, so that the light from the lamp shone from behind him, and he wondered if the picture had been condemned to hang with its face to the wall because it typified the existent rather than the past. He looked more closely, and drew back step by step, until he was in the proper focus to bring out every expression in the lovely face. In the picture he saw each moment a greater resemblance to Jeanne. The eyes, the hair, the sweetness of the mouth, the smile, brought to him a vision of Jeanne herself. The woman in the picture was older than Jeanne, and his first thought was that it must be a sister, or her mother. It came to him in the next breath that this would be impossible, for Jeanne had been found by Pierre in the deep snows, on her dead mother's breast. And this was a painting of life, of youth, of beauty, and not of death and starvation.

He returned the forbidden picture to the position in which he had found it against the wall, half ashamed of the act and thoughts into which his curiosity had led him. And yet, after all, it was not curiosity. He told himself that as he washed himself and groomed his disheveled clothes.

An hour had passed when he heard a low tap at the door, and Pierre came in. In that time the half-breed had undergone a transformation. He was dressed in an exquisite coat of yellow buckskin, with the same old-fashioned cuffs he had worn when Philip first saw him, trousers of the same material, buckled below the knees, and boot-moccasins with flaring tops. He wore a new rapier at his waist, and his glossy black hair was brushed smoothly back, and fell loose upon his shoulders. It was the courtier, and not Pierre the half-breed, who bowed to Philip.

"M'sieur, are you ready?" he asked.

"Yes," replied Philip.

"Then we will go to M'sieur d'Arcambal, the master of Fort o' God."

They passed out into the hall, which was faintly illumined now, so that Philip caught glimpses of deep shadows and massive doors as he followed behind Pierre. They turned into a second hall, at the end of which was an open door through which came a flood of light. At this door Pierre stopped, and with a bow allowed his companion to pass in ahead of him. The next moment Philip stood in a room twice as large as the one he had left. It was brilliantly lighted by three or four lamps; he had only an instant's vision of numberless shelves loaded with books, of walls covered with pictures, of a ponderous table in front of him, and then he heard a voice.

A man stepped out from beside the door, and he stood face to face with the master of Fort o' God.

XVII

He was an old man. Beard and hair were white. He was as tall as Philip; his shoulders were broader; his chest massive; and as he stood under the light of one of the hanging lamps, his face shining with a pale glow, one hand upon his breast, the other extended, it seemed to Philip that all of the greatness and past glory of Fort o' God, whatever they may have been, were personified in the man he beheld. He was dressed in soft buckskin, like Pierre. His hair and beard grew in wild disorder, and from under shaggy eyebrows there burned a pair of deep-set eyes of the color of blue steel. He was a man to inspire awe; old, and yet young; white-haired, gray-faced, and yet a giant. One might have expected from between his bearded lips a voice as thrilling as his appearance; a rumbling voice, deep-chested, sonorous—and it would have caused no surprise. It was the voice that surprised Philip more than the man. It was low, and trembling with an agitation which even strength and pride could not control.

"Philip Whittemore, I am Henry d'Arcambal. May God bless you for what you have done!"

A hand of iron gripped his own. And then, before Philip had found words to say, the master of Fort o' God suddenly placed his arms about his shoulders and embraced him. Their shoulders touched. Their faces were close. The two men who loved Jeanne d'Arcambal above all else on earth gazed for a silent moment into each other's eyes.

"They have told me," said D'Arcambal, softly. "You have brought my Jeanne home through death. Accept a father's blessing, and with it—this!"

He stepped back, and swept his arms about the great room.

"Everything—everything—would have gone with her," he said. "If you had let her die, I should have died. My God, what peril she was in! In saving her you saved me. So you are welcome here, as a son. For the first time since my Jeanne was a babe Fort o' God offers itself to a man who is a stranger and its hospitality is yours so long as its walls hang together. And as they have done this for upward of two hundred years, M'sieur Philip, we may conclude that our friendship is to be without end."

He clasped Philip's hands again, and two tears coursed down his gray cheeks. It was difficult for Philip to restrain the joy his words produced, which, coming from the lips of Jeanne's father, lifted him suddenly into a paradise of hope. For many reasons he had come to expect a none too warm reception at Fort o' God; he had looked ahead to the place with a grim sort of fear, scarcely definable; and here Jeanne's father was opening his arms to him. Pierre was unapproachable; Jeanne herself was a mystery, filling him alternately with hope and despair; D'Arcambal had accepted him as a son. He could find no words adequate to his emotion; none that could describe his own happiness, unless it was in a bold avowal of his love for the girl he had saved. And this his good sense told him not to make, at the present moment.

"Any man would have done as much for your daughter," he said at last, "and I am happy that I was the fortunate one to render her assistance."

"You are wrong," said D'Arcambal, taking him by the arm. "You are one out of a thousand. It takes a MAN to go through the Big Thunder and come out at the other end alive. I know of only one other who has done that in the last twenty years, and that other is Henry d'Arcambal himself. We three, you, Jeanne, and I, have alone triumphed over those monsters of death. All others have died. It seems like a strange pointing of the hand of God."

Philip trembled.

"We three!" he exclaimed.

"We three," said the old man, "and for that reason you are a part of Fort o' God."

He led Philip deeper into the great room, and Philip saw that almost all the space along the walls of the huge room was occupied by shelves upon shelves of books, masses of papers, piles of magazines shoulder-high, scores of maps and paintings. The massive table was covered with books; there were piles on smaller tables; chairs, and the floor itself, covered with the skins of a score of wild beasts, were littered with them. At the far end of the room he saw deeper and darker shelves, where gleamed faintly in the lamplight row upon row of vials and bottles and strange instruments of steel and glass. A scientist in the wilderness—a student exiled in a desolation! These were the thoughts that leaped into his mind, and he knew that in this room Jeanne had been created; that here, between these centuries-old walls, amid an environment of strange silence, of whispering age, her visions of the world had come. Here, separated from all her kind, God, Nature, and a father had made her of their handiwork.

The old man pointed Philip to a chair near the large table, and sat down close to him. At his feet was a stool covered with silvery lynx-skin, and D'Arcambal looked at this, his strong, grim face relaxing into a gentle smile of happiness.

"There is where Jeanne sits—at my feet," he said. "It has been her place for many years. When she is not there I am lost. Life ceases. This room has been our world. To-night you are in Fort o' God; to-morrow you will see D'Arcambal House. You have heard of that, perhaps, but never of Fort o' God. That belongs to Jeanne and me, to Pierre—and you. Fort o' God is the heart, the soul, the life's blood of D'Arcambal House. It is this room and two or three others. D'Arcambal House is our barrier. When strangers come, they see D'Arcambal House; plain rooms, of rough wood; quarters such as you have seen at posts and stations; the mask which gives no hint of what is hidden within. It is there that we live to the world; it is here that we live to ourselves. Jeanne has my permission to tell you whatever she wishes, a little later. But I am curious, and being an old man must be humored first. I am still trembling. You must tell me what happened to Jeanne."

For an hour they talked, and Philip went over one by one the events as they had occurred since the fight on the cliff, omitting only such things as he thought that Jeanne and Pierre might wish to keep secret to themselves. At the end of that hour he was certain that D'Arcambal was unaware of the dark cloud that had suddenly come into Jeanne's life. The old man's brow was knitted with deep lines, and his powerful jaws were set hard, as Philip told of the ambush, of the wounding of Pierre, and the flight of his assailants with his daughter. It was to get money, the old man thought. The half-breed had suggested that, and Jeanne herself had given it as her opinion. Why else should they have been attacked at Churchill? Such things had occurred before, he told Philip. The little daughter of the factor at Nelson House had been stolen, and held for ransom. With a hundred questions he wrung from Philip every detail of the second fight and of the struggle for life in the rapids. He betrayed no physical excitement, even in those moments of Philip's description when Jeanne hung between life and death; but in his eyes there was the glow of red-hot fires. At last there came to interrupt them the low, musical tinkling of a bell under the table.

D'Arcambal's face lighted up suddenly.

"Ah, I had forgotten," he exclaimed. "Pardon me, Philip. Dinner has been awaiting us this last half-hour; and besides—"

He reached out and touched a tiny button, which Philip had not observed before.

JAMES OLIVER CURWOOD

"I am selfish."

He had hardly ceased speaking when footsteps sounded in the hall, and in spite of every resolution he had made to guard himself against any betrayal of the emotions burning in his breast, Philip sprang to his feet. Jeanne had come in under the glow of the lamps and stood now a dozen feet from him, a vision so exquisitely lovely that he saw nothing of those who entered behind her, nor heard D'Arcambal's low, happy laugh at his side. It seemed to him for a moment as if there had suddenly appeared before him the face of the picture that was turned against the wall, only more beautiful now, radiant with the glow of living flesh and blood. But there was something even more startling than this resemblance. In this moment Jeanne was the fulfilment of his dream; she had come to him from out of another world. She was dressed in an old-fashioned gown of pure white, a fabric so delicate that it seemed to float about her slender form, responsive to every breath she drew. Her white shoulders revealed themselves above masses of filmy lace that fell upon her bosom; her slender arms, girlish rather than womanly in their beauty, were bare. Her hair was bound up in shining coils about her head, with a single flower nestling amid a little cluster of curls that fell upon her neck. After his first movement, Philip recovered himself by a strong effort. He bowed low to conceal the flush in his face. Jeanne swept him a little courtesy, and then ran past him, with the eagerness of any modern child, into the outstretched arms of her father.

Laughter and joy rumbled in the beard of the master of Fort o' God as he looked over Jeanne's head at Philip.

"And this is what you have saved for me," he said.

Then he looked beyond, and for the first time Philip realized there were others in the room. One was Pierre; the other a pretty, dark-faced girl, with hair that glistened like a raven's wing in the lamp-glow.

Jeanne left her father's arms and gave her hand to Philip.

"M'sieur Philip, this is my sister, Mademoiselle Couchee," she cried.

Pierre's sister gave Philip her hand, and behind them D'Arcambal laughed softly in his beard again, and said:

"To-morrow, in D'Arcambal House, you may call her Otille, Philip. But to-night we are in Fort o' God. Oh, Jeanne, Jeanne, what a witch you are!"

"An angel!" breathed Philip, but no one heard him.

"And this witch," added the old man, "you are to take in to supper, M'sieur Philip. To night I suppose that I must call you m'sieur, but to-morrow, when I have on my leather leggings and my skin cap, I will call you Phil, or Tom, Dick, or Harry, just as I please. This is the first time, sir, that my Jeanne has ever gone in to dinner on another arm than mine or Pierre's. And so I may be a little jealous. Proceed."

As Jeanne's hand rested in his arm, and they went into the hall, Philip could not restrain himself from whispering:

"I am glad—of that."

"And the dress, M'sieur Philip!" exclaimed D'Arcambal behind them, in the voice of a happy boy. "It is an honor to escort that, to say nothing of the silly girl that's in it. That dress, sir, belonged to a beautiful lady who was called Camille, and who died over a century ago."

"Father, please do be good!" protested Jeanne. "Remember!"

"Ah, so I will," said her father. "I had forgotten that you were to tell M'sieur Philip these things."

They entered another room illuminated by a single huge lamp suspended above a table spread with silver and fine linen. The room was as great a surprise as the other two had been. It contained no chairs. What Philip mentally designated as benches, with deep cushion seats of greenish leather, were arranged about the table. These same curious seats furnished other parts of the room. From the pictures on the walls to the ancient helmet and cuirass that stood up like a legless sentinel in one corner, this room, like the others, breathed of extreme age. Over a big open fireplace, in which half a dozen birch logs were burning, hung a number of old-fashioned weapons; a flintlock, a pair of obsolete French dueling pistols, a short rapier similar to that which Pierre wore, and two long swords. Philip noticed that about each of the dueling pistols was tied a bow of ribbon, dull and faded, as though the passing of generations had robbed them of beauty and color, to be replaced by the somberness of age.

During the meal Philip could not but observe that Jeanne was laboring under some mysterious strain. Her cheeks were brilliantly flushed, and her eyes were filled with a lustrous brightness that he had never seen in them before. Their beauty was almost feverish. Several times he caught a strange little tremor of her white shoulders, as though a sudden chill had passed through her. He discovered, too, that Pierre was observing these things, and that there was something forced in the half-breed's cheerfulness. But D'Arcambal and Otille seemed completely oblivious of any change. Their happiness overflowed. Philip thought of his last supper at Churchill, with Eileen Brokaw and her father. Miss Brokaw had acted strangely then, and had struggled to hide some secret grief or excitement, as Jeanne was struggling now.

He was glad when the meal was finished, and the master of Fort o' God rose from his seat. At D'Arcambal's movement his eyes caught Jeanne's, and then he saw that Pierre was looking sharply at him.

"Jeanne owes you an apology—and an explanation, M'sieur Philip," said D'Arcambal, resting a hand upon Jeanne's head. "We are going to retire, and she will initiate you into the fold of Fort o' God."

Pierre and Otille followed him from the room. For the first time in an hour Jeanne laughed frankly at Philip.

"There isn't much to explain, M'sieur Philip," she said, rising from her seat. "You know pretty nearly all there is to know about Fort o' God now. Only I am sure that I did not appear to value your confidence very much—a little while ago. It must have seemed ungrateful in me, indeed, to have told you so little about myself and my home, after what you did for Pierre and me. But I have father's permission now. It is the second time that he has ever given it to me."

"And I don't want to hear," exclaimed Philip, bluntly. "I have been more or less of a brute, Miss Jeanne. I know enough about Fort o' God. It is a glorious place. You owe me nothing, and for that reason—"

"But I insist," interrupted the girl. "Do you mean to say that you do not care to listen, when this is the second time in my life that I have had the opportunity of talking about my home? And the first—didn't give me any pleasure. This will."

A shadow came into Jeanne's eyes. She motioned him to a seat beside her in front of the fire. Her nearness, the touch of her dress, the sweet perfume of her presence, thrilled him. He felt that the moment was near when the whole world as he knew it was to slip away from him, leaving him in a paradise, or a chaos of despair. Jeanne looked up at the dueling pistols. The firelight trembled in the soft folds of lace over her bosom; it glistened in her hair, and lighted her face with a gentle glow.

"There isn't much to explain," she said again, in a voice so low that it was hardly more than a whisper. "But what little there is I want you to know, so that when you go away you will understand. More than two hundred years ago a band of gentlemen adventurers were sent over into this country by Prince Rupert to form the Hudson's Bay Company. That is history, and you know more of it, probably, than I. One of these men was Le Chevalier Grosellier. One summer he came up the Churchill, and stopped at the great rock on which we saw the sun setting to-night, and which was called the Sun Rock by the Indians. He was struck by the beauty of the place, and when he went back to France it was with the plan of returning to build himself a chateau in the wilderness. Two or three years later he did this, and called the place Fort o' God. For more than a century, M'sieur, Fort o' God was a place of revel and pleasure in the heart of this desolation. Early in the nineteenth century it passed into the hands of a man by the name of D'Arcy, and it is said that at one time it housed twenty gentlemen and as many ladies of France for one whole season. Its history is obscure, and mostly lost. But for a long time after D'Arcy came it was a place of adventure, of pleasure, and of mystery, very little of which remains to-day. Those are his pistols above the fire. He was killed by one of them out there beside the big rock, in a quarrel with one of his guests over a woman. We think—here—from letters that we have found, that her name was Camille. There is a chest in my room filled with linen that bears her name. This dress came from that chest. I have to be careful of them, as they tear very easily. After D'Arcy the place was almost forgotten and remained so until nearly forty years ago when my father came into possession of it. That, M'sieur, is the very simple story of Fort o' God. Its old name is forgotten. It lives only with us. Others know it as D'Arcambal House."

"Yes, I have heard of that," said Philip.

He waited for Jeanne, and saw that her fingers were nervously twisting a bit of ribbon in her lap.

"Of course, that is uninteresting," she continued. "You can almost guess the rest. We have lived here—alone. Not one of us has ever felt the desire to leave this little world of ours. It is curious—you may scarcely believe what I say—but it is true that we look out upon your big world and laugh at it and dislike it. I guess—that I have been taught to hate it—since I can remember."

There was a little tremble in Jeanne's voice, an instant's quivering of her chin. Philip looked from her face into the fire, and stared hard, choking back words which were ready to burst from his lips. In place of them he said, with a touch of bitterness in his voice:

"And I have grown to hate my world, Jeanne. It has compelled me to hate it. That is why I spoke to you that night on the cliff at Churchill."

"I have sometimes thought that I have been very wrong," said the girl. "I have never seen this other world. I know nothing of it, except as I have been taught. I have no right to hate it, and yet I do. I have never wanted to see it. I have never cared to know the people who lived in it. I wish that I could understand, but I cannot; except that father has made for us, for Pierre and Otille and me, this little world at Fort o' God, and has taught us to fear the other. I know that there is no other man in the whole world like my father, and that what he has done must be best. It is his pride that we bring your world to our doors, but that we never go to it; he says that we know more about that world than the people who live there, which of course cannot be so. And so we have grown up amid the old memories, the pictures, and the dead romances of Fort o' God. We have taken pleasure in living as we do—in making for ourselves our own little social codes, our childish aristocracy, our make-believe world. It is the spirit of Fort o' God that lives with us, and makes us content; the shadow-faces of men and women who once filled these rooms with life and pleasure, and whose memory seems to have passed into our keeping alone. I know them all; many of their names, all of their faces. I have a daguerreotype of Camille Poitiers, and she must have been very beautiful. There are the tiniest slippers in the world in her chest, and ribbons like those which are tied about the pistols. There is a painting of D'Arcy in your room. It is the picture next to the one that has its face turned to the wall."

She rose to her feet, and Philip stood beside her. There was a mist in her eyes as she held out her hand to him.

"I—I—would like to have you—see that picture," she whispered.

Philip could not speak. He held the hand Jeanne had given him as they passed through the long, dimly lighted halls. At the open door to his room they stopped, and he could feel Jeanne trembling.

"You will tell me—the truth?" she begged, like a child. "You will tell me what you think—of the picture?"

"Yes."

She went in ahead of him and turned the frame so that the face in the picture smiled down upon them in all of its luring loveliness. There was something pathetic in the girl's attitude now. She stood under the picture, facing Philip, and there was a tense eagerness in her eyes, a light that was almost supplication, a crying out of her soul to him in a breathless moment that seemed hovering between pain and joy. It was Jeanne, an older Jeanne, that looked from out of the picture, smiling, inviting admiration, bewildering hi her beauty; it was Jeanne, the child, waiting for him in flesh and blood to speak, her eyes big and dark, her breath coming quickly, her hands buried in the deep lace on her bosom. A low word came to Philip's lips, and then he laughed softly. It was a laugh, almost under his breath, which sweeps up now and then from a soul in a joy—an emotion—which is unutterable in words. But to Jeanne it was different. Her dark eyes grew hurt and wounded, two great tears ran down her paling cheeks, and suddenly she buried her face in her hands and with a sobbing cry turned from him, with her head bowed under the smiling face above.

"And you—you hate it, too!" she sobbed. "They all hate it—Pierre—father—all—all hate it. It must—it must be bad. They hate her—every one—but me. And—I love her so!"

Her slender form shook with sobs. For a moment Philip stood like one struck dumb. Then he sprang to her and caught her close in his arms.

"Jeanne—Jeanne—listen," he cried. "To-night I looked at that picture before I went to see your father, and I loved it because it is like you. Jeanne, my darling, I love you—I love you—"

She was panting against his breast. He covered her face with kisses. Her sweet lips were not turned from him, and there filled her eyes a sudden light that made him almost sob in his happiness.

"I love you, I love you," he repeated, again and again, and he could find no other words than those.

For an instant her arms clung about his shoulders, and then, suddenly, they strained against him, and she tore herself free, and, with a cry so pathetic that it seemed as though her heart had broken in that moment, she fled from him, and out of the room.

JAMES OLIVER CURWOOD

XVIII

Philip stood where Jeanne had left him, his arms half reaching out to the vacant door through which she had fled, his lips parted as if to call her name, and yet motionless, dumb. A moment before he was intoxicated by a joy that was almost madness. He had held Jeanne in his arms; he had looked into her eyes, filled with surrender under his caresses and his avowal of love. For a moment he had possessed her, and now he was alone. The cry that had wrung itself from her lips, breaking in upon his happiness like a blow, still rang in his ears, and there was something in the exquisite pain of it that left him in torment. Heart and soul, every drop of blood in him, had leaped in the joy of that glorious moment, when Jeanne's eyes and sweet lips had accepted his love, and her arms had clung about his shoulders. Now these things had been struck dead within him. He felt again the fierce pressure of Jeanne's arms as she had thrust him away, he saw the fright and torture that had leaped into her eyes as she sprang from him, as though his touch had suddenly become a sacrilege. He lowered his arms slowly, and went to the hall. It was empty. He heard no sound, and closed the door.

It was so still that he could hear the excited throbbing of his own heart. He looked at the picture again, and a strange fancy impressed him with the idea that it was no longer smiling at him, but that its eyes were turned to the door through which Jeanne had disappeared. He moved his position, and the illusion was gone. It was Jeanne looking down upon him again, an older and happier Jeanne than the one whom he loved. For the first time he examined it closely. In one corner of the canvas he found the artist's name, Bourret, and after it the date, 1888. Could it be the picture of Jeanne's mother? He told himself that it was impossible, for Jeanne's mother had been found dead in the snow, five years later than the date of the canvas, and Pierre, the half-breed, had buried her somewhere out on the barren, so that she was a mystery to all but him. Even the master of Fort o' God, to whom he had brought the child, had never seen the woman upon whose cold breast Pierre had found the little Jeanne.

With nervous hands he replaced the picture with its face to the wall, and began to pace up and down the room, wondering if D'Arcambal would send for him. He had hope of seeing Jeanne again that night. He felt sure that she had gone to her room, and that even D'Arcambal might not know that he was alone. In that event he had a long night ahead of him, filled with hours of sleeplessness and torment. He waited for three-quarters of an hour, and then the idea came to him that he might discover some plausible excuse for seeking out his host. He was about to act upon this mental suggestion when he heard a low rustling in the hall, followed by a distinct and yet timid knock. It was not a man's knock, and filled with the hope that Jeanne had returned, Philip hastened to the door and opened it.

He heard soft footsteps retreating rapidly down the hall, but the lights were out, and he could see nothing. Something had fallen at his feet, and he bent down to pick it up. The object was a small, square envelope; and re-entering his room he saw his own name written across it in Jeanne's delicate hand. His heart beat with hope as he opened the note. What he read brought a gray pallor into his face:

MONSIEUR PHILIP,

If you cannot forget what I have done, please at least try to forgive me. No woman in the world could value your love more than I, for circumstances have proven to me the strength and honor of the man who gives it. And yet it is as impossible for me to accept it as it would be for me to give up Fort o' God, my father, or my life, though I cannot tell you why. And this, I know, you will not ask. After what has happened to-night it will be impossible for me to see you again, and I must ask you, as one who values your friendship among the highest things in my life, to leave Fort o' God. No one must know what has passed between us. You will go—in the morning. And with you there will always be my prayers.

JEANNE

The paper dropped from between Philip's fingers and fell to the floor. Three or four times in his life Philip had received blows that had made him sick—physical blows. He felt now as though one of these blows had descended upon him, turning things black before his eyes. He staggered to the big chair and dropped into it, staring at the bit of white paper on the floor. If one had spoken to him he would not have heard. Gregson, in these moments, might have laughed a little nervously, smoked innumerable cigarettes, and laid plans for a continuance of the battle to-morrow. But Philip was a fighter of men, and not of women.

He had declared his love, he had laid open his soul to Jeanne, and to a heart like his own, simple in its language, boundless in its sincerity, this was all that could be done. Jeanne's refusal of his love was the end—for him. He accepted his fate without argument. In an instant he would have fought ten men—a hundred, naked-handed, if such a fight would have given him a chance of winning Jeanne; he would have died, laughing, happy, if it had been in a struggle for her. But Jeanne herself had dealt him the blow.

For a long time he sat motionless in the chair facing the picture on the wall. Then he rose to his feet, picked up the note, and went to one of the little square windows that looked out into the night. The moon had risen, and the sky was full of stars. He knew that he was looking into the north, for the pale shimmer of the aurora was in his face. He saw the black edge of the spruce forest; the barren stretched out, pale and ghostly, into the night shadows.

He made an effort to open the window, but it was wedged tightly in its heavy sill. He crossed the room, opened the door, and went silently down the hall to the door through which Pierre had led him a few hours before. It was not locked, and he passed out into the night. The fresh air was like a tonic, and he walked swiftly out into the moonlit spaces, until he found himself in the deep shadow of the Sun Rock that towered like a sentinel giant above his head. He made his way around its huge base, and then stopped, close to where they had landed in the canoe. There was another canoe drawn up beside Pierre's, and two figures stood out clear in the moonlight.

One of these was a man, the other a woman, and as Philip stopped, wondering at the scene, the man advanced to the woman and caught her in his embrace. He heard a voice, low and expostulating, which sounded like Otille's, and in spite of his own misery Philip smiled at this other love which had found its way to Fort o' God. He turned back softly, leaving the lovers as he had found them; but he had scarce taken half a dozen steps when he heard other steps, and saw that the girl had left her companion and was hurrying toward him. He drew back close into the shadow of the rock to avoid possible discovery, and the girl passed through the moonlight almost within arm's reach of him. At that moment his heart ceased to beat. He choked back the groaning cry that rose to his lips. It was not Otille who passed him. It was Jeanne.

In another moment she was gone. The man had shoved his canoe into the narrow stream, and was already lost in the gloom. Then, and not until then, did the cry of torture fall from Philip. And as if in echo to it he heard the sobbing break of another voice, and stepping out into the moonlight he stood face to face with Pierre Couchee.

It was Pierre who spoke first.

"I am sorry, M'sieur," he whispered, hoarsely. "I know that it has broken your heart. And mine, too, is crushed."

Something in the half-breed's face, in the choking utterance of his voice, struck Philip as new and strange. He had seen the eyes of dying animals filled with the wild pain that glowed in Pierre's, and suddenly he reached out and gripped the other's hand, and they stood staring into each other's face. In that look, the cold grip of their hands, the strife in their eyes, the bare truth revealed itself.

"And you, too—you love her, Pierre," said Philip.

"Yes, I love her, M'sieur," replied Pierre, softly. "I love her, not as a brother, but as a man whose heart is broken."

"Now—I understand," said Philip.

He dropped Pierre's hand, and his voice was cold and lifeless.

"I received a note—from her, asking me to leave Fort o' God in the morning," he went on, looking from Pierre out beyond the rock into the white barren. "I will go to-night."

"It is best," said Pierre.

"I have left nothing in Fort o' God, so there is no need of even returning to my room," continued Philip. "Jeanne will understand, but you must tell her father that a messenger came suddenly from Blind Indian Lake, and that I thought it best to leave without awakening him. Will you guide me for a part of the distance, Pierre?"

"I will go with you the whole way, M'sieur. It is only twenty miles, ten by canoe, ten by land."

They said no more, but both went to the canoe, and were quickly lost in the gloom into which the other canoe had disappeared a few minutes ahead of them. They saw nothing of this canoe, and when they came to the Churchill Pierre headed the birch-bark down-stream. For two hours not a word passed between them. At the end of that time the half-breed turned in to shore.

"We take the trail here, M'sieur," he explained.

He went on ahead, walking swiftly, and now and then when Philip caught a glimpse of his face he saw in it a despair as great as his own. The trail led along the backbone of a huge ridge, and then twisted down into a broad plain; and across this they traveled, one after the other,

JAMES OLIVER CURWOOD

two moving, silent shadows in a desolation that seemed without end. Beyond the plain there rose another ridge, and half an hour after they had struck the top of it Pierre halted, and pointed off into the ghostly world of light and shadow that lay at their feet.

"Your camp is on the other side of this plain, M'sieur," he said. "Do you recognize the country?"

"I have hunted along this ridge," replied Philip. "It is only three miles from here, and I will strike a beaten trail half a mile out yonder. A thousand thanks, Pierre."

He held out his hand.

"Good-by, M'sieur."

"Good-by, Pierre."

Their voices trembled. Their hands gripped hard. A choking lump rose in Philip's throat, and Pierre turned away. He disappeared slowly in the gray gloom, and Philip went down the side of the mountain. From the plain below he looked back. For an instant he saw Pierre drawn like a silhouette against the sky.

"Good-by, Pierre," he shouted.

"Good-by, M'sieur," came back faintly.

Light and silence dropped about them.

XIX

To be alone, even after the painful parting with Pierre, was in one way a relief to Philip, for with the disappearance of the lonely half-breed over the mountain there had gone from him the last physical association that bound him to Jeanne and her people. With Pierre at his side, Jeanne was still with him; but now that Pierre was gone there came a change in him—one of those unaccountable transmutations of the mind which make the passing of yesterdays more like a short dream than a long and full reality. He walked slowly over the plain, and, when he came to the trail beaten by the hoofs of his own teams he followed it mechanically. In his measurement of things now, it seemed only a few hours since he had traveled over this trail on his way to Fort Churchill; it might, have been that morning, or the morning before. The weeks of his absence had passed with marvelous swiftness, now that he looked back upon them. They seemed short and trivial. And yet he knew that in those weeks he had lived more of his life than he had ever lived before, or would ever live again. For a brief spell life had been, filled with joy and hope—a promise of happiness which a single moment in the shadow of the Sun Rock had destroyed forever. He had seen Jeanne in another man's arms; he had read the confirmation of his fears in Pierre's grief-distorted face, in the strange tremble of his voice, in the words that he had spoken. He was sorry for Pierre. He would have been glad if that other man had been the lovable half-breed; if Jeanne, in the poetry of life and love, had given herself to the one who had saved the spark of life in her chilled little body years and years ago. And yet in his own grief he unconsciously rejoiced that it was a man like Pierre who suffered with him.

This thought of Pierre strengthened him, and he walked faster, and breathed more deeply of the clear night air. He had lost in the fight for Jeanne as he had lost in many other fights; but, after all, there was another and bigger fight ahead of him, which he would begin to-morrow. Thoughts of his men, of his camps, and of this struggle through which he must pass to achieve success raised him above his depression, and stirred his blood with a growing exhilaration. And Jeanne—was she hopelessly lost to him? He dared to ask himself the question half an hour after he had separated from Pierre, and his mind flew back to the portrait-room where he had told Jeanne of his love, and where for a moment he had seen in her eyes and face the sweet surrender that had given him a glimpse of his paradise. But what did the sudden change mean? And after that—the scene in the starlight?

A quickening of his pulse was the answer to these questions. Jeanne had told him there were only two men at Fort o' God, Pierre and her father. Then who could be this third? A lover, whom she met clandestinely? He shivered, and began loading his pipe as he walked. He was certain that the master of Fort o' God did not know of the tryst beyond the rock, and he was equally certain that the girl was unaware of Pierre's knowledge of the meeting. Pierre had remained hidden, like himself, and he had given Philip to understand that it was not the first time he had looked upon the meetings of Jeanne and the man they had seen from the shadow of the rock. And yet, in spite of all evidence, he could not lose faith in Jeanne.

Suddenly he saw something ahead of him which changed for a moment the uncomfortable trend of his thoughts. It was a pale streak, rising above the level of the trail, and stretching diagonally across the plain to the east. With an exclamation of surprise Philip hastened his steps, and a moment later stood among the fresh workings of his men. When he had left for Churchill this streak, which was the last stretch of road-bed between them and the surveyed line of the Hudson's Bay Railway, had ended two miles to the south and west. In a little over a month MacDougall had pushed it on the trail, and well across it in the direction of Gray Beaver Lake. In that time he had accomplished a work which Philip had not thought possible to achieve that autumn. He had figured that the heavy snows of winter would cut them off at the trail. And MacDougall was beyond the trail, with three weeks to spare!

Something rose up in his blood, warming him with an elation which sent him walking swiftly toward the end of the road-bed. A quarter of a mile out on the plain he came to the working end. About him were scattered half a dozen big scoop shovels and piles of working tools. The embers of a huge log fire still glowed where dinner had been cooked for the men. Philip stood for a few moments, looking off into the distance. Another mile and a half out there was the Gray Beaver, and from the Gray Beaver there lay the unbroken waterway to the point of their conjunction with the railway coming up from the south. A sudden idea occurred to Philip. If MacDougall had built two and a quarter miles of road-bed in five weeks they could surely complete this other mile and a half before winter stopped them. In that event, they would have fifteen miles of road, linking seven lakes, which would give them a splendid winter trail for men, teams, and dogs to the Gray Beaver. And from the Gray Beaver they would have smooth ice for twenty miles, to the new road. He had not planned to begin fishing operations until spring, but he could see no reason now why they should not commence that winter, setting their nets through the ice. At Lobstick Creek, where the new road would reach them sometime in April or May, they could freeze their fish and keep them in storage. Five hundred tons in stock, and perhaps a thousand, would not be a bad beginning. It would mean from forty to eighty thousand dollars, a half of which could be paid out in dividends.

He turned back, whistling softly. There was new life in him, burning for action. He was eager to see MacDougall, and he hoped that Brokaw would not be long in reaching Blind Indian Lake. Before he reached the trail he was planning the accommodation stations, where men and animals could find shelter. There would be one on the shore of the Gray Beaver, and from there he would build them at regular intervals of five miles on the ice.

He had come to the trail, and was about to turn in the direction of the camp, when he saw a shadowy figure making its way slowly across the plain which he had traversed half an hour before. The manner in which this person was following in his footsteps, apparently with extreme caution, caused Philip to move quickly behind the embankment of the road-bed. Two or three minutes later a man crossed into view. Philip could not see his face distinctly, but by the tired droop of the stranger's shoulders and his shuffling walk he guessed that what he had first taken for caution was in reality the tedious progress of a man nearing exhaustion. He wondered how he had missed him in his own journey over the trail from the ridge mountains, for he had made twice the progress of the stranger, and must surely have passed him somewhere within the last mile or so. The fact that the man had come from the direction of Fort o' God, that he was exhausted, and that he had evidently concealed himself a little way back to avoid discovery, led Philip to cut out diagonally across the plain so that he could follow him and keep him in sight without being observed. Twice in the next mile the nocturnal traveler stopped to rest, but no sooner had he reached the first scattered shacks of the camp than he quickened his steps, darting quickly among the shadows, and then stopped at last before the door of a small log cabin within a pistol-shot of Philip's own headquarters. The cabin was newly built, and Philip gave a low whistle of surprise as he noted its location. He had, to a certain degree, isolated his own camp home, building it a couple of hundred yards back from the shore of the lake, where most of the other cabins were erected. This new cabin was still a hundred yards farther back, half hidden in a growth of spruce. He heard the click of a key in a lock and the opening and closing of a door. A moment later a light flared dimly against a curtained window.

Philip hurried across the open to the cabin occupied by himself and MacDougall, the engineer. He tried the door, but it was barred. Then he knocked loudly, and continued knocking until a light appeared within. He heard the Scotchman's voice, close to the door.

"Who's there?" it demanded.

"None of your business!" retorted Philip, falling into the error of a joke at the welcome sound of MacDougall's voice. "Open up!"

A bar slipped within. The door opened slowly. Philip thrust himself against it and entered. In the pale light of the lamp he was confronted by the red face of MacDougall, and a pair of little eyes that gleamed menacingly. And on a line with MacDougall's face was an ugly-looking revolver.

Philip stopped with a sudden uncomfortable thrill. MacDougall lowered his gun.

"Lord preserve us, but that's the time you almost drew a perforation!" he exclaimed. "It isn't safe to cut-up in these diggings any more—not with Sandy MacDougall!"

He held out a hand with a relieved laugh, and the two men shook in a grip that made their fingers ache.

"Is this the way you welcome all of your friends, Mac?"

MacDougall shrugged his shoulders and laid his gun on a table in the center of the room.

"Can't say that I've got a friend left in camp," he said, with a curious grimace. "What in thunder do you mean, Phil? I've tried to reason something out of it, but I can't!"

Philip was hanging up his cap and coat on one of a number of wooden pegs driven into the long wall. He turned quickly.

"Reason something out of what?" he said.

"Your instructions from Churchill," replied MacDougall, picking up a big, black-bowled pipe from the table.

Philip sat down with a restful sigh, crossed his legs, loaded his pipe, and lighted it.

"Thought I made myself lucid enough, even for a Scotchman, Sandy," he said. "I learned at Churchill that the big fight is going to be pulled off mighty soon. It's about time for the fireworks. So I told you to put the sub-camps in fighting shape, and arm every responsible man in this camp. There's going to be a whole lot of gun-work before you're many days older. Great Scott, man, don't you understand Now? What's the matter?"

MacDougall was staring at him as if struck dumb.

"You told me—to arm—the camps?" he gasped.

"Yes, I sent you full instructions two weeks ago."

"MacDougall tapped his forehead suspiciously with a stubby forefinger.

"You're mad—or trying to pull off a poor brand of joke!" he exclaimed. "If you're dreaming, come out of it. Look here, Phil," he cried, a little heatedly, "I've been having a hell of a time since you left the camp, and I want to talk seriously."

It was Philip who stared now. He fairly thrust himself upon the engineer.

"Do you mean to say you didn't get my letter telling you to put the camps in fighting shape?"

"No, I didn't get it," said MacDougall. "But I got the other."

"There was no other!"

MacDougall jumped to his feet, darted to his bunk, and came back a moment later with a letter. He thrust it almost fiercely into Philip's hands. A sweat broke out upon his face as he saw its effect upon his companion. Philip's face was deadly pale when he looked up from the letter.

"My God! you haven't done this?" he gasped.

"What else could I do?" demanded MacDougall. "It's down there in black and white, isn't it? It charges me to outfit six prospecting parties of ten men each, arm every man with a rifle and revolver, victual them for two months, and send them to the points named there. That letter came ten days ago, and the last party, under Tom Billinger, has been gone a week. You told me to send your very best men, and I have. It has fairly stripped the camp of the men we depended upon, and there are hardly enough guns left to kill meat with."

"I didn't write this letter," said Philip, looking hard at MacDougall. "The signature is a fraud. The letter which I sent to you, revealing my discoveries at Churchill, has been intercepted and replaced by this. Do you know what it means?"

MacDougall was speechless. His square jaw was set like an iron clamp, his heavy hands doubled into knots on his knees.

"It means—fight," continued Philip. "To-night—to-morrow—at any moment now. I can't guess why the blow hasn't fallen before this."

He quickly related to MacDougall the chief facts he had gathered at Fort Churchill. When he had finished, the young Scotchman reached over to the table, seized his revolver, and held the butt end of it out to Philip.

"Pump me full of lead—for God's sake, do, Phil," he pleaded.

Philip laughed, and gripped his hand.

"Not while I need a few fighters like yourself, Sandy," he objected. "We're on to the game in time. By to-morrow morning we'll be prepared for the war. We haven't an hour—perhaps not a minute—to lose. How many men can you get hold of to-night whom we can depend upon to fight?"

"Ten or a dozen, no more. The road gang that we were expecting up from the Grand Trunk Pacific came three days after you started for Churchill—twenty-eight of 'em. They're a tough-looking outfit, but devilish good workers. I believe you could HIRE that gang to do anything. They won't take a word from me. It's all up to Thorpe, the foreman who brought 'em up, and they won't obey an order unless it comes through him. Thorpe could get them to fight, but they haven't anything to fight with, except a few knives. I've got eight guns left, and I can scrape up eight men who'll handle them for the glory of it. Thorpe's gang would be mighty handy in close quarters, if it came to that."

MacDougall moved restlessly, and ran a hand through his tawny hair.

"I almost wish we hadn't invited that bunch up here," he added. "They look to me like a lot of dollar thugs, but they work like horses. Never saw such men with the shovel and pick. And fight? They've cleaned up on a half of the men in camp. If we can get Thorpe—"

"We'll see him to-night," interrupted Philip. "Or to be correct, this morning. It's one o'clock. How long will it take to round up our best men?"

"Half an hour," said MacDougall, promptly, jumping to his feet. "There are Roberts, Henshaw, Tom Cassidy, Lecault, the Frenchman, and the two St. Pierre brothers. They're all crack gun-men. Give 'em each an automatic and they're worth twenty ordinary men."

A few moments later MacDougall extinguished the light, and the two men left the cabin. Philip drew his companion's attention to the dimly lighted window of the cabin to which he had followed the stranger a short time before.

"That's Thorpe's," said the young engineer. "I haven't seen him since morning. Guess he must be up."

"We'll sound him first," said Philip, starting off.

At MacDougall's knock there was a moment's silence inside, then heavy footsteps, and the door was flung open. Sandy entered, followed by Philip. Thorpe stepped back. He was of medium height, yet so athletically built that he gave the impression of being two inches taller than he actually was. He was smooth-shaven, and his hair and eyes were black. His whole appearance was that of a person infinitely superior to what Philip had expected to find in the gang-foreman. His first words, and the manner in which they were spoken, added to this impression.

"Good evening, gentlemen."

"Good morning," replied MacDougall, nodding toward Philip. "This is Mr. Whittemore, Thorpe. We saw your light, and thought you wouldn't mind a call."

Philip and Thorpe shook hands.

"Just in time to have a cup of coffee," invited Thorpe, pleasantly, motioning toward a steaming pot on the stove. "I just got in from a long hike out over the new road-bed. Been looking the ground over along the north shore of the Gray Beaver, and was so interested that I didn't start for home until dark. Won't you draw up, gentlemen? There are mighty few who can beat me at making coffee."

MacDougall had noted a sudden change in Philip's face, and as Thorpe hastened to lift the over-boiling pot from the stove he saw his chief make a quick movement toward a small table, and pick up an object which looked like a bit of cloth. In an instant Philip had hidden it in the palm of his hand. A flush leaped into his cheeks. A strange fire burned in his eyes when Thorpe turned.

"I'm afraid we can't accept your hospitality," he said. "I'm tired, and want to get to bed. In passing, however, I couldn't refrain from dropping in to compliment you on the remarkable work your men are doing out on the plain. It's splendid."

"They're good men," said Thorpe, quietly. "Pretty wild, but good workers."

He followed them to the door. Outside, Philip's voice trembled when he spoke to MacDougall.

"You go for the others, and bring them to the office, Sandy," he said. "I said nothing to Thorpe because I have no confidence in liars, and Thorpe is a liar. He was not out to the Gray Beaver to-day; for I saw him when he came in—from the opposite direction. He is a liar, and he will bear watching. Mind that, Sandy. Keep your eyes on this man Thorpe. And keep your eyes on his gang. Hustle the others over to the office as soon as you can."

They separated, and Philip returned to the cabin which they had left a few minutes before. He relighted the lamp, and with a sharp gasp in his breath held out before his eyes the object which he had taken from Thorpe's table. He knew now why Thorpe had come from over the mountains that night, why he was exhausted, and why he had lied. He clasped his head between his hands, scarcely believing the evidence of his eyes. A deeper breath, almost a moan, fell from his twisted lips. For he had discovered that Thorpe, the gang-foreman, was Jeanne's lover. In his hand he held the dainty handkerchief, embroidered in blue, which he had seen in Jeanne's possession earlier that evening—crumpled and discolored, still damp with her tears!

XX

For many minutes Philip did not move, or look from the bit of damp fabric which he held between his fingers. His heart was chilled. He felt sick. Each moment added to the emotion which was growing in him, an emotion which was a composite of disgust and of anguish. Jeanne—Thorpe! An eternity of difference seemed to lie between those two—Jeanne, with her tender beauty, her sweet life, her idyllic dreams, and Thorpe, the gang-driver! In his own soul he had made a shrine for Jeanne, and from his knees he had looked up at her, filled with the knowledge of his own unworthiness. He had worshiped her, as Dante might have worshiped Beatrice. To him she was the culmination of all that was sweet and lovable in woman, transcendently above him. And from this love, this worship of his, she had gone that very night to Thorpe, the gang-man. He shivered. Going to the stove he thrust in a handful of paper, dropped the handkerchief in with it, and set the whole on fire.

A few moments later the door opened and MacDougall came in. He was followed by the two swarthy-faced St. Pierres, the camp huntsmen. Philip shook hands with them, and they passed after the engineer through a narrow door leading into a room which was known as the camp office, Cassidy, Henshaw, and the others followed within the next ten minutes. There was not a man among them whose eyes faltered when Philip put up his proposition to them. As briefly as possible he told them a part of what he had previously revealed to MacDougall, and frankly conceded that the preservation of property and life in the camp depended almost entirely upon them.

"You're not the sort of men to demand pay in a pinch like this," he finished, "and that's just the reason I've confidence enough in you to ask for your support. There are fifty men in camp whom we could hire to fight, but I don't want hired fighters. I don't want men who will run at the crack of a few rifles, but men who are willing to die with their boots on. I won't offer you money for this, because I know you too well. But from this hour on you're going to be a part of the Great Northern Fish and Development Company, and as soon as the certificates can be signed I'm going to turn over a hundred shares of stock to each of you. Remember that this isn't pay. It's simply a selfish scheme of mine to make you a part of the company. There are eight of us. Give us each an automatic and I'll wager that there isn't a combination in this neck of the woods strong enough to do us up."

In the pale light of the two oil-lamps the men's faces glowed with enthusiasm. Cassidy was the first to grip Philip's hand in a pledge of fealty.

"When hell freezes over, we're licked," he said. "Where's me automatic?"

MacDougall brought in the guns and ammunition.

"In the morning we will begin the erection of a new building close to this one," said Philip. "There is no reason for the building, but that will give me an excuse for keeping you men together on one job, within fifty feet of your guns, which we can keep in this room. Only four men need work at a shift, and I'll put Cassidy in charge of the operations, if that is satisfactory to the others. We'll have a couple of new bunks put in here so that four men can stay with MacDougall and me every night. The other four, who are not on the working shift, can hunt not far from the camp, and keep their eyes peeled. Does that look good?"

"Can't be beat," said Henshaw, throwing open the breech of his gun. "Shall we load?"

"Yes."

The room became ominous with the metallic click of loaded cartridge clips and the hard snap of released chambers.

Five minutes later Philip stood alone with MacDougall. The loaded rifles, each with a filled cartridge belt hanging over the muzzle, were arranged in a row along one of the walls.

"I'll stake everything I've got on those men," he exclaimed. "Mac, did it ever strike you that when you want REAL men you ought to come north for them? Every one of those fellows is a northerner, except Cassidy, and he's a fighter by birth. They'll die before they go back on their word."

MacDougall rubbed his hands and laughed softly.

"What next, Phil?"

"We must send the swiftest man you've got in camp after Billinger, and get word to the other parties you sent out as quickly as we can. They'll probably get in too late. Billinger may arrive in time."

"He's been gone a week. It's doubtful if we can get him back within three," said MacDougall. "I'll send St. Pierre's cousin, that young Crow Feather, after him as soon as he can get a pack ready. You'd better go to bed, Phil. You look like a dead man."

Philip was not sure that he could sleep, notwithstanding the physical strain he had been under during the past twenty-four hours. He was filled with a nervous desire for continued action. Only action kept him from thinking of Jeanne and Thorpe. After MacDougall had gone to stir up young Crow Feather he undressed and stretched out in his bunk, hoping that the Scotchman would soon return. Not until he closed his eyes did he realize how tired he was. MacDougall came in an hour later, and Philip was asleep. It was nine o'clock when he awoke. He went to the cook's shanty, ate a hot breakfast of griddle-cakes and bacon, drank a pint of strong coffee, and hunted up MacDougall. Sandy was just coming from Thorpe's house.

"He's a queer guinea, that Thorpe," said the engineer, after their first greeting. "He doesn't pretend to do a pound's work. Notice his hands when you see him again, Phil. They look as though he had been drumming a piano all his life. But love o' mighty, how he does make the OTHERS work. You want to go over and see his gang throw dirt."

"That's where I'm going," said Philip. "Is Thorpe at home?"

"Just leaving. There he is now!"

At MacDougall's whistle Thorpe turned and waited for Philip.

"Goin' over?" he asked, pleasantly, when Philip came up.

"Yes. I want to see how your men work without a leader," replied Philip. He paused for a moment to light his pipe, and pointed to a group of men down on the lake shore. "See that gang?" he asked. "They're building a scow. Take away their foreman and they wouldn't be worth their grub. They're men we brought up from Winnipeg."

Thorpe was rolling a cigarette. Under his arm he held a pair of light gloves.

"Mine are different," he laughed, quietly.

"I know that," rejoined Philip, watching the skill of his long white fingers. "That's why I want to see them in action, when you're away."

"My policy is to know to a cubic foot what a certain number of men are capable of doing in a certain time," explained Thorpe, as they walked toward the plain. "My next move is to secure the men who will achieve the result, whether I am present or not. That done, my work is done. Simple, isn't it?"

There was something likable about Thorpe. Even in his present mood Philip could not but concede that. He was surprised in Thorpe, in more ways than one. His voice was low, and filled with a certain companionable quality that gave one confidence in him immediately.

He was apparently a man of education and of some little culture, in spite of his vocation, which usually possesses a vocabulary of its own as hard as rock. But Philip's greatest surprise came when he regarded Thorpe's personal appearance. He judged that he was past forty, perhaps forty-five, and the thought made him shudder inwardly. He was twice—almost three times—as old as Jeanne. And yet there was about him something irresistibly attractive, a fascination which had its influence upon Philip himself. His nails dug into tie flesh of his hands when he thought of this man—and Jeanne.

Thorpe's gang was hard at work when they came to the end of the rock-bed. Scarcely a man seemed to take notice when he appeared. There was one exception, a wiry, red-faced little man who raised a hand to his cap when he saw the foreman.

"That's the sub-foreman," explained Thorpe. "He answers to me." The little man had given a signal, and Thorpe added, "Excuse me for a moment. He's got something on his mind."

He drew a few steps aside, and Philip walked along the line of laboring-men. He grinned and nodded to them, one after another. MacDougall was right. They were the toughest lot of men he had ever seen in one gang.

Loud voices turned him about, and he saw that Thorpe and the sub-foreman had approached a huge, heavy-shouldered man, with whom they seemed to be in serious altercation. Two or three of the workmen had drawn near, and Thorpe's voice rang out clear and vibrant.

"You'll do that, Blake, or you'll shoulder your kit back home. And what goes with you goes with your clique. I know your kind, and you can't worry me. Take that pick and dig—or hike. There's no two ways about it."

Philip could not hear what the big man said, but suddenly Thorpe's fist shot out and struck him fairly on the jaw. In another instant Thorpe had jumped back, and was facing half a dozen angry, threatening men. He had drawn a revolver, and his white teeth gleamed in a cool and menacing smile.

"Think it over, boys," he said, quietly. "And if you're not satisfied come in and draw your pay this noon. We'll furnish you with outfits and plenty of grub if you don't like the work up here. I don't care to hold men like you to your contracts."

He came to meet Philip, as though nothing unusual had happened.

"That will delay the completion of our work for a week at least," he said, as he thrust his revolver into a holster hidden under his coat. "I've been expecting trouble with Blake and four or five of his pals for some time. I'm glad it's over. Blake threatens a strike unless I give him a sub-foremanship and increase the men's wages from six to ten dollars a day. Think of it. A strike—up here! It would be the beginning of history, wouldn't it?"

He laughed softly, and Philip laughed from sheer admiration of the man's courage.

"You think they'll go?" he asked, anxiously.

"I'm sure of it," replied Thorpe. "It's the best thing that can happen."

An hour later Philip was back in camp. He did not see Thorpe again until after dinner, and then the gang-foreman hunted him up. His face wore a worried look.

"It's a little worse than I expected," he said. "Blake and eight others came in for their pay and outfits this noon. I didn't think that more than three or four would have the nerve to quit."

"I'll furnish you with men to take their places," said Philip.

"There's the hitch," replied Thorpe, rolling a cigarette. "I want my men to work by themselves. Put half a dozen of your amateur road-men among them and it will mean twenty per cent. less work done, and perhaps trouble. They're a tough lot. I concede that. I've thought of a way to offset the loss of Blake and the others. We can set a gang of your men at work over at Gray Beaver Lake, and they can build up to meet us."

Philip saw MacDougall soon after his short talk with Thorpe. The engineer did not disguise his pleasure at the turn which affairs had taken.

"I'm glad they're going," he declared. "If there's to be trouble I'll feel easier with that bunch out of camp. I'd give my next month's salary if Thorpe would take his whole outfit back where they came from. They're doing business with the road-bed all right, but I don't like the idea of having 'em around when there are throats to be cut, one side or t'other."

Philip did not see Thorpe again that day. He selected his men for the Gray Beaver work, and in the afternoon despatched a messenger over the Fort Churchill route to meet Brokaw. He was confident that Brokaw and his daughter would show up during the next few days, but at the same time he instructed the messenger to go to Churchill if he should not meet them on the way. Other men he sent to recall the prospecting parties outfitted by MacDougall. Early in the evening the St. Pierres, Lecault, and Henshaw joined him for a few minutes in the office. During the day the four had done scout work five miles on all sides of the camp. Lecault had shot a moose three miles to the south, and had hung up the meat. One of the St. Pierres saw Blake and his gang on the way to the Churchill. Beyond these two incidents they brought in no news. A little later MacDougall brought in two other men whom he could trust, and armed them with muzzle-loaders. They were the two last guns in the camp.

With ten men constantly prepared for attack, Philip began to feel that he had the situation well in hand. It would be practically impossible for his enemies to surprise the camp, and after their first day's scout duty the men on the trail would always be within sound of rifle-shots, even if they did not discover the advance of an attacking force in time to beat them to camp. In the event of one making such a discovery he was to signal the others by a series of shots, such as one might fire at a running moose.

Philip found it almost impossible to fight back his thoughts of Jeanne. During the two or three days that followed the departure of Blake he did not allow himself an hour's rest from early dawn until late at night. Each night he went to bed exhausted, with the hope that sleep would bury his grief. The struggle wore upon him, and the faithful MacDougall began to note the change in his comrade's face. The fourth day Thorpe disappeared and did not show up again until the following morning. Every hour of his absence was like the stab of a knife in Philip's heart, for he knew that the gang-foreman had gone to see Jeanne. Three days later the visit was repeated, and that night MacDougall found Philip in a fever.

"You're overdoing," he told him. "You're not in bed five hours out of the twenty-four. Cut it out, or you'll be in the hospital instead of in the fighting line when the big show comes to town."

Days of mental agony and of physical pain followed. Neither Philip nor MacDougall could understand the mysterious lack of developments. They had expected attack before this, and yet ceaseless scout work brought in no evidence of an approaching crisis. Neither could they understand the growing disaffection among Thorpe's men. The numerical strength of the gang dwindled from nineteen down to fifteen, from fifteen to twelve. At last Thorpe voluntarily asked Philip to cut his salary in two, because he could not hold his men. On that same day the little sub-foreman and two others left him, leaving only nine men at work. The delay in Brokaw's arrival was another puzzle to Philip. Two weeks passed, and in that time Thorpe left camp three times. On the fifteenth day the Fort Churchill messenger returned. He was astounded when he found that Brokaw was not in camp, and brought amazing news. Brokaw and his daughter had departed from Fort Churchill two days after Pierre had followed Jeanne and Philip. They had gone in two canoes, up the Churchill. He had seen no signs of them anywhere along the route.

No sooner had he received the news than Philip sent the messenger after MacDougall. The Scotchman's red face stared at him blankly when he told him what had happened.

"That's their first move in the real fight," said Philip, with a hard ring in his voice. "They've got Brokaw. Keep your men close from this hour on, Sandy. Hereafter let five of them sleep in our bunks during the day, and keep them awake during the night."

Five days passed without a sign of an enemy.

About eight o'clock on the night of the sixth MacDougall came into the office, where Philip was alone. The young Scotchman's usually florid face was white. He dropped a curse as he grasped the back of a chair with both hands. It was the third or fourth time that Philip had heard MacDougall swear.

"Damn that Thorpe!" he cried, in a low voice.

"What's up?" asked Philip, his muscles tightening.

MacDougall viciously beat the ash from the bowl of his pipe.

"I didn't want to worry you about Thorpe, so I've kept quiet about some things," he growled. "Thorpe brought up a load of whisky with him. I knew it was against the law you've set down for this camp, but I figured you were having trouble enough without getting you into a mix-up with him, so I didn't say anything. But this other—is damnable! Twice he's had a woman sneak in to visit him. She's there again to-night!"

A choking, gripping sensation rose in Philip's throat. MacDougall was not looking, and did not see the convulsive twitching of the other's face, or the terrible light that shot for an instant into his eyes.

"A woman—Mac—"

"A YOUNG woman," said MacDougall, with emphasis. "I don't know who she is, but I do know that she hasn't a right there or she wouldn't sneak in like a thief. I'm going to be blunt—damned blunt. I think she's one of the other men's wives. There are half a dozen in camp."

"Haven't you ever looked—to see if you could recognize her?"

"Haven't had the chance," said MacDougall. "She's been wrapped up both times, and as it was none of my business I didn't lay in wait. But now—it's up to you!"

Philip rose slowly. He felt cold. He put on his coat and cap, and buckled on his revolver. His face was deadly white when he turned to MacDougall.

"She is over there to-night?"

"Sneaked in not half an hour ago, I saw her come out of the edge of the spruce."

"From the trail that leads out over the plain?"

"Yes."

Philip walked to the door.

"I'm going over to call on Thorpe," he said, quietly. "I may not be back for some time, Sandy."

In the deep shadows outside he stood gazing at the light in Thorpe's cabin. Then he walked slowly toward the spruce. He did not go to the door, but leaned with his back against the building, near one of the windows. The first shuddering sickness had gone from him. His temples throbbed. At the sound of a voice inside which was Thorpe's the chill in his blood turned to fire. The terrible fear that had fallen upon him at MacDougall's words held him motionless, and his brain worked upon but one idea—one determination. If it was Jeanne who came in this way, he would kill Thorpe. If it was another woman, he would give Thorpe that night to get out of the country. He waited. He heard the gang-man's voice frequently, once in a loud, half-mocking laugh. Twice he heard a lower voice—a woman's. For an hour he watched. He walked back and forth in the gloom of the spruce, and waited another hour. Then the light went out, and he slipped back to the corner of the cabin.

After a moment the door opened, and a hooded figure came out, and walked rapidly toward the trail that buried itself amid the spruce. Philip ran around the cabin and followed. There was a little open beyond the first fringe of spruce, and in this he ran up silently from behind and overtook the one he was pursuing. As his hand fell upon her arm the woman turned upon him with a frightened cry. Philip's hand dropped. He took a step back.

"My God! Jeanne—it is you!"

His voice was husky, like a choking man's. For an instant Jeanne's white, terrified face met his own. And then, without a word to him, she fled swiftly down the trail.

Philip made no effort to follow. For two or three minutes he stood like a man turned suddenly into hewn rock, staring with unseeing eyes into the gloom where Jeanne had disappeared. Then he walked back to the edge of the spruce. There he drew his revolver, and cocked it. The starlight revealed a madness in his face as he approached Thorpe's cabin. He was smiling, but it was such a smile as presages death; a smile as implacable as fate itself.

XXI

As Philip approached the cabin he saw a figure stealing away through the gloom. His first thought was that he had returned a minute too late to wreak his vengeance upon the gang-foreman in his own home, and he quickened his steps in pursuit. The man ahead of him was cutting direct for the camp supply-house, which was the nightly rendezvous of those who wished to play cards or exchange camp gossip. The supply-house, aglow with light, was not more than two hundred yards from Thorpe's, and Philip saw that if he dealt out the justice he contemplated he had not a moment to lose. He began to run, so quickly that he approached within a dozen paces of the man he was pursuing without being heard. It was not until then that he made a discovery which stopped him. The man ahead was not Thorpe. Suddenly, looking beyond him, he saw a second figure pass slowly through the lighted door of the supply-house. Even at that distance he recognized the gang-foreman. He thrust his revolver under his coat and fell a little farther behind the man he had mistaken for Thorpe so that when the latter passed within the small circle of light that came from the supply-house windows he was fifty instead of a dozen paces away. Something in the other's manner, something strangely and potently familiar in his slim, lithe form, in the quick, half-running movement of his body, drew a sharp breath from Philip. He was on the point of calling a name, but it died on his lips. A moment more and the man passed through the door. Philip was certain that it was Pierre Couchee who had followed Thorpe.

He was filled with a sudden fear as he ran toward the store. He had scarcely crossed the threshold when a glance showed him Thorpe leaning upon a narrow counter, and Pierre close beside him. He saw that the half-breed was speaking, and Thorpe drew himself erect. Then, as quick as a flash, two things happened. Thorpe's hand went to his belt, Pierre's sent a lightning gleam of steel back over his shoulder. The terrible drive of the knife and the explosion of Thorpe's revolver came in the same instant. Thorpe crumpled back over the counter, clutching at his breast. Pierre turned about, staggering, and saw Philip. His eyes lighted up, and with a moaning cry he stretched out his arms as Philip sprang to him. Above the sudden tumult of men's feet and excited voices he gasped out Jeanne's name. Half a dozen men had crowded about them. Through the ring burst MacDougall, a revolver in his hand. Pierce had become a dead weight in Philip's arms.

"Help me over to the cabin with him, Mac," he said. He looked around among the men. It struck him as curious, even then, that he saw none of Thorpe's gang. "Is Thorpe done for?" he asked.

"He's dead," replied some one.

With an effort Pierre opened his eyes.

"Dead!" he breathed, and in that one word there was a tremble of joy and triumph.

"Take Thorpe over to his cabin," commanded Philip, as he and MacDougall lifted Pierre between them. "I will answer for this man."

They could hear Pierre's sobbing breath as they hurried across the open. They laid him on Philip's bunk and Pierre opened his eyes again. He looked at Philip.

"M'sieur," he whispered, "tell me—quick—if I must die!"

MacDougall had studied medicine and surgery before engineering, and took the place of camp physician. Philip drew back while he ripped open the half-breed's garments and bared his breast. Then he darted to his bunk for the satchel in which he kept his bandages and medicines, throwing off his coat as he went. Philip bent over Pierre. Blood was oozing slowly from the wounded man's right breast. Over his heart Philip noticed a blood-stained locket, fastened by a babiche string about his neck.

Pierre's hands groped eagerly for Philip's.

"M'sieur—you will tell me—if I must die?" he pleaded. "There are things you must know—about Jeanne—if I go. It will not hurt. I am not afraid. You will tell me—"

"Yes," said Philip.

He could scarcely speak, and while MacDougall was at work stood so that Pierre could not see his face. There was a sobbing note in Pierre's breath, and he knew what it meant. He had heard that same sound more than once when he had shot moose and caribou through the lungs. Five minutes later MacDougall straightened himself. He had done all that he could. Philip followed him to the back part of the room. Almost without sound his lips framed the words, "Will he die?"

"Yes," said MacDougall. "There is no hope. He may last until morning."

Philip took a stool and sat down beside Pierre. There was no fear in the wounded man's face. His eyes were clear. His voice was a little stronger.

"I will die, M'sieur," he said, calmly.

"I am afraid so, Pierre."

Pierre's damp fingers closed about his own. His eyes shone softly, and he smiled.

"It is best," he said, "and I am glad. I feel quite well. I will live for some time?"

"Perhaps for a few hours, Pierre."

"God is good to me," breathed Pierre, devoutly. "I thank Him. Are we alone?"

"Do you wish to be alone?"

"Yes."

Philip motioned to MacDougall, who went into the little office room.

"I will die," whispered Pierre, softly, as though he were achieving a triumph. "And everything would die with me, M'sieur, if I did not know that you love Jeanne, and that you will care for her when I am gone. M'sieur, I have told you that I love her. I have worshiped her, next to my God. I die happy, knowing that I am dying for her. If I had lived I would have suffered, for I love alone. She does not dream that my love is different from hers, for I have never told her. It would have given her pain. And you will never let her know. As Our Dear Lady is my witness, M'sieur, she has loved but one man, and that man is you."

Pierre gave a great breath. A warm flood seemed suddenly to engulf Philip. Did he hear right? Could he believe? He fell upon his knees beside Pierre and brushed his dark hair back from his face.

"Yes, I love her," he said, softly. "But I did not know that she loved me."

"It is not strange," said Pierre, looking straight into his eyes. "But you will understand—now—M'sieur. I seem to have strength, and I will tell you all—from the beginning. Perhaps I have done wrong. You will know—soon. You remember Jeanne told you the story of the baby—of the woman frozen in the snow. That was the beginning of the long fight—for me. This—what I am about to tell you—will be sacred to you, M'sieur?"

"As my life," said Philip.

Pierre was silent for a few moments. He seemed to be gathering his thoughts, so that he could tell in few words the tragedy of years. Two brilliant spots burned in his cheeks, and the hand which Philip held was hot.

"Years ago—twenty, almost—there came a man to Fort o' God," he began. "He was very young, and from the south. D'Arcambal was then middle-aged, but his wife was young and beautiful. Jeanne says that you saw her picture—against the wall. D'Arcambal worshiped her. She was his life. You understand what happened. The man from the south—the young wife—they went away together."

Pierre coughed. A bit of blood reddened his lips. Philip wiped it away gently with his handkerchief, hiding the stain from Pierre's eyes.

"Yes," he said, "I understand."

"It broke D'Arcambal's heart," resumed Pierre. "He destroyed everything that had belonged to the woman. He turned her picture to the wall. His love turned slowly to hate. It was two years later that I came over the barrens one night and found Jeanne and her dead mother. The woman, M'sieur—Jeanne's mother—was D'Arcambal's wife. She was returning to Fort o' God, and God's justice overtook her almost at its doors. I carried little Jeanne to my Indian mother, and then made ready to carry the woman to her husband. It was then that a terrible thought came to me. Jeanne was not D'Arcambal's daughter. She was a part of the man who had stolen his wife. I worshiped the little Jeanne even then, and for her sake my mother and I swore secrecy, and buried the woman. Then we took the babe to Fort o' God as a stranger. We saved her. We saved D'Arcambal. No one ever knew."

Pierre stopped for breath.

"Was it best?"

"It was glorious," said Philip, trembling.

"It would have come out right—in the end—if the father had not returned," said Pierre. "I must hurry, M'sieur, for it hurts me now to talk. He came first a year ago, and revealed himself to Jeanne. He told her everything. D'Arcambal was rich; Jeanne and I both had money. He threatened—we bought him off. We fought to keep the terrible thing from D'Arcambal. Our money sent him away for a time. Then he returned. It was news of him I brought up the river to Jeanne—from Churchill. I offered to kill him—but Jeanne would not listen to that. But the Great God willed that I should. I killed him to-night—over there!"

A great joy surged above the grief in Philip's heart. He could not speak, but pressed Pierre's hand harder, and looked into his glistening eyes.

Pierre's next words broke his silence, and wrung a low cry from his lips.

"M'sieur, this man Thorpe—Jeanne's father—is the man whom you know as Lord Fitzhugh Lee."

He coughed violently, and with sudden fear Philip lifted his head so that it rested against his shoulder. After a moment he lowered it again. His face was as white as Pierre's after that sudden fit of coughing.

"I talked with him—alone—on the afternoon of the fight on the rock," continued Pierre, huskily. "He was hiding in the woods near Churchill, and left for Fort o' God on that same day. I did not tell Jeanne—until after what happened, and I came up with you on the river. Thorpe was waiting for us at Fort o' God. It was he whom Jeanne saw that night beside the rock, but I could not tell you the truth—then. He came often after that—two, three times a week. He tortured Jeanne. My God! he taunted her, M'sieur, and made her let him kiss her, because he was her father. We gave him money—all that we could get; we promised him more, if he would leave—five thousand dollars—in three years. He agreed to go—after he had finished his work here. And that work—M'sieur—was to destroy you. He told Jeanne, because it made her fear him more. He compelled her to come to his cabin. He thought she was his slave, that she would do anything to be free of him. He told her of his plot—how he had fooled you in the sham fight with one of his men—how those men were going to attack you a little later, and how he had intercepted your letter from Churchill and sent in its place the other letter which made your camp defenseless. He was not afraid of her. She was in his power, and he laughed at her horror, and tortured her as a cat will a bird. But Jeanne—"

A spasm of pain shot over Pierre's face. Fresh blood dyed his lips, and a shiver ran through his body.

"My God!—water—something—M'sieur," he gasped. "I must go on!"

Philip raised him again in his arms. He saw MacDougall's head appear through the door.

"You will rest easier this way, Pierre," he said.

After a few moments Pierre spoke in a gasping whisper.

"You must understand. I must be quick," he said. "We could not warn you of what Jeanne had discovered. That would have revealed her father. D'Arcambal would have known—every one. Thorpe plans to dress his men—like Indians. They are to attack your camp to-morrow night. Ten days ago we went to the camp of old Sachigo, the Cree, who loves Jeanne as his own daughter. It was Jeanne's idea—to save you. Jeanne told him of Thorpe's plot to destroy you, and to lay the blame on Sachigo's people. Sachigo is out there—in the mountains—hiding with thirty of his tribe. Two days ago Jeanne learned where her father's men were hiding. We had planned everything. To-morrow night—when they move to attack—we were to start a signal-fire on the big rock mountain at the end of the lake. Sachigo starts at the signal, and lays in ambush for the others in the ravine between the two mountains. None of Thorpe's men will come out alive. Sachigo and his people will destroy them, and none will ever know how it happened, for the Crees keep their secrets. But now—it is too late—for me. When it happens—I will be gone. The signal-pile is built—birch-bark—at the very top of the rock. Jeanne will wait for me out on the plain—and I will not come. You must fire the signal, M'sieur—as soon as it is dark. None will ever know. Jeanne's father is dead. You will keep the secret—of her mother—always—"

"Forever," said Philip.

MacDougall came into the room, He brought a glass, partly filled with a colored liquid, and placed it to Pierre's lips. Pierre swallowed with an effort, and with a significant hunch of his shoulders for Philip's eyes alone the engineer returned to the little room.

"Mon Dieu, how it burns!" said Pierre, as if to himself. "May I lie down again, M'sieur?"

Philip lowered him gently. He made no effort to speak in these moments. Pierre's eyes were dark and luminous as they sought his own. The draught he had taken gave him a passing strength.

"I saw Thorpe again this afternoon," he said, more calmly. "D'Arcambal thought I had taken Jeanne to visit a trapper's wife down the Churchill. I saw Thorpe—alone. He had been drinking. He laughed at me, and said that Jeanne and I were fools—that he would not leave as he had said he would—but that he would remain—always. I told Jeanne, and asked her again to let me kill him. But she said no—and I had taken my oath to her. Jeanne saw him again to-night. I was near the cabin, and saw you. I told him I would kill him if he did not go. He laughed again, and struck me. When I came to my feet he was half across the open; I followed. I forgot my oath. Rage filled my heart. You know what happened. You will tell Jeanne—so that she will understand—"

"Can we not send for her?" asked Philip. "She must be near."

"No, M'sieur," he replied, softly. "It would only give her great pain to see me—like this. She was to meet me to-night—at twelve o'clock—on the trail where the road-bed crosses. You will meet her in my place. When she understands all that has happened you may bring her here, if she wishes to come. Then—to-morrow night—you will go together to fire the signal."

"But Thorpe is dead," said Philip. "Will they attack without him?"

"There is another, besides him," said Pierre. "That is one secret which Thorpe has kept from Jeanne—who the other is—the one who is paying to have you destroyed. Yes—they will attack."

Philip bent low over Pierre.

"I have known of this plot for a long time, Pierre," he said, tensely. "I know that this Thorpe, who for some reason has passed as Lord Fitzhugh Lee, is but the agent of a more powerful force behind him. Have you told me all, Pierre? Do you know nothing more?"

"Nothing, M'sieur."

"Was it Thorpe who attacked you on the cliff at Churchill?"

"No, I am sure that it was not he. If the attack had not failed—it would have meant loss—for him. I have laid it to the ruffians who wanted to kill me—and secure Jeanne. You understand—"

"Yes, but I do not believe that was the motive for the attack, Pierre," said Philip. "Did Thorpe go to see any one in Churchill?"

"I don't know. He was concealing himself in the forest."

A convulsive shudder ran through Pierre's body. He gave a low cry of pain, and his hand clutched at the babiche cord which held the locket about his neck.

"M'sieur," he whispered, quickly, "this locket—was on the little Jeanne—when I found her in the snow. I kept it because it bears the woman's initials. I am foolish, M'sieur. I am weak. But I would like to have it buried with me—under the old tree—where Jeanne's mother lies. And if you could, M'sieur—if you only could—place something of Jeanne's in my hand—I would rest easier."

Philip bowed his head in silence, while his eyes grew blinding hot. Pierre pressed his hand.

"She loves you—as I love her," he whispered, so low that Philip could scarcely hear. "You will love her—always. If you do not—the Great God will let the curse of Pierre Couchee fall upon you!"

Choking back the great sobs that rose in his breast, Philip sank upon his knees beside Pierre, and buried his face in his arms like a heartbroken boy. For several moments there was a silence, punctuated by the rasping breath of the wounded man. Suddenly this sound ceased, and Philip felt a cold fear leap through him. He listened, neither breathing nor lifting his head. In that interval of pulseless quiet a terrible cry came from Pierre's lips, and when Philip looked up the dying half-breed had struggled to a sitting posture, blood staining his lips again, his eyes blazing, his white face damp with the clammy touch of death, and was staring through the cabin window. It was the window that looked out over the lake, toward the rock mountain half a mile away. Philip turned, horrified and wondering. Through the window he saw a glow in the sky—the glow of a fire, leaping up in a crimson flood from the top of the mountain!

Again that terrible, moaning cry fell from Pierre's lips, and he reached out his arms toward the signal that was blazing forth its warning in the night.

"Jeanne—Jeanne—" he sobbed. "My Jeanne—"

He swayed, and fell back. His words came in choking gasps.

"The signal!" he struggled, fighting to make Philip understand him. "Jeanne—saw—Thorpe—to-night. He—must—changed—plans. Attack—to-night. Jeanne—Jeanne—my Jeanne—has lighted—the signal—fire!"

A tremor ran through his body, and he lay still. MacDougall ran across from the half-open door, and put his head to Pierre's breast.

"Is he dead?" asked Philip.

"Not yet."

"Will he become conscious again?"

"Possibly."

Philip gripped MacDougall by the arm.

"The attack is to be made to-night, Mac," he exclaimed. "Warn the men. Have them ready. But you—You, MacDougall, attend to this man, And Keep Him Alive!"

Without another word he ran to the door and out into the night. The signal-fire was leaping to the sky. It lighted up the black cap of the mountain, and sent a thousand aurora fires flashing across the lake. And Philip, as he ran swiftly through the camp toward the narrow trail that led to that mountain-top, repeated over and over again the dying words of Pierre—

"Jeanne—my Jeanne—my Jeanne—"

JAMES OLIVER CURWOOD

XXII

News of the double tragedy had swept through the camp, and there was a crowd in front of the supply-house. Philip passed close to Thorpe's house to avoid discovery, ran a hundred yards up the trail over which Jeanne had fled a short time before, and then cut straight across through the thin timber for the head of the lake. He felt no effort in his running. Low bush whipped him in the face and left no sting. He was not conscious that he was panting for breath when he came out in the black shadow of the mountain. This night in itself had been a creation for him, for out of grief and pain it had lifted him into a new life, and into a happiness that seemed to fill him with the strength and the endurance of five men. Jeanne loved him! The wonderful truth cried itself out in his soul at every step he took, and he murmured it aloud to himself, over and over again, as he ran.

The glow of the signal-fire lighted up the sky above him, and he climbed up, higher and higher, scrambling swiftly from rock to rock, until he saw the tips of the flames licking up into the sky. He had come up the steepest and shortest side of the ridge, and when he reached the top he lay upon his face for a moment, his breath almost gone.

The fire was built against a huge dead pine, and the pine was blazing a hundred feet in the air. He could feel its heat. The monster torch illumined the barren cap of the rock from edge to edge, and he looked about him for Jeanne. For a moment he did not see her, and her name rose to his lips, to be stilled in the same breath by what he saw beyond the burning pine. Through the blaze of the heat and fire fie beheld Jeanne, standing close to the edge of the mountain, gazing into the south and west. He called her name. Jeanne turned toward him with a startled cry, and Philip was at her side. The girl's face was white and strained. Her lips were twisted in pain at sight of him. She spoke no word, but a strange sound rose in her throat, a welling-up of the sudden despair which the fire-light revealed in her eyes. For one moment they stood apart, and Philip tried to speak. And then, suddenly, he reached out and drew her quickly into his arms—so quickly that there was no time for her to escape, so closely that her sweet face lay imprisoned upon his breast, as he had held it once before, under the picture at Fort o' God. He felt her straining to free herself; he saw the fear in her eyes, and he tried to speak calmly, while his heart throbbed with the passion of love which he wished to pour into her ears.

"Listen, Jeanne," he said. "Pierre has sent me to you. He has told me everything—everything, my sweetheart. There is nothing to keep from me now. I know. I understand. And I love you—love you—love you—my own sweet Jeanne!"

She trembled at his words. He felt her shuddering in his arms, and her eyes gazed at him wonderingly, filled with a strange and incredulous look, while her lips quivered and remained speechless. He drew her nearer, until his face was against her own, and the warmth of her lips, her eyes, and her hair entered into him, and near stifled his heart with joy.

"He has told me everything, my little Jeanne," he said again, in a whisper that rose just above the crackling of the pine. "Everything. He told me because he knew that I loved you, and because—"

The words choked in his throat. At this hesitation Jeanne drew her head back, and, with her hands pressing against his breast, looked into his face. There were in her eyes the same struggling emotions, but with them now there came also a sweet faltering, a piteous appeal to him, a faith that rose above her terrors, and the tremble of her lips was like that of a crying child. He drew her face back, and kissed the quivering lips, and suddenly he felt the strain against him give way, and Jeanne's head sobbed upon his breast. In that moment, looking where the roaring pine sent its pinnacles of flame leaping up into the night, a word of thanks, of prayer, rose mutely to his lips, and he held Jeanne more closely, and whispered over and over again in his happiness, "Jeanne—Jeanne—my sweetheart Jeanne."

Jeanne's sobs grew less and less, and Philip strengthened himself to tell her the terrible news of Pierre. He knew that in the selfishness of his own joy he had already wasted precious minutes, and very gently he took Jeanne's wet face between his two hands and turned it a little toward his own.

"Pierre has told me everything, Jeanne," he repeated. "Everything—from the day he found you many years ago to the day your father returned to torture you." He spoke calmly, even as he felt her shiver in pain against him. "To-night there was a little trouble down in the camp, dear. Pierre is wounded, and wants you to come to him. Thorpe—is—dead."

For an instant Philip was frightened at what happened. Jeanne's breath ceased. There seemed to be not a quiver of life in her body, and she lay in his arms as if dead. And then, suddenly, there came from her a terrible cry, and she wrenched herself free, and stood a step from him, her face as white as death.

"He—is—dead—"

"Yes, he is dead."

"And Pierre—Pierre killed him?"

Philip held out his arms, but Jeanne did not seem to see them. She saw the answer in his face.

"And—Pierre—is—hurt—" she went on, never taking her wide, luminous eyes from his face.

Before he answered Philip took her trembling hands in his own, as though he would lighten the blow by the warmth and touch of his great love.

"Yes, he is hurt, Jeanne," he said. "We must hurry, for I am afraid there is no time to lose."

"He is—dying?"

"I fear so, Jeanne."

He turned before the look that came into her face, and led her about the circle of fire to the side of the mountain that sloped down into the plain. Suddenly Jeanne stopped for an instant. Her fingers tightened about his. Her face was turned back into the endless desolation of night and forest that lay to the south and west. Far out—a mile—two miles— an answering fire was breaking the black curtain that hid all things beyond them. Jeanne lifted her face to him. Grief and love, pain and joy, shone in her eyes.

"They are there!" she said, chokingly. "It is Sachigo, and they are coming—coming—coming—"

Once again before they began the descent of the mountain Philip drew her close in his arms, and kissed her. And this time there was the sweet surrender to him of all things in the tenderness of Jeanne's lips. Silent in their grief, and yet communing in sympathy and love in the firm clasp of their hands, they came down the mountain, through the thin spruce forest, and to the lighted cabin where Pierre lay dying. MacDougall was in the room when they entered, and rose softly, tiptoeing into the little office. Philip led Jeanne to Pierre's side, and as he bent over him, and spoke softly, the half-breed opened his eyes. He saw Jeanne. Into his fading eyes there came a wonderful light. His lips moved, and his hands strove to lift themselves above the crumpled blanket. Jeanne dropped upon her knees beside him, and as she clasped his chilled hands to her breast a glorious understanding lighted up her face; and then she took Pierre's face between her hands, and bowed her own close down to it, so that the two were hidden under the beauteous halo of her hair. Philip gripped at his throat to hold back a sob. A terrible stillness came into the room, and he dared not move. It seemed a long time before Jeanne lifted her head, slowly, tenderly, as if fearing to awaken a sleeping child. She turned to him, and he read the truth in her face before she had spoken. Her voice was low and calm, filled with the sweetness and tenderness and strength that come only to a woman in the final moment of a great sorrow.

"Leave us, Philip," she said. "Pierre is dead."

XXIII

For a moment Philip bowed his head, and then he turned and went noiselessly from the room, without speaking. As he closed the door softly behind him he looked back, and from her attitude beside Pierre he knew that Jeanne was whispering a prayer. A vision flashed before him, so quick that it had come like a ray of light—a vision of another hour, years and years ago, when Pierre had knelt beside HER, and when he had lifted up his wild, half-thought prayer out in the death-chill of the snowy barrens. And this was his reward, to have Jeanne kneel beside him as the soul which had loved her so faithfully took its flight.

Philip could not see when he turned his face to the light of the office. For the first time the grief which he had choked back escaped in a gasping break in his voice, and he wiped his eyes with his pocket-handkerchief. He knew that MacDougall was looking upon his weakness, but he did not at first see that there was another person in the room besides the engineer. This second person rose to meet him, while MacDougall remained in his seat, and as he came out into the clearer light of the room Philip could scarce believe his eyes.

It was Gregson!

"I am sorry that I came in just at this time, Phil," he greeted, in a low voice.

Philip stared, still incredulous. He had never seen Gregson as he looked now. The artist advanced no farther. He did not hold out his hand. There was none of the joy of meeting in his face. His eyes shifted to the door that led into the death-chamber, and they were filled with the gloom of a condemned man. With a low word Philip held out his hand to meet his old comrade's. Gregson drew back.

"No—not now," he said. "Wait—until you have heard me."

Something in his cold, passionless voice stopped Philip. He saw Gregson glance toward MacDougall, and understood what he meant. Going to the engineer, he placed a hand on his shoulder, and spoke so that only he could hear.

"She is in there, Mac—with Pierre. She wanted to be alone with him for a few minutes. Will you wait for her—outside—at the door, and take her over to Cassidy's wife? Tell her that I will come to her in a little while."

He followed MacDougall to the door, speaking to him in a low voice, and then turned to Gregson. The artist had seated himself at one side of the small office table, and Philip sat down opposite him, holding out his hand to him again.

"What is the matter, Greggy?"

"This is not a time for long explanations," said the artist, still holding back his hand. "They can come later, Phil. But to-night—now—you must understand why I cannot shake hands with you. We have been friends for a good many years. In a few minutes we will be enemies— or you will be mine. One thing, before I go on, I must ask of you. I demand it. Whatever passes between us during the next ten minutes, say no word against Eileen Brokaw. I will say what you might say—that for a time her soul wandered, and was almost lost. But it has come back to her, strong and pure. I love her. Some strange fate has ordained that she should love me, worthless as I am. She is to be my wife."

Philip's hand was still across the table.

"Greggy—Greggy—God bless you!" he cried, softly. "I know what it is to love, and to be loved. Why should I be your enemy because Eileen Brokaw's heart has turned to gold, and she has given it to you? Greggy, shake!"

"Wait," said Gregson, huskily. "Phil, you are breaking my heart. Listen. You got my note? But I did not desert you so abominably. I made a discovery that last night of yours in Churchill. I went to Eileen Brokaw, and to-morrow—some time—if you care I will tell you of all that happened. First you must know this. I have found the 'power' that is fighting you down below. I have found the man who is behind the plot to ruin your company, the man who is responsible for Thorpe's crimes, the man who is responsible—for—that—in—there."

He leaned across the table and pointed to the closed door.

"And that man—"

For a moment he seemed to choke.

"Is Brokaw, the father of my affianced wife!"

"Good God!" cried Philip. "Gregson, are you mad?"

"I was almost mad, when I first made the discovery," said Gregson, as cold as ice. "But I am sane now. His scheme was to have the government annul your provisional license. Thorpe and his men were to destroy this camp, and kill you. The money on hand from stock, over six hundred thousand dollars, would have gone into Brokaw's pockets. There is no need of further detail—now—for you can understand. He knew Thorpe, and secured him as his agent. It was merely a whim of Thorpe's to take the name of Lord Fitzhugh instead of something less conspicuous. Three months before Brokaw came to Churchill he wished to get detailed instructions to Thorpe which he dared not trust to a wilderness mail service. He could find no messenger whom he dared trust. So he sent Eileen. She was at Fort o' God for a week. Then she came to Churchill, where we saw her. The scheme was that Brokaw should bribe the ship's captain to run close into Blind Eskimo Point, at night, and signal to Thorpe and Eileen, who would be waiting. It worked, and Eileen and Thorpe came on with the ship. At the landing—you remember—Eileen was met by the girl from Fort o' God. In order not to betray herself to you she refused to recognize her. Later she told her father, and Thorpe and Brokaw saw in it an opportunity to strike a first blow. Brokaw had brought two men whom he could trust, and Thorpe had four or five others at Churchill. The attack on the cliff followed, the object being to kill the man, but take the girl unharmed, A messenger was to take the news of what happened to Fort o' God, and lay the crime to men who had run up to Churchill from your camp. Chance favored you that night, and you spoiled their plan. Chance favored me, and I found Eileen. It is useless for me to go into detail as to what happened after that, except to say this—that Eileen knew nothing of the proposed attack, that she was ignorant of the heinousness of the plot against you, and that she was almost as much a tool of her father as you. Phil—"

For the first time there came a pleading light into Gregson's eyes as he leaned across the table.

"Phil, if it wasn't for Eileen I would not be here. I thought that she would kill herself when I told her as much of the story as I knew. She told me what she had done; she confessed for her father. In that hour of her agony I could not keep back my love. We plotted. I forged a letter, and made it possible to accompany Brokaw and Eileen up the Churchill. It was not my purpose to join you, and so Eileen professed to be taken ill. We camped, back from the river, and I sent our two Indians back to Churchill, for Eileen and I wished to be alone with Brokaw in the terrible hour that was coming. That is all. Everything is revealed. I have come to you as quickly as I could, to find that Thorpe is dead. In my own selfishness I would have shielded Brokaw, arguing that he could pay Thorpe, and work honorably henceforth. You would never have known. It is Eileen who makes this confession, not I. Phil, her last words to me were these: 'You love me. Then you will tell him all this. Only after this, if he shows us a mercy which we do not deserve, can I be your wife.'

"There is only one other thing to add. I have shown Brokaw a ray of hope. He will hand over to you all his rights in the company and the six hundred thousand in the treasury. He will sign over to you, as repurchase money for whatever stock you wish to call in, practically his whole fortune—five hundred thousand. He will disappear, completely and forever. Eileen and I will hunt out our own little corner in a new world, and you will never hear of us again. This is what we have planned to do, if you show us mercy."

Philip had not spoken during Gregson's terrible recital. He sat like one turned to stone. Rage, wonder, and horror burned so fiercely in his heart that they consumed all evidence of emotion. And to arouse him now there came an interruption that sent the blood flushing back into his face—a low knock at the closed door, a slow lifting of the latch, the appearance of Jeanne. Through her tears she saw only the man she loved, and sobbing aloud now, like a child, she stretched out her arms to him; and when he sprang to her and caught her to his breast, she whispered his name again and again, and stroked his face with her hands. Love, overpowering, breathing of heaven, was in her touch, and as she lifted her face to him of her own sweet will now, entreating him to kiss her and to comfort her for what she had lost, he saw Gregson moving with bowed head, like a stricken thing, toward the outer door. In that moment the things that had been in his heart melted away, and raising a hand above his head, he called, softly:

"Tom Gregson, my old chum, if you have found a love like this, thank your God. My own love I would lose if I destroyed yours. Go back to Eileen. Tell Brokaw that I accept his offers. And when you come back in a few days, bring Eileen. My Jeanne will love her."

And Jeanne, looking from Philip's face, saw Gregson, for the first time, as he passed through the door.

XXIV

Both Philip and Jeanne were silent for some moments after Gregson had gone; their only movement was the gentle stroking of Philip's hand over the girl's soft hair. Their hearts were full, too full for speech. And yet he knew that upon his strength depended everything now. The revelations of Gregson, which virtually ended the fight against him personally, were but trivial in his thoughts compared with the ordeal which was ahead of Jeanne. Both Pierre and her father were dead, and, with the exception of Jeanne, no one but he knew of the secret that had died with them. He could feel against him the throbbing of the storm that was passing in the girl's heart, and in answer to it he said nothing in words, but held her to him with a gentleness that lifted her face, quiet and beautiful, so that her eyes looked steadily and questioningly into his own.

"You love me," she said, simply, and yet with a calmness that sent a curious thrill through him.

"Beyond all else in the world," he replied.

She still looked at him, without speaking, as though through his eyes she was searching to the bottom of his soul.

"And you know," she whispered, after a moment.

He drew her so close she could not move, and crushed his face down against her own.

"Jeanne—Jeanne—everything is as it should be," he said. "I am glad that you were found out in the snows. I am glad that the woman in the picture was your mother. I would have nothing different than it is, for if things were different you would not be the Jeanne that I know, and I would not love you so. You have suffered, sweetheart. And I, too, have had my share of sorrow. God has brought us together, and all is right in the end. Jeanne—my sweet Jeanne—"

Gregson had left the outer door slightly ajar. A gust of wind opened it wider. Through it there came now a sound that interrupted the words on Philip's lips, and sent a sudden quiver through Jeanne. In an instant both recognized the sound. It was the firing of rifles, the shots coming to them faintly from far beyond the mountain at the end of the lake. Moved by the same impulse, they ran to the door, hand in hand.

"It is Sachigo!" panted Jeanne. She could hardly speak. She seemed to struggle to get breath, "I had forgotten. They are fighting—"

MacDougall strode up from his post beside the door, where he had been waiting for the appearance of Jeanne.

"Firing—off there," he said. "What does it mean?"

"We must wait and see," replied Philip. "Send two of your men to investigate, Mac. I will rejoin you after I have taken Miss d'Arcambal over to Cassidy's wife."

He moved away quickly with Jeanne. On a sudden rise of the wind from the south the firing came to them more distinctly. Then it died away, and ended in three or four intermittent shots. For the space of a dozen seconds a strange stillness followed, and then over the mountain top, where there was still a faint glow in the sky, there came the low, quavering, triumphal cry of the Crees: a cry born of the forest itself, mournful even in its joy, only half human—almost like a far-away burst of tongue from a wolf pack on the hunt trail. And after that there was an unbroken silence.

"It is over," breathed Philip.

He felt Jeanne's fingers tighten about his own.

"No one will ever know," he continued. "Even MacDougall will not guess what has happened out there—to-night."

He stopped a dozen paces from Cassidy's cabin. The windows were aglow, and they could hear the laughter and play of Cassidy's two children within. Gently he drew Jeanne to him.

"You will stay here to-night, dear," he said. "To-morrow we will go to Fort o' God."

"You must take me home to-night," whispered Jeanne, looking up into his face. "I must go, Philip. Send some one with me, and you can come—in the morning—with Pierre—"

She put her hand to his face again, in the sweet touch that told more of her love than a thousand words.

"You understand, dear," she went on, seeing the anxiety in his eyes. "I have the strength—to-night. I must return to father, and he will know everything—when you come to Fort o' God."

"I will send MacDougall with you," said Philip, after a moment. "And then I will follow—"

"With Pierre."

"Yes, with Pierre."

For a brief space longer they stood outside of Cassidy's cabin, and then Philip, lifting her face, said gently:

"Will you kiss me, dear? It is the first time."

He bent down, and Jeanne's lips reached his own.

"No, it is not the first time," she confessed, in a whisper. "Not since that day—when I thought you were dying—after we came through the rapids—"

Five minutes later Philip returned to MacDougall. Roberts, Henshaw, Cassidy, and Lecault were with the engineer.

"I've sent the St. Pierres to find out about the firing," he said. "Look at the crowd over at the store. Every one heard it, and they've seen the fire on the mountain. They think the Indians have cornered a moose or two and are shooting them by the blaze."

"They're probably right," said Philip. "I want a word with you, Mac."

He walked a little aside with the engineer, leaving the others in a group, and in a low voice told him as much as he cared to reveal about the identity of Thorpe and Gregson's mission in camp. Then he spoke of Jeanne.

"I believe that the death of Thorpe practically ends all danger to us," he concluded. "I'm going to offer you a pleasanter job than fighting, Mac. It is imperative that Miss d'Arcambal should return to D'Arcambal House before morning, and I want you to take her, if you will. I'm choosing the best man I've got because—well, because she's going to be my wife, Mac. I'm the happiest man on earth to-night!"

MacDougall did not show surprise.

"Guessed it," he said, shortly, thrusting out a hand and grinning broadly into Philip's face "Couldn't help from seeing, Phil. And the firing, and Thorpe, and that half-breed in there—"

Understanding was slowly illuminating his face.

"You'll know all about them a little later, Mac," said Philip softly. "To-night we must investigate nothing—very far. Miss d'Arcambal must be taken home immediately. Will you go?"

"With pleasure."

"She can ride one of the horses as far as the Little Churchill," continued Philip. "And there she will show you a canoe. I will follow in the morning with the body of Pierre, the half-breed."

A quarter of an hour later MacDougall and Jeanne set out over the river trail, leaving Philip standing behind, watching them until they were hidden in the night. It was fully an hour later before the St. Pierres returned. Philip was uneasy until the two dark-faced hunters came into the little office and leaned their rifles against the wall. He had feared that Sachigo might have left some trace of his ambush behind. But the St. Pierres had discovered nothing, and could give only one reason for the burning pine on the summit of the mountain. They agreed that Indians had fired it to frighten moose from a thick cover to the south and west, and that their hunt had been a failure.

It was midnight before Philip relaxed his caution, which he maintained until then in spite of his belief that Thorpe's men, under Blake, had met a quick finish at the hands of Sachigo and his ambushed braves. His men left for their cabins, with the exception of Cassidy, whom he asked to spend the remainder of the night in one of the office bunks. Alone he went in to prepare Pierre for his last journey to Fort o' God.

A lamp was burning low beside the bunk in which Pierre lay. Philip approached and turned the wick higher, and then he gazed in wonder upon the transfiguration in the half-breed's face. Pierre had died with a smile on his lips; and with a curious thickening in his throat Philip thought that those lips, even in death, were craved in the act of whispering Jeanne's name. It seemed to him, as he stood in silence for many moments, that Pierre was not dead, but that he was sleeping a quiet, unbreathing sleep, in which there came to him visions of the great love for which he had offered up his life and his soul. Jeanne's hands, in his last moments, had stilled all pain. Peace slumbered in the pale shadows of his closed eyes. The Great God of his faith had come to him in his hour of greatest need on earth, and he had passed away into the Valley of Silent Men on the sweet breath of Jeanne's prayers. The girl had crossed his hands upon his breast. She had brushed back his long hair. Philip knew that she had imprinted a kiss upon the silent lips before the soul had fled, and in the warmth and knowledge of that kiss Pierre had died happy.

And Philip, brokenly, said aloud:

"God bless you, Pierre, old man!"

He lifted the cold hands back, and gently drew the covers which had hidden the telltale stains of death from Jeanne's eyes. He turned down Pierre's shirt, and in the lamp-glow there glistened the golden locket. For the first time he noticed it closely. It was half as large as the palm of his hand, and very thin, and he saw that it was bent and twisted. A shudder ran through him when he understood what had happened. The bullet that had killed Pierre had first struck the locket, and had burst it partly open. He took it in his hand. And then he saw that through the broken side there protruded the end of a bit of paper. For a brief space the discovery made him almost forget the presence of death. Pierre had never opened the locket, because it was of the old-fashioned kind that locked with a key, and the key was gone. And the locket had been about Jeanne's neck when he found her out in the snows! Was it possible that this bit of paper had something to do with the girl he loved?

Carefully, so that it would not tear, he drew it forth. There was writing on the paper, as he had expected, and he read it, bent low beside the lamp. The date was nearly eighteen years old. The lines were faint. The words were these:

My Husband,

God can never undo what I have done. I have dragged myself back, repentant, loving you more than I have ever loved you in my life, to leave our little girl with you. She is your daughter, and mine. She was born on the eighth day of September, the seventh month after I left Fort o' God, She is yours, and so I bring her back to you, with the prayer that she will help to fill the true and noble heart that I have broken. I cannot ask your forgiveness, for I do not deserve it. I cannot let you see me, for I should kill myself at your feet. I have lived this long only for the baby. I will leave her where you cannot fail to find her, and by the time you have read this I will have answered for my sin—my madness, if you can have charity regard it so. And if God is kind I will hover about you always, and you will know that in death the old sweetheart, and the mother, has found what she could never again hope for in life.

Your Wife

Philip rose slowly erect and gazed down into the still, tranquil face of Pierre, the half-breed.

"Why didn't you open it?" he whispered. "Why didn't you open it? My God, what it would have saved—"

For a full minute he looked down at Pierre, as though he expected that the white lips would move and answer him. And then he thought of Jeanne hurrying to Fort o' God, and of the terrible things which she was to reveal to her father that night. She was D'Arcambal's own daughter. What pain—what agony of father and child he might have saved if he had examined the locket a little sooner! He looked at his watch and found that Jeanne had been gone three hours. It would be impossible to overtake MacDougall and the girl unless something had occurred to delay them somewhere along the trail. He hurried back into the little room, where he had left Cassidy. In a few words he explained that it was necessary for him to follow Jeanne and the engineer to D'Arcambal House without a moment's delay, and he directed Cassidy to take charge of camp affairs, and to send Pierre's body with a suitable escort the next day.

"It isn't necessary for me to tell you what to do," he finished, "You understand."

Cassidy nodded. Six months before he had buried his youngest child under a big spruce back of his cabin.

Philip hastened to the stables, and, choosing one of the lighter animals, was soon galloping over the trail toward the Little Churchill. In his face there blew a cold wind from Hudson's Bay, and now and then he felt the sting of fine particles in his eyes. They were the presage of storm. A shifting of the wind a little to the east and south, and the fine particles would thicken, and turn into snow. By morning the world would be white. He came into the forests beyond the plain, and in the spruce and the cedar tops the wind was half a gale, filling the night with wailing and moaning sounds that sent strange shivers through him as he thought of Pierre in the cabin. In such a way, he imagined, had the north wind swept across the cold barrens on the night that Pierre had found the woman and the babe; and now it seemed, in his fancies, as though above and about him the great hand that had guided the half-breed then was bringing back the old night, as if Pierre, in dying, had wished it so. For the wind changed. The fine particles thickened, and changed to snow. And then there was no longer the wailing and the moaning in the tree-tops, but the soft murmur of a white deluge that smothered him in a strange gloom and hid the trail. There were two canoes concealed at the end of the trail on the Little Churchill, and Philip chose the smallest. He followed swiftly after MacDougall and Jeanne. He could no longer see either side of the stream, and he was filled with a fear that he might pass the little creek that led to Fort o' God. He timed himself by his watch, and when he had paddled for two hours he ran in close to the west shore, traveling so slowly that he did not progress a mile in half an hour. And then suddenly, from close ahead, there rose through the snow-gloom the dismal howl of a dog, which told him that he was near to Fort o' God. He found the black opening that marked the entrance to the creek, and when he ran upon the sand-bar a hundred yards beyond he saw lights burning in the great room where he had first seen D'Arcambal. He went now where Pierre had led him that night, and found the door unlocked. He entered silently, and passed down the dark hall until, on the left, he saw a glow of light that came from the big room. Something in the silence that was ahead of him made his own approach without sound, and softly he entered through the door.

In the great chair sat the master of Fort o' God, his gray head bent; at his feet knelt Jeanne, and so close were they that D'Arcambal's face was hidden in Jeanne's shining, disheveled hair. No sooner had Philip entered the room than his presence seemed to arouse the older man. He lifted his head slowly, looking toward the door, and when he saw who stood there he raised one of his arms from about the girl and held it out to Philip.

"My son!" he said.

In a moment Philip was upon his knees beside Jeanne, and one of D'Arcambal's heavy hands fell upon his shoulder in a touch that told him he had come too late to keep back any part of the terrible story which Jeanne had bared to him. The girl did not speak when she saw him beside her. It was as if she had expected him to come, and her hand found his and nestled in it, as cold as ice.

"I have hurried from the camp," he said. "I tried to overtake Jeanne. About Pierre's neck I found a locket, and in the locket—was this—"

He looked into D'Arcambal's haggard face as he gave him the blood-stained note, and he knew that in the moment that was to come the master of Fort o' God and his daughter should be alone.

"I will wait in the portrait-room," he said, in a low voice, and as he rose to his feet he pressed Jeanne's hand to his lips.

The old room was as he had left it weeks before. The picture of Jeanne's mother still hung with its face to the wall. There was the same elusive movement of the portrait over the volume of warm air that rose from the floor. In this room he seemed to breathe again the presence of a warm spirit of life, as he had felt it on the first night—a spirit that seemed to him to be a part of Jeanne herself, and he thought of the last words of the wife and mother—of her promise to remain always near those whom she loved, to regain after death the companionship which she could never hope for in life. And then there came to him a thought of the vast and wonderful mystery of death, and he wondered if it was her spirit that had been with him more than one lonely night, when his camp-fire was low; if it was her presence that had filled him with transcendent dreams of hope and love, coming to him that night beside the rock at Churchill, and leading him at last to Jeanne, for whom she had given up her life. He heard again the rising of the wind outside and the beating of the storm against the window, and he went softly to see if his vision could penetrate into the white, twisting gloom beyond the glass. For many minutes he stood, seeing nothing. And then he heard a sound, and turned to see Jeanne and her father standing in the door. Glory was in the face of the master of Fort o' God. He seemed not to see Philip—he seemed to see nothing but the picture that was turned against the wall. He strode across the room, his great shoulders straightened, his shaggy head erect, and with the pride of one revealing first to human eyes the masterpiece of his soul and life he turned the picture so that the radiant face of the wife and mother looked down upon him. And was it fancy that for a fleeting moment the smile left the beautiful lips, and a light, soft and luminous, pleading for love and forgiveness, filled the eyes of Jeanne's mother? Philip trembled. Jeanne came across to him silently, and crept into his arms. And then, slowly, the master of Fort o' God turned toward them and stretched out both of his great arms.

"My children!" he said.

XXV

All that night the storm came out of the north and east. Hours after Jeanne and her father had left him Philip went quietly from his room, passed down the hall, and opened the outer door. He could hear the gale whistling over the top of the great rock, and moaning in the spruce and cedar forest, and he closed the door after him, and buried himself in the darkness and wind. He bowed his head to the stinging snow, which came like blasts of steeled shot, and hurried into the shelter of the Sun Rock, and stood there after that listening to the wildness of the storm and the strange whistling of the wind cutting itself to pieces far over his head. Since man had first beheld that rock such storms as this had come and gone for countless generations. Two hundred years and more had passed since Grosellier first looked out upon a wondrous world from its summit. And yet this storm—to-night— whistling and moaning about him, filling all space with its grief, its triumph, and its madness, seemed to be for him—and for him alone. His heart answered to it. His soul trembled to the marvelous meaning of it. To-night this storm was his own. He was a part of a world which he would never leave. Here, beside the great Sun Rock of the Crees, he had found home, life, happiness, his God. Here, henceforth through all time, he would live with his beloved Jeanne, dreaming no dreams that went beyond the peace of the mountains and the forests. He lifted his face to where the storm swept above him, and for an instant he fancied that high up on the ragged edge of the rock there might have stood Pierre, with his great, gaping, hungry heart, filled with pain and yearning, staring off into the face of the Almighty. And he fancied, too, that beside him there hovered the wife and mother. And then he looked to Fort o' God. The lights were out. Quiet, if not sleep, had fallen upon all life within. And it seemed to Philip, as he went back again through the storm, that in the moaning tumult of the night there was music instead of sadness.

He did not sleep until nearly morning. And when he awoke he found that the storm had passed, and that over a world of spotless white there had risen a brilliant sun. He looked out from his window, and saw the top of the Sun Rock glistening in a golden fire, and where the forest trees had twisted and moaned there were now unending canopies of snow, so that it seemed as though the storm, in passing, had left behind only light, and beauty, and happiness for all living things.

Trembling with the joy of this, Philip went to his door, and from the door down the hall, and where the light of the sun blazed through a window near to the great room where he expected to find the master of Fort o' God, there stood Jeanne. And as she heard him coming, and turned toward him, all the glory and beauty of the wondrous day was in her face and hair. Like an angel she stood waiting for him, pale and yet flushing a little, her eyes shining and yearning for him, her soul in the tremble of the single word on her sweet lips.

"Philip—"

"Jeanne—"

No more—and yet against each other their hearts told what it was futile for their lips to attempt. They looked out through the window. Beyond that window, as far as the vision could reach, swept the barrens, over which Pierre had brought the little Jeanne. Something sobbing rose in the girl's throat. She lifted her eyes, swimming with love and tears, to Philip, and from his breast she reached up both hands gently to his face.

"They will bring Pierre—to-day—" she whispered.

"Yes—to-day."

"We will bury him out yonder," she said, stroking his face, and he knew that she meant out in the barren, where the mother lay.

He bowed his face close down against hers to hide the woman's weakness that was bringing a misty film into his eyes.

"You love me," she whispered. "You love me—love me—and you will never take me away, but will stay with me always. You will stay here—dear—in my beautiful world—we two—alone—"

"For ever and for ever," he murmured.

They heard a step, firm and vibrant with the strength of a new life, and they knew that it was the master of Fort o' God.

"Always—we two—forever," whispered Philip again.

THE END

JAMES OLIVER CURWOOD

A NOTE ABOUT THE AUTHOR

James Oliver Curwood (1878–1927) was an American writer and conservationist popular in the action-adventure genre. Curwood began his career as a journalist, and was hired by the Canadian government to travel around Northern Canada and publish travel journals in order to encourage tourism. This served as a catalyst for his works of fiction, which were often set in Alaska or the Hudson Bay area in Canada. Curwood was among the top ten best-selling authors in the United States during the early and mid 1920s. Over one-hundred and eighty films have been inspired by or based on his work. With these deals paired with his record book sales, Curwood earned an impressive amount of wealth from his work. As he grew older, Curwood became an advocate for conservationism and environmentalism, giving up his hunting hobby and serving on conservation committees. Between his activism and his literary work, Curwood helped shape the popular perception of the natural world.

A NOTE FROM THE PUBLISHER

Spanning many genres, from non-fiction essays to literature classics to children's books and lyric poetry, Mint Edition books showcase the master works of our time in a modern new package. The text is freshly typeset, is clean and easy to read, and features a new note about the author in each volume. Many books also include exclusive new introductory material. Every book boasts a striking new cover, which makes it as appropriate for collecting as it is for gift giving. Mint Edition books are only printed when a reader orders them, so natural resources are not wasted. We're proud that our books are never manufactured in excess and exist only in the exact quantity they need to be read and enjoyed.

bookfinity™

Discover more of your favorite classics with Bookfinity™.

- Track your reading with custom book lists.
- Get great book recommendations for your personalized Reader Type.
- Add reviews for your favorite books.
- AND MUCH MORE!

Visit **bookfinity.com** and take the fun Reader Type quiz to get started.

Enjoy our classic and modern companion pairings!